SPY SOCIETY

SPY SOCIETY

ROBIN BENWAY

SIMON AND SCHUSTER

First published in Great Britain in 2013 by Simon and Schuster UK Ltd
A CBS COMPANY

First published in the USA in 2013 by Walker Books for Young Readers,
an imprint of Bloomsbury Publishing inc.

Copyright © 2013 Robin Benway
Book design by Nicole Gastonguay
Typeset by Westchester Book Composition

1 3 5 7 9 10 8 6 4 2

Simon & Schuster UK Ltd
1st Floor, 222 Gray's Inn Road
London
WC1X 8HB

Simon & Schuster Australia, Sydney
Simon & Schuster India, New Delhi

A CIP catalogue record for this book
is available from the British Library.

PB ISBN: 978-1-47111-674-2
eBook ISBN: 978-1-47111-675-9

This book is a work of fiction. Names, characters,
places and incidents are either the product of the author's imagination
or are used fictitiously. Any resemblance to actual people living or dead,
events or locales is entirely coincidental.

Printed and bound by CPI Group (UK) Ltd, Croydon, CR0 4YY

www.simonandschuster.co.uk
www.simonandschuster.com.au

"Perchance you wonder at this show;
But wonder on, till truth make all things plain."
WILLIAM SHAKESPEARE,
A Midsummer Night's Dream

"It's just you and me against me. . ."
DANGER MOUSE AND DANIELE LUPPI,
Two Against One

SPY SOCIETY

CHAPTER 1

I cracked my first lock when I was three.

I know that sounds like I'm bragging, but really, it wasn't that hard. It was a Master Lock, the same combination lock that you probably have on your locker or bike. Anyone with Internet access and too much time on his or her hands can crack a Master Lock. I'm serious. Google it. I'll wait.

See? Easy.

My parents were the ones who gave me the lock. They still swear up and down that they weren't testing me, that I really wanted to play with it and they were just trying to keep me from having some sort of toddler meltdown. But really? I'm not buying it. How many of you had a Master Lock for a toy?

My parents weren't surprised that I cracked the lock. I think they'd have been more surprised if I *hadn't* opened it. It would probably be hugely disappointing for two spies to have a completely inept kid, you know? Even my name—*Margaret*, ugh—was chosen because it has so many different nicknames: Peggy, Maisie, Molly, Margie, Meg—the list is endless. My parents have called me Maggie since I was born, but I have twelve birth certificates that all say something different.

Maybe I should explain.

My family works for the Collective. You've never heard of the Collective, but you've definitely read about our work. Tobacco executives on trial because of damning evidence? Human smuggling rings being broken up? The fall of that Peruvian dictator? That's us.

I have to admit, I'm still not sure who or what the Collective even *is*. I know only a few details: there are about two hundred spies stationed around the globe, moving to wherever we're needed. Some of us are forgers (more on that later), computer hackers, statisticians, weapons experts, and I think a few assassins, too, but my parents won't answer my questions about them. I don't know how many safecrackers there are, but my family moves a lot because of me. Apparently a lot of safes need cracking.

We don't ever take things that aren't ours. The Collective may be secretive, but we're not sneaky. The whole point is to right wrongs, not create them. When I was little, I thought the Collective was like Santa Claus, giving out presents but never being seen. Now I know, of course, that the Collective is based in London, not the North Pole, but whether it's run by dozens of guilty-conscienced millionaires working toward a noble cause or one crazy Howard Hughes–type dude, I have no idea.

The Collective had stationed us in Reykjavík, Iceland, over the summer. We were getting ready to head to New York tonight after finishing this job, which could not end soon enough for me. The summer had been painfully boring (and painfully bright, because Reykjavík gets twenty-four hours of sunlight during the summer), since my parents were both busy trying to figure out the case, and school wasn't in session. I spent a lot of time practicing my safe-cracking skills on safes that the Collective sent to our house, but even that got old after a while. I started keeping an eye on the family across the street, even though there was nothing suspicious about them. They were painfully normal, especially their son. Especially their *cute* son. I even managed to mortify myself by having a long-running and completely one-sided "How *you* doin'?" imaginary conversation with Cute Boy.

Where'd we move from? Oh, nowhere you'd know. So what do you do around here for fun?

Ice cream? Yeah, I love ice cream. With you? Of course! No, my parents are totally cool with me dating.

See? Pathetic. As you can tell, I've never had a boyfriend, but whatever. It's cool. After all, most girls who have boyfriends probably can't say that they helped to bring down the Peruvian government, right?

So, after a long and lazy summer spent safecracking and slowly going crazy over Cute Boy, I was ready for New York, ready for a change.

I was ready for something to *happen*.

* * *

The first rule of being a spy: Listen. Our family friend Angelo always says that a good spy never asks questions, that people will always tell you what you need to know.

I've known Angelo my entire life. He was friends with my parents back when they were all in Berlin together, and they've stayed in contact ever since. Angelo works for the Collective, too, but I think he's semiretired now, or at least that's what he says. For all I know, he's getting ready to be knighted by the queen or about to go spelunking somewhere in the Galapagos. He always gives good advice, too, especially about safecracking and lock picking. It's like if Tim Gunn and James Bond had a baby, and that baby was Yoda. Angelo's response? "Who's Yoda?"

I sent him the Star Wars DVDs for Christmas. And a DVD player.

Angelo's a forger. I have twelve passports and just as many birth certificates, and they're all Angelo's handiwork. He handles most of the paperwork for the Collective, including duplicate documents. Like, let's say that someone wants to sell the original Gettysburg Address on the black market and use that money to buy guns for crazy despots. (It's been known to happen.) Angelo forges the document, switches them out, and then the bad guy ends up with no money, and the Gettysburg Address gets returned to its original home. There are probably about a million more steps involved, things like finding the right paper pulp and hiding printing presses, but Angelo doesn't like to discuss details. He can be quite secretive that way, but I understand. We all work in different ways. As long as he keeps using flattering pictures on my passport photos, I'm happy.

As soon as I started writing, Angelo taught me how to forge signatures. In fact, the first name I wrote wasn't mine, it was my mom's, a near-perfect imitation of her signature. And when I was tall enough to reach his front door, Angelo taught me how to pick locks. Once his front door got too easy, we moved on to Gramercy Park, which is in Manhattan. Angelo has a key to that park, but it's no fun when you have to use the key. I love my parents, I do, but neither of them could open a lock if their lives depended on it. And since our lives *do*, in fact, depend on it, that's usually where I come in.

Here's an example of how it works:

At the beginning of the summer, my parents and I got sent to Iceland to investigate one of their largest banks. The CEO's family was suddenly driving imported cars, sending their kids to Swiss private schools, and buying homes in Spain with no money down, yet there wasn't an uptick in the CEO's yearly income.

That usually means someone's hiding something, something like cold hard cash, and let's just say I'm really good at hide-and-seek.

So, my mom gets a job as part of the bank building's cleaning crew, which pretty much gives her access to everyone's office, including the CEO's. She's an amazing computer hacker, which I think sort of rankles my dad. He's useless when it comes to electronics. One time, we were in Boston and they got into this huge fight because my dad thought my mom was taking too long to do her job. She just handed him the TiVo remote and said, "Tell me how this works." And of course he couldn't, so she was all, "Don't tell me how to do my job," and believe me, he doesn't anymore. He really loves watching *Planet Earth* on Discovery Channel.

Anyway, my mom gets into the CEO's office and, of course, has access to his computer. It's so, so easy to get into someone's computer, I can't even tell you. Password protected? *Whatever*. All you ever need to hack someone's computer is a copy of their birth certificate and, sometimes, not even that. If the person's really famous, they've probably already talked about their mom in the news, so boom, there's the mother's maiden name. Pets, children's names, the street where they grew up, their place of birth? They're all password clues, and most people use the same password for everything.

Including the CEO of this company.

(I think my mom was actually sort of disappointed. She likes when she has to do the serious hacking. She says it keeps her young.)

So my mom goes into his computer and sets up a Trojan Horse virus that lets her look at the CEO's computer from her laptop at home. Sneaky, right? Meanwhile my dad starts looking at the company's financial records and notices that there were a lot of bank accounts being opened with tiny bits of cash in them, which is what money launderers do to avoid being caught.

And judging from the names on the accounts—all female, all young, and not an Icelandic surname among them—there was an excellent chance that this CEO was involved in human trafficking. What a degenerate, right?

There was definitely a paper trail somewhere—all the

e-mails pointed to that—and that paper trail was about to be shredded. My mom hurried up and jammed the shredder the next night, but it meant we had to work fast.

It meant that *I* had to work fast.

I went down the hall toward the CEO's office, the fluorescent lights barely lit overhead as I crept past rows and rows of cubicles. It was almost eleven at night, so the employees were long gone by now—there weren't even any overachieving stragglers. The only sound came from my shoes sliding over the cheap carpet as I stayed close to the walls and turned the corner. I was in total game mode after hanging around for three months; I was ready to play.

Here's the boring part of my job: I don't really get to do a lot. I mean, I open safes and I can forge signatures pretty well, but that usually happens at the very end. I've never had a case that was all mine, that rested on my shoulders rather than my parents'. I had spent most of my time in Iceland admiring the scenery, rather than kicking ass and taking names. It was cool, I guess, but it was sort of like being stuck in elementary school while everyone else goes to college. I wanted something more.

The CEO's office door was open just like it was supposed to be, and I could hear the cleaning crew down the hall. My mother was working with the crew tonight as planned; she was the reason the door was unlocked. Personally, I would have rather jimmied the lock open because hi, let's play to our strengths, but my parents are always about doing things the simple way. It gets annoying sometimes, I can't lie. "If we wanted to do things the right way, then why are we spies?"

I sometimes point out, but I know they're correct. It's not about creating excitement; it's about getting the job done.

That's the second rule of being a spy: Be beige. Be beiger than beige. Be as average as possible. Be like the cashiers in your grocery store. Could you describe them? Chances are, no. Did you see them? Of course. Do you know their names, even if they were wearing name tags? Probably not. It's like that.

I know in the movies, spies always have this really cool look, like Angelina Jolie. I'm sorry, but Angelina Jolie would be the worst spy in the world. Who wouldn't remember looking at someone like Angelina Jolie? My mom always gets really upset whenever we watch movies about espionage. "This is so unrealistic!" she always yells. "Why would you dye your hair pink if you're trying to stay undercover? Why is she using a drill to open that safe? All that noise and time!" (My dad and I sometimes joke that the unofficial third rule of being a spy is: "Never mention *Austin Powers* to Mom." She doesn't know about that joke, but we think it's hilarious.)

But she's right about the drill. You just can't use it any old time you want, not when the clock's ticking and your arm's tired and there's building security ambling around just one floor below you. A lot of safes, at least ones that I've seen, have cobalt shields, and let me tell you, trying to drill through that is the most boring thing in the world and it takes *forever*. I'm sixteen—I don't have that kind of time! And if you miss and hit the wrong spot, then you can trigger a bunch of extra locks, which means that you are never,

ever going to open up that safe. I'll spare you the technical details, but trust me when I tell you that it's bad, very bad. You will not be getting the Safecracker of the Year Award if that happens.

So no drills. Or explosives. Or sledgehammers. Sledgehammers are not beige, to say the least.

The office was dark and hummed with electrical energy, computers and outlets all downloading and backing up hard drives and whatnot. I'm not sure how all that works. I didn't inherit my mom's computer genius. Besides, my experience in this job has taught me that most CEOs don't know how it all works, either. They hire some guy to come in and set up security, but they have no idea if it's actually secure. That's why CEOs are always getting busted.

Well, that, and because of people like us.

I glanced out the windows as I slipped into the office, past empty orange-lit parking lots and homes and shopping centers and the tall steeple of a church. Everything seemed stagnant, running into the horizon with no end in sight. If I squinted hard enough, Iceland appeared to be flatlining.

If I focused my eyes differently, I could see myself in the window, looking out on the Icelandic night. I was wearing black jeans and a black sweater underneath a dark denim coat that had a shearling lining. (It may have been September in Iceland, but it was already getting cold out.) Some spies get to wear cool outfits and change their hair up, but as a safecracker, all that mattered was that I did my job. No one cared about my shoes.

My hair was just as boring as my clothes: long and brown and way past my shoulders. "You need a haircut," my mom kept telling me, sounding like she did when I was four years old. My bangs hung directly across my forehead, and I tugged at them self-consciously, trying to make them hang straight.

When I turned around, I saw Kandinsky's *Composition VII* on the wall, the chaotic bull's-eye of the office. This CEO probably thought it was an original, but I knew it wasn't. I knew this because I had seen the original painting at the State Tretyakov Gallery in Moscow. This was two years ago, back when we were doing some research on local elections and their effect on Prime Minister Putin. In Russia. In the winter. Imagine sitting in a tub of ice cubes. That's Moscow in the winter. I still shiver when I think about it.

But I didn't care about Moscow or Kandinsky or even *Composition VII*. I cared about what was behind it. My mom had been cleaning these offices for the past three months, every night during the summer, and every night she would notice that the painting was off-balance in a different direction. No one moves a painting that often.

Not unless they want to get to the wall behind it.

I lifted the painting off the wall, struggling a little with the weight of the glass, and set it down before turning back to the safe that was set into the wall.

"Hello there." I grinned. "Come to Mama."

Okay. I've tried to explain safecracking to my parents several times, but their eyes start to glaze over and finally my dad says something like, "Sweetie, we're just so *proud* of you," and my mom smiles and nods, so I've stopped trying. But the basics are this: For every number in the combination, there's a corresponding wheel within the safe's lock. Find out how many wheels there are, then find out all the possible notches in each wheel and their corresponding numbers by going through the numbers on the dial in groups of three. Find out where the numbers match up by graphing them, then start trying to open the lock using all the different combinations of those numbers.

As you can imagine, if there are only three numbers in the combination, then it's Easy Street. If there are eight numbers, it's Oh Crap City. And since our plane was due at the airport in less than an hour, I needed Easy Street. Judging from the knockoff Kandinsky, I was about to get there. When the painting's an original, the safe behind it is always difficult. Like the designer Mies van der Rohe said, "God is in the details."

The office was musty from too much paper, dust, and time, and I sort of wanted to cough, but I didn't. The last thing I needed was to blow this whole thing because of a tickle in my throat. Instead, I pulled on gloves (yes, I wear gloves, mostly because I never know who's touched the safe before me and whether or not they had the Death Flu) and got to work.

It was a standard fireproof wall safe, thank goodness. Fireproof safes are always easier to crack, because they're not made of steel. Steel melts too quickly in a fire, as I learned after that unfortunate incident in Prague (that fire,

I would like to go on record as saying, was not my fault), which makes it useless if you want to protect paperwork.

Angelo loves to watch me crack safes. He always presses his lips together and nods his head and says, "Hmmm." He says it's because he's never seen a safecracker remember all the numbers in her head without having to graph them. "How do you do it?" he once asked me, but I didn't know how to explain it.

"I can just see them," I finally said. "Like a picture. Graphing takes up too much time." He thinks I have a photographic memory, which is fine by me. Whatever gets me in and out of there is great.

This particular safe had three numbers in its combination, which is *terrible* security if you're ever trying to hide damning documents, just FYI. I clicked the dial back and forth, listening, listening, listening. The clicks were as soft as a mouse's footsteps, but I could feel them against my fingers. I've been doing this since I was a baby.

The best is when you get into the Zone, as I call it. It's almost like the numbers are singing to me, calling me to them. I don't feel anything except those numbers and my heartbeat, and we work in synchronicity, like the best orchestra in the world. That dial is the baton in my hand, and we're playing toward the final crashing crescendo, to the cymbal sounds of justice.

18-6-36.

It clicked open.

"Gotcha," I whispered.

I swung open the door carefully, just in case it was like

a jack-in-the-box (small traumatic childhood incident, too long to explain), but all that was in there was a large envelope. I picked it up and used the dim lights outside the office to examine its contents.

Jackpot. Dozens of passports were inside, all belonging to young women, along with a Post-it note stuck on top, reading: "TO SHRED."

"Not anymore," I whispered, as I put them back in their manila envelope and tucked it underneath my shirt. I shut the safe, the knock-off Kandinsky went back on the wall, and I was about to leave when a noise stopped me.

At first, I thought that my pulse was so loud I could hear it, but it wasn't my pulse. It was the sound of footsteps in the hall. They were a man's, heavy and assured. Women's shoes make *tap-tap-tap* sounds. Men's shoes go *clunk-clunk-clunk*. They got closer and my heart sped up with them, clunking along at a breakneck pace. There was only one person who would be coming toward the office this late at night, and he was the one person I didn't want to see: the CEO.

I hit the floor, the paperwork still hidden against me as I thought fast. I hate thinking fast like this—there are too many opportunities for mistakes—but I happen to work well under pressure. Still, it's not fun, especially when you're trying to suppress a sneeze because the floor's all dusty and clearly my mom hasn't been cleaning *this* office and . . .

I had an idea.

By the time the CEO came through the door, I had

slammed on the lights and was using a tissue to wipe down the Kandinsky's frame, praying he wouldn't notice that I was shaking a little from adrenaline. "Can I help you?" I said in Icelandic. "Are you looking for someone?" My dad had taught me those sentences, as well as "Hello" and "More coffee, please."

The CEO looked like the most average man in the world, not someone who had conspired to make money off human trafficking. "This is my office," he replied in perfect English, brow furrowing in concentration. (I love to watch them squirm; it's so satisfying.) "What are *you* doing—?"

"Oh, I'm so sorry!" My mom appeared suddenly, pushing her cleaning cart and wearing her janitorial outfit. "I have a new assistant; we're training her."

I smiled. "There's a lot of dust in here. Have you thought about getting an air filt—"

The CEO cut me off. "I need. My office back." He spoke the same way my dad did whenever he was annoyed with me. Short sentences. Because the effort. Of Talking. Is just. Too much.

"No problem," I said, balling up my tissue and skirting past my mom. "Only three hundred more offices to go, right? The night is young!"

I went out the door, the passports now scratchy and warm against my skin, and took off for the elevator bank while my mom apologized to the CEO once again. I was glad she was busy because she would *freak* if she knew I was taking the elevator. My parents are always like, "Take the stairs!" but to me, the stairs are usually foolish, especially if you're on a high floor. If you're being chased, you've basically trapped yourself in a spiral, and running down twenty-eight flights of stairs is way too time-consuming. The elevator is best.

Plus elevator music can be very calming. I'm just saying.

The doors were just opening when I heard a *"Psst!"* sound behind me. My mom poked her head around the corner, glaring at me. "Stairs," she mouthed, and pointed at the large EXIT sign hanging over the door.

I took the stairs.

By the time I got into the empty lobby, I was breathing hard but still moving, almost on autopilot. I could feel the security guard's eyes on me as I went toward the revolving doors. "All good?" he asked nonchalantly, sipping at coffee while flipping through the local paper.

"We're good, Dad," I said, keeping my eyes straight ahead. "See you in ten."

"*What* have we told you about taking the elevator?" my mom screeched at me eleven minutes later as my dad pulled our car out of the parking lot, backing over all of the SIM cards from our disposable cell phones and crushing them into smithereens. Another mission accomplished.

"I know, I know!" I said, trying to put on my seatbelt. "I just don't like stairs!"

"You took the elevator?" my dad said, looking at me in the rearview mirror.

"She tried to, but she almost got caught," my mom said. "Seriously, Maggie."

"*Merde*," my dad muttered.

Aside from being a statistician, my dad's also great with languages. He knows how to say "You're grounded!" twelve different ways.

¡Estás castigado!

Tu es privée de sortie!

Ты наказана. Ты не можешь выходить из дому!

あなたは、接地している!

"Yeah, hey, by the way, guess who cracked the safe?" I pulled the envelope out of my shirt and handed it to my mom, ready to change the subject. "Check it out, he's *so* guilty!"

She flicked through the passports, then gave me a smile over her shoulder. "How many numbers in the combination?"

"Three," I said smugly.

"Amateur," my mom and dad said at the same time.

We zipped through the wet streets toward the airport. Our car was a late-model sedan, black exterior, tan interior, just like every third car on the road today. Someday I'm hoping we get a Maserati or something cool like that. My dad taught me how to drive when I was ten, back when we lived in Germany near the autobahn. I'm pretty good at doing 180s and I'm awesome at driving a stick shift, which makes it all the more disappointing when we end up with Toyotas. The speedometer doesn't even go past 160 mph. Not that we'd have to drive that fast, but it'd be nice if the car had *some* power.

We pulled in to the executive airport, and my dad parked the car in the lot. He got our overnight bags out of the car (even spies like to brush their teeth before bed), and I went to work on the license plates, unscrewing them and handing them to my mom as I took them off the car.

"Plane's waiting," my dad said.

"New York's not going anywhere," my mom replied, but she grinned and followed him into the airport and through the concierge area. She took my hand and squeezed it as we walked, and I let her. My parents always get weirdly overprotective whenever we leave a town. It's best just to let them get it out of their system.

The Collective started using private planes after 9/11, but to be honest, I really miss commercial airports. I hear that airport security is the biggest nightmare in the world, but an airport is a spy's best friend. Disposable cell phones at every kiosk, coffee every ten feet, and international newspapers. (You can use your phone to read the *Washington Post* or *Le Monde*, I know, but sometimes you have to go offline, and a spy without access to information is a cranky spy.) You can even get a delicious soft pretzel. Okay, that last one may be important just for me. I love pretzels.

I grabbed some juice from the concierge area and followed my parents onto the tarmac. The rain was picking up now, a little bit cooler than it had been all summer. Autumn was definitely on its way, and I suddenly felt tired. The adrenaline was leaving now, and when it goes, it's hard to find something else to take its place.

There was one flight attendant and a pilot. We rarely talk to them, but I'm pretty sure they work for the Collective, too. Our whole thing is secrecy, so what are we going to say? "We just got paperwork to bring down an evil-doer! Booyah!" That definitely wouldn't be keeping in line with the "stay beige" rule.

My mom handed the license plates and the manila folder to the flight attendant. "Thanks, Zelda," she said. They must have worked together before. I wondered where. All I really know about my parents is that they were both orphaned young and met in Paris. Maybe Zelda was with them in Paris, too. Maybe Angelo was, as well. I wondered who my friends were going to be when I got older. Judging from my summer with Cute Boy, they would probably be imaginary.

Great.

Still, I knew I was expected to eventually go out on my own once I turned twenty-one. I hoped that I would meet awesome people, people who wanted to drive Maseratis instead of Toyotas, people who knew how to change the world, like me.

And I also hoped that they were terrible safecrackers. A girl has a reputation to uphold, after all.

I curled up in a seat near the window and stretched out across from my parents, who were sitting at the table. They probably wouldn't sleep, but I was exhausted. "It's late," my mom said. "Get some rest, okay? Busy day tomorrow. Another life ahead."

"Our family is weird," I replied as I took the blanket from Zelda, the mysterious flight attendant. "I'm the only spy in the world who has someone telling them to go to bed."

"We all start somewhere," my dad said. "Catch some winks."

The plane's engines started to rev as the doors closed.

The lights overhead were soft and muted, probably for my benefit, and I pulled the blanket up to my chin and kicked off my shoes. I hoped I had cute shoes waiting for me in New York. I was tired of wearing flip-flops from Old Navy. It had been almost five years since I had last been in New York, but I knew you could get away with a lot, clothes-wise, in Manhattan. I mean, I'm a spy, but even spies watch *Gossip Girl* once in a while. I hoped for boots. I hoped the assignment was good. I was ready for a major change.

The plane started to pick up speed, its force pushing me back into my makeshift bed before lifting us up into the sky. I almost peeked out the window to see Iceland disappear below us, but I didn't.

Because that's the third rule of being a spy:

Never look back.

CHAPTER 2

If Iceland was flatlining, then New York looked like it was having a heart attack.

We landed at JFK somewhere around three thirty in the morning, and I didn't remember the car ride to our new place. We were living downtown this time, deposited in a Soho loft five stories above Prince Street. I was so tired that I barely saw it on my way to what I guessed was my bedroom. I even fell asleep in my new bed with my shoes on, which explained all the scuff marks on the clean white sheets.

Occupational hazard, I guess.

It took me a few seconds to remember where I was when I woke up the next morning. My new bedroom was smaller than the one in Reykjavík, but this one had a wall of exposed brick and a window that faced west. If I stood on my bed, I could probably see the Hudson River. The white curtains were nice, as was the brass bedframe, but I already knew not to get too attached to things like bedroom furniture. When I was five, I had to leave a princess-style canopy bed behind in Sydney, and I'm not exaggerating when I say that it was *tragic*. I think I'm still grieving for that bed.

My parents were already at the kitchen table when I stumbled out to join them around eleven, bagels and coffee spread out over the wide butcher-block table. It was a pretty nice kitchen, lots of shiny stainless-steel things that did stuff, and I knew immediately that Angelo had picked out our place for us. He told me once that he had always wanted to be a chef, even though I've never seen him cook a thing.

The microwave looked all fancy. It would be great for heating up takeout, at least.

"What's the story, morning glory?" I said to my dad, who pushed a cup of coffee at me.

"Hey, sleepyhead," he said. "Did you remember where you were?"

"Of course," I teased. "I love New Jersey."

He grinned and passed over a bagel. I started picking off the sesame seeds with my fingernails, yawning hard. "So what's the word? What's the deal? What are we up to?"

My parents exchanged glances. My dad's hair was starting to go a little gray at the temples, but it was still mostly dark brown, just like mine. My mom's hair was black and just barely touched her shoulders, but she and I had the same pale skin.

"Uh-oh," I said around a mouthful of dough and sesame seeds. "Does Mom have to clean offices again?" That hadn't been a popular assignment for her, to say the least.

"No, thankfully," she said, then passed my dossier over to me.

We each had one, manila envelopes that had probably been left in our new place a minute before we walked through the door. That's how it's always been; we move and our new identities are there to greet us.

Colton Hooper is the reason we have new identities every time. He's been in charge of our safety since before I can remember, moving my family and me to secure locations and slipping shiny new passports under the door. Angelo may forge them, but Colton puts them into our hands.

Neither my parents nor I have ever met Colton. It's safer that way, not knowing what people look like or where they are. Colton seems like he'd be cool to hang out with, though. Over the phone, he always sounds smooth and relaxed, like some playboy billionaire without a care in the world. He calls me "the infamous Maggie," which I like. It sounds like he trusts me as much as he trusts my parents, and since our lives are often in his hands, we trust him right back.

I opened up my folder and flipped through it. "Ooh, I get to keep my first name!" I said as soon as I saw the school ID. "Maggie Sil—wait, what?"

My parents exchanged another glance.

"I get to go to high school?" I said. "No more home-schooling? Do I . . . do I finally get an assignment?"

"All last summer, you kept saying that you were bored and wanted to talk to people who didn't remember being at the fall of the Berlin Wall," my dad pointed out.

"Holy crap!" I said. "Hallelujah, it's a miracle! I finally get to do something besides watch everyone else have fun!" I raised my bagel in the air like an award, then pretended to wipe away tears. "This just means so much to me! I'd like to thank all the little people that I crushed on my way to the top."

"You are ridiculous," my mother said, her smile tight.

I took a bite of bagel, then washed it down with coffee. "These high school kids won't know what hit them. Who do I get to emotionally destroy?"

I shook the rest of the manila folder, waiting for some piece of crucial information to fall out, but there was nothing. Just my new birth certificate, social security card, school ID, all with the name Maggie Silver, and a cell phone that I knew was for speaking with anyone *not* in the Collective. My last name was completely new—I'd have to get used to it.

"So am I breaking into lockers and looking for drugs?" I asked. "Is it a performing arts high school? I don't know that I'm good with singing and dancing. It might be hard to assimilate."

"No singing and dancing," my dad said. "But please remember that that's exactly what a spy does. We assimilate."

"Like I had any say in *that* decision," I muttered. "What if I have to go to a *pep rally*?"

My dad raised an eyebrow. "It's a private high school in Greenwich Village," he pointed out. "Do you really think there's a football team?"

"I'm sure they have pep about something!" I cried.

And then it hit me.

"Wait. Did you say it's *private*?" I asked. "Are there uniforms?"

My parents' faces went decidedly blank.

"*I have to wear a uniform?*" I screamed. "Are you *serious*?"

"The blouse is so darling," my mom said.

I whirled around and ran back to my room, throwing open the closet doors. I hadn't even looked at my clothes yet, but sure enough, there were five identical private school uniforms: white blouses (who even says "blouses" anymore?) and dark blue plaid skirts. There were also some jeans, sweaters, and really cute gray suede boots, but I couldn't focus on them. I grabbed a uniform off the hanger and carried it back to my parents.

"Look at this!" I said, shaking it in front of them. "I've waited my whole life to go to high school and now I have to wear *this*?"

My mom spread cream cheese on her bagel. My dad sipped his coffee and nodded.

"Are you okay with me walking the streets of downtown New York looking like Lolita?" I pressed on. I could feel my argument going nowhere, and for the first time in years, I felt nervous. If this didn't work, I'd be starting high school the very next morning showing more leg than I had ever shown before. "This looks obscene. Someone should call *Dateline*."

"You'll probably need a sweater," my mom replied. "It's a little chilly out."

"Cheer up, buttercup," my dad added. "It's your first job. You've got bigger and better things ahead." He pushed the envelope at me. "Here, sit down. Time to work."

I slumped back into my chair, the wind out of my sails already. "I just hope that for your sakes, I don't get caught up in a sexting scandal," I told them.

"Duly noted," my mom said. "Anyone want more coffee?"

That's the thing with having spies for parents. They don't get upset about much. Sometimes it's awesome, and sometimes it does not work in my favor.

I sighed once more and reached for my coffee cup. It was white and modern, almost too heavy in my hand. I sort of missed the I BRAKE FOR CAFFEINE mug that we had in our old house. I wondered if another spy had that mug now, or if it had been destroyed. When I was younger, I used to take one thing from each house we lived in, but after a while, they just made me homesick for homes that I would never see again and that had never really been mine anyway.

The dossier was straightforward. Maggie Silver, sixteen years old, transferring from Andover in New Hampshire to the Harper School in Greenwich Village. The school's pamphlet looked pretty straightforward: a happy, smiling, multicultural, "Yay, we're so smart!" student body, reading their books and enjoying their study groups. Liberal arts education, a focus on the individual, blah blah blah.

Booor-ring. I picked up the dossier page labeled *OBJEC-TIVE* and started to scan through.

"Jesse Oliver, sixteen years old, son of Armand Oliver, editor in chief of *Memorandum* magazine. Student, the Harper School."

I sat back in my chair and sighed. "I have to seduce someone," I announced to my parents. "High school is already destroying my moral code and I haven't even set foot on the campus yet."

My mom peeked at my dossier. "I think 'befriend' is the word you're looking for," she said after a minute.

Sometimes she's no fun.

The three of us sat at the table for a good hour, going over the new assignment. My job was to make friends with (or seduce, depending on your interpretation) Jesse Oliver at school and then use that friendship to get access to Armand Oliver's computer and e-mails. "So," my dad said, and then he and my mom put on their Serious Parenting Time faces. "We think that Armand is going to publish a story about the Collective and it's going to name names."

I froze when they said that. "What?" I asked. "How would he even know who we are?"

"No one's quite sure," my dad said. "Someone may be selling information or they might have heard rumors. Either way, we need to stop it. *You* need to stop it."

"Wait a minute," I said as I read through the assignment. "If you just want to kill the article, why doesn't Mom just go work in the IT department at *Memorandum* or something?"

"Because Armand's paranoid," my mom said. "His

hiring process takes months. He's notorious for it." She held up her hand. "He demands fingerprints."

Fingerprints. The one thing a spy can't change.

"So you get in through Jesse," my dad said to me. "This one's on you, kiddo."

"I have to go to school while you two get to stay home?" I glared at both my parents. "You're so lucky."

"Hey, I did my time in high school," my dad said.

"But Maggie," my mom added, her voice cautious. "You know this means that you aren't *actually* making friends. You're getting to know people to gain information, but it can be more difficult if you get attached."

"Duh," I said, flipping through the paperwork and wondering if I could possibly retake my school ID photo. "This is not a friendly business, I get it."

I could feel my parents exchange glances over my head, but I ignored them. "Besides, the people in this pamphlet look lame. These aren't the kind of friends I'd want to have, anyway."

"Well, once you get the paperwork, then your mom and I will do our analysis. *Et fin.*" He stood up and went to gather up the dossiers. "Everybody got it?"

My mom and I handed him all the objectives and mission statements, which he took to the sink. One lit match and two minutes later, our assignments were burned to a crisp. We used to shred everything, but even cross-cut shred isn't that safe anymore. No one can tape together ashes.

I started to gather up everything else: my new social

security card, birth certificate, school ID, and cell phone. "I have to go to work now," I told my parents. "I have to start *assimilating*. I hope you're proud."

"Bursting with pride," my dad said, not even looking up from his bagel.

"Glowing," my mom added.

"You're no fun," I told them, then went back to my new bedroom.

I spent my first day in New York huddled over my laptop, gathering as much information as I could about Jesse Oliver and the Harper School. You'd think we'd get a vacation between jobs, right? Wrong. Oh, so very wrong. Sometimes I think it'd be amazing to just sit on a beach or, I don't know, go to Disney World or something touristy like that, but then I remember that I burn instead of tan, and giant crowds of people wearing Goofy hats just sounds scary. Still, it'd be nice to have a few days without being inherently suspicious of the world at large. Including Jesse Oliver.

And when it came to Jesse Oliver, I was suspicious.

"He's a delinquent!" I yelled out to my parents. "He was arrested for shoplifting last year!"

No response.

"I just want you to know that I'm going to be hanging out with someone who has a criminal record!" I cried.

"Let's not forget that our family can never reenter Luxembourg without being arrested!" my dad yelled back.

Touché.

The truth of the matter was, Jesse Oliver sounded kind

of lame, like the rebel-without-a-cause in a really bad made-for-TV movie. The *New York Daily News* reported that he had been busted for trying to steal a copy of *The Catcher in the Rye* from the Union Square Barnes & Noble, and I lowered my head and banged it gently against the computer keyboard. Shoplifting a paperback and getting caught? Amateur. Wanting to be Holden Caulfield? Poseur.

Jesse Oliver also knew nothing about protecting his Facebook profile from strangers and third-party phishing schemes, judging from how quickly I was able to see it. My mom came in to check on me right when I pulled up his profile picture, which just goes to show that parents have eternally terrible timing.

"Well," my mom said with a grin. "He'll be easy on the eyes."

"Mom!" I cried. "Please do not ever say that again!"

"What? He's cute!"

The worst part was that my mom was right: Jesse Oliver, damn him, was really cute. Dark brown hair that curled over his ears and forehead, hazel eyes, dark olive skin, and teeth that had either been borne from amazing genes or seen a boatload of orthodontia, judging from how straight they were.

But there was no way I was admitting this to my mom.

"He looks entitled," I said, craning my neck to look up at her. "He got caught stealing *Catcher in the Rye*. What does that tell you?"

"That you're more criminally adept than he is," she replied.

"Exactly." I clicked through to his information page. "His interests are 'hanging out' and 'doing stuff.' Is it too late to go back to Reykjavík?"

Even Jesse Oliver's photo page was banal. Hanging out with friends in one shoot, giving the finger in another, hugging a golden retriever in the third. (I had to admit that the dog photo made me jealous. I've always wanted a pet, but even a goldfish is inconvenient when you're constantly moving around the world.) Maybe the golden retriever would be the best part of getting to meet Jesse Oliver.

By the time I was in bed that night, I had a headful of information about Jesse Oliver and one thought that stood out above the rest: I had to stop calling him Jesse Oliver. I mean, *really*.

I woke up the next morning at 5:44, fifteen seconds before my alarm went off. As you can imagine, spies are morning people, except when we have to pull our version of an all-nighter, in which case we become night owls. Basically, we are very amenable twenty-four hours a day.

Still, 5:45 in the morning is 5:45 in the morning, and I felt like I had been hit by a truck. Sleep hadn't been easy that night, and I tried to tell myself that it was because of the new bed and the fact that New York was a hell of a lot louder than Reykjavík.

But I knew the real reason: I was nervous about my first day of school.

It was time for the mirror pep talk.

"Okay, Maggie," I said to myself after my shower, wiping

the steam off the medicine cabinet. "You could eat these kids for breakfast. You won't, though, because that would be cannibalistic and wrong."

Even talking to myself, I was easily distracted. Not a good sign.

"Focus," I told myself. "You are there to get information about Jesse Oliv—*Jesse*. That is it. You're not there to make friends or look cool or whatever you're supposed to be doing. You have a job. You don't have time to worry about your bangs and whether or not they'll stay straight all day. That is not the objective."

I nodded firmly at my reflection.

Then I plugged in my hair straightener.

After breakfast (coffee and leftover bagels), I prepared myself to leave the safe haven of the loft.

"Hasta!" I yelled to my parents. "Don't worry about me, I'm fine!"

I started to climb into the freight elevator, but just before I pulled the gate, my dad ran up and handed me a twenty. "Cab it," he said. "At least until you know your way around."

"Will do," I said, then pressed the button to go down. We've never had our own private elevator before. That was kinda nice. Now we didn't have to share with neighbors.

I wondered if we even *had* neighbors.

There were already tourists and residents in front of our building, streaming through Soho at seven in the morning. I put my hands in my blazer pockets and stuck my elbows out slightly to keep anyone from getting too close. I'm not anti-people at all, but it's instinctive at this point. Still, I figured I was pretty safe. Tourists are generally harmless.

Except when they stop walking in the middle of the street to look up at all the buildings. That just bugs. Architectural walking tours are the *worst*. A brick wall is easier to pass than those groups.

I pocketed the cab money from my dad and hoofed it over to West Fourth and headed north instead. My parents are always, "Safety first!" but it's important to get to know a city when you're assigned to live there, and there's no better way to do that than walking.

The pep talk resumed during the ten-block walk to the Harper School. "You can do this," I said to myself, grateful for being in New York, where it's perfectly acceptable to talk to yourself in public. "You're considered a fugitive in *Luxembourg*, remember? This is the cotton candy of assignments. Fluffy, airy, bad for you."

I really had to work on my pep talks.

The Harper School was on a tree-, squirrel-, and brownstone-lined street, over on Jane Street in the West Village. Red brick buildings lined the streets like antebellum soldiers at attention, and I sort of felt like saluting them as I walked up West Fourth toward the school.

As soon as I reached it, I could tell I had made a tactical error. I was just wearing my normal, semi-inappropriate school uniform, nothing flashy or cool, along with the suede boots I had found in my closet. Everyone else, though, had accessorized to the teeth. (Literally. One kid had a gold cap on his front tooth when he grinned. It made him look like an entitled pirate, but still, A+ for effort.)

Girls were wearing tights, necklaces, and gaudy brooches on the lapels of their blazers. I was wearing none of that. If this school were a circus, these girls would be the trapeze artists and I would look like the sucker who had to clean up after the elephant act.

Well, *shit*.

I had a backpack, too, something black and simple that traveled well, but everyone else had messenger bags or purses slung over their shoulders. I might as well have had a neon sign over my head that flashed, NEW KID! NEW KID! as I walked up the concrete steps, and I could feel everyone looking at me, which was so uncomfortable that I wanted to turn around and run back to our loft. Or Reykjavík. Either place seemed better than the front stoop of the Harper School.

Was this what teenagers did at school? I glanced down at my uniform and then back at the girls, realizing how boring and, well, *beige* I looked. Beige is great when you're opening a safe, but in a world of neon and color, beige was suddenly anything but.

At least I had worn my gray suede boots. That had to count for something, right?

I pressed on. It's rule number three, after all: Never look back.

The hallways inside were filled with kids my age and I took a deep breath. I hadn't been around this many teenagers in . . . well, *ever*. It was sort of claustrophobic and reminded me of that one time we got stuck at O'Hare in Chicago during a blizzard and almost missed our flight to Amsterdam. (Now *that* is a story for another time, but I will say that it involved the mutiny of the airport Starbucks employees and a nun who turned out to be an undercover cop.) "You survived O'Hare, you'll survive this," I muttered to myself.

I let the crowd carry me toward the office, which was blessedly empty. I wondered if I could just stay in here all day, maybe tell them that I had a contagious disease that flared up whenever I was near people my own age. "Hi," I said to the woman behind the front desk. "I'm Maggie Silver, it's my first day."

I don't know what I had been expecting, but this woman barely blinked. I mean, she didn't have to fire a confetti cannon or cue the tap-dancing elephants, but a smile would have been nice.

If there's one thing I've learned from being part of a spy family, it's that you have to give to get. If you want someone to talk to you, you have to talk to them. So I grinned at her, a full-banana smile that made my cheeks hurt, and turned on the charm. "I am just so *nervous*," I told her. (For some reason, I had also adopted a slight Southern accent, but whatever.) "First-day jitters. Any advice?"

She looked at me like I was crazy. She would be amazing during an interrogation. "Study hard," she told me, then handed me my class schedule.

I nodded as I took it, doing a quick scan of the office. Three secretaries; four closed doors, which probably led to various principals' offices; and three computers. One of the doors near the very back had a Simplex vertical push-button lock on it. Most people set a three-number combination: just push the buttons in the correct order and the door clicks open. I smiled to myself when I saw it because they're pretty much the easiest locks in the *world* to crack. All you need is a thirty-dollar magnet. (I got mine on Craigslist two years ago.) Hold the magnet up to the lock and BOOM! The lock pops open.

Seeing that lock sort of flipped a switch in me, and I smiled even wider.

"Good luck," she said to me.

"Right back atcha," I said, taking my class schedule and sauntering out.

Bring it, Harper School.

The Harper School definitely brought it.

By the time lunch rolled around, I felt like I was ready to retire. What had I been thinking, cursing my lazy summer in Iceland? I would give anything to be on my couch, surrounded by combination locks and practice safes, making up imaginary conversations with Cute Boy.

It wasn't that the schoolwork was hard. I had been put in geometry, which was outrageous because I had learned geometry three years ago, and French, which was going to be ugly because my accent was terrible. They should've put me in calculus and Latin, but I would take care of that later. And it wasn't that any of the students were mean to me, either.

No, it was that everyone kept *looking at me*.

I've never stood out so much in my life. I mean, my whole job is to make sure that people aren't looking at me. If people notice anything strange, the jig is up, and what's stranger than a new kid at school? I was sure that everyone was on to me by now, that my family and I would be outed and our lives over. The Collective should have enrolled me on the first day, not three weeks into the semester. What were they even thinking? I didn't know who made up the Collective, but clearly, there wasn't a teenage girl among them.

Right off, I noticed that no one else was alone: students traveled in packs of two, three, or four through the halls, not moving out of the way for anyone else. At one point, I actually had to duck under someone's arm and almost got an accidental elbow to the eye. Wild animals also traveled in packs, I realized. That was usually how they surrounded and devoured their prey.

I probably shouldn't have watched so many nature shows in Iceland. They were starting to mess with my head.

Another problem: everyone was sizing me up, checking me out, taking me in. Sometime between second and third period, I could feel the sweat start to creep up the back of my neck, and by the time we got to lunch, I was on the fast track to full-blown paranoid.

And I still hadn't seen Jesse Oliver.

I needed some air.

As soon as the lunch bell rang (and having a bell going off every hour wasn't helping the situation), I walked outside into the autumn afternoon sun and took a deep breath, pushing my hair out of my face and willing my heart to slow down to a more manageable beat. The air was nice and cool in the courtyard and there were groups of students gathered by different tables, mostly girls huddled around one another, none of them acknowledging me. At first it was a nice change of pace, but I started to realize that standing by myself wasn't exactly subtle.

That was it. I was going to quit spying. I didn't care what my parents said, this was just insane. I was a sitting duck, and frankly, I'd rather be on trial in *Luxembourg* because at least then I could—

"Are you going to stand there all day?"

I turned around to see a blond girl sitting by herself at a table behind me, regarding me with an expression that could be described only as haughty. It reminded me of that time when the Queen of England—

"You seriously are going to just stand there, aren't you." She laughed to herself. "Jesus, you're like a bleeding gazelle in the middle of the grassland."

"Excuse me?" I said. "Do I know you?"

She took a huge bite of her apple and spoke around it. "Nope."

She was familiar, though. Not necessarily in looks, just in the way she sat, like she was waiting for something to happen. Her uniform was on inside out, which, I am sorry to tell you, looked really cool, and she was dangling the apple from her fingers like she didn't care whether or not she dropped it.

"Then why are you—?"

"Look," she interrupted. "First rule of New York: Don't just stand there. Keep moving. We don't like it when you stand there. It makes us *angry*."

I was sure I knew her! Maybe she was a spy, too. Maybe the Collective had two of us infiltrating the system. That would be a first, but hey, it wasn't any crazier than enrolling me in geometry.

The girl started to laugh, only it was more of a cackle. "Fine." She shrugged. "Have it your way. Enjoy the lion stampede."

And then I realized why she was so familiar. She reminded me of *me*. That was my attitude, my voice, my exact thoughts. I had been so nervous that they got lost in the shuffle, but seeing them all in this girl made those qualities come rushing back.

I was a *spy*.

"I'll stand if I want to," I told her, squaring my shoulders and instantly feeling my posture fall back into place like an old friend. *Oh, hi again,* my body seemed to be saying. *Thanks for finally getting your game face on.* "You're the one who can keep following the herd."

She didn't even blink. "I'm not a follower."

"That's funny, because you're sitting *behind* me." I picked an invisible piece of lint off my blazer.

"It all depends on perception," she retorted.

"It all depends on who's perceiving," I shot back.

She finally grinned. "Well, it's about time someone cool showed up." She nodded at the seat across from her. "I'm Roux."

"Roo?" I said. "As in Kan—?"

"If you say Kanga, I will throw this apple at your head." She just set it down, though. "It's R-O-U-X. My mom had a brief fling with the French language when I was born."

"Maggie," I replied, wishing *my* mother had had an affair with the French language, too. Next to Roux, Maggie sounded like some wide-hipped farmhand who thought the Moulin Rouge was a new type of makeup. "It's my first day."

Roux widened her eyes dramatically. *"No!"*

"I'm as thrilled as you are," I replied.

The easiest way to talk to someone new is to say what you think they want you to say. It was even easier when that's what you would have said anyway. Roux was making this a piece of cake.

"Junior?" she guessed, and I nodded. "Yeah, me too. You know you can go off-campus for lunch, right?"

I shrugged. "Why? You just told me not to be a follower."

She grinned for real this time. "You're a quick learner."

"Roux," I said, "you have no idea."

Within fifteen minutes, I learned that she was left-handed, hated school, and wore her uniform inside out after fighting a three-month battle with the school board. "I'm still *wearing* it," she pointed out. "I just like to toy with their heads." Then she glanced up and down at my plain uniform. "What are you going to do with this unfortunate situation?"

She didn't need to know that I had the accessorizing

abilities of a paralyzed flea. "Keep it as is." I shrugged. "I have bigger things to worry about."

She narrowed her eyes at me. "Well, at least the boots are good."

"The uniform's scandalous enough," I pointed out, motioning to the skirt. I would have killed for a pair of tights, especially now that the sun was slipping behind some clouds. "Did they buy these things on Canal Street?"

She snorted, but I saw her hand go protectively to her Balenciaga motorcycle bag. *Knockoff,* I thought. "They've all got a jones for the Lolita look," she agreed. "And polyester."

I drummed my unpolished fingernails on the table, realizing that a manicure was going to have to happen pretty soon. "So, where do you live?"

"Upper East Side. Worst side ever. One subway line for two million people. Germ central. You?"

"Soho," I said, jerking a thumb over my shoulder like she didn't know where it was. "It's right on Prince."

"Nice. Loft?"

I nodded.

"We've got this ridiculous prewar thing. It's so ugly and old." She wrinkled her nose. "My dad refuses to move, but he travels all the time, so it's not like he's even there to see the 'classic crown moldings.'" She made finger quotes around the last words, then sighed. "I want a loft on Prince."

I just nodded again, but inside I was doing cartwheels. This girl was so *easy*! Most people don't start talking like this, which told me one thing: she was lonely. The fact that she had been sitting by herself only added to my suspicions.

I was pretty sure I had just made my first friend.

"So," she said brightly, "who do you think is cute here?"

No time like the present.

"You know who I really want to meet?" I told her, leaning in like a conspirator and dropping my voice a little. "Jesse Oliver."

Roux looked unimpressed. "Are you kidding me? You have a bad-boy thing?"

Honesty was definitely the best policy here. "I tend to thrive in exciting situations."

She rolled her eyes. "Jesse's the equivalent of beige housepaint that thinks it's really neon pink." She paused before adding, "But he *is* cute."

The word "beige" made me sit up a little, but not as much as the word "cute." "So you like him?" I asked. The last thing I needed was a rivalry with some faux-French, knockoff-bagged high school girl over a guy that I didn't even want in the first place. That sort of thing was just *not* in my wheelhouse.

"Oh, God, no." Roux waved away the idea with her hand. "I've known him since we were, like, four."

Phew.

"So will you introduce me?" I asked. I knew I sounded a little eager, but one morning of high school had taught me the importance of getting this assignment over with as fast as possible. "He's cute. He's just my type."

He was *so* not my type.

"Sure," Roux said. "I don't know where he is today, though. He ditches a lot."

Excellent news! If my target ditched school, that meant I could, too! "Cool." I shrugged. "Whenever. It's cool."

The sooner, the better.

CHAPTER 3

After a mind-numbing afternoon filled with a chemistry teacher who clearly knew nothing about chemicals and a US history class pop quiz that I aced even without reading the source material, I was ready to go home.

I followed the herd down the stairs toward the wrought-iron gates. I saw something taped to one of the spires: a plain white business card with the letter *A* directly in the middle. On the back was a drawing of a pagoda.

I grinned. I would know that card anywhere.

Angelo was in town.

Union Square was a sensory mess, so many people and stores and styles. It was like a spy's fantasy. Even if I ran around screaming, "I'm a spy! I'm an international safecracker and your safety is in my hands, *mwah-ha-ha*!" everyone would probably ignore me. Or throw spare change, who knows?

The streets got calmer and the trees got closer together as I walked up Irving Place and passed a tea-and-coffee bar. Angelo liked espressos, so I stopped in and used my dad's twenty-dollar bill to buy two doubles. If he didn't like them anymore, more for me. I needed a caffeine kick, anyway. The first day of school had flattened me.

I knew where Angelo would be even before I saw him: on the northwest side of Gramercy Park, near my favorite birdhouse. (It's shaped like a pagoda, which cracks me up. Like the birds can even appreciate architecture.) The heavy gate was locked, of course, and I set down one of the espressos so I could dig a paper clip out of my backpack. The lock looked old, but I knew it wasn't. They changed the locks every January 1. The key alone costs $350, and a replacement is $1,000.

It's so funny that anyone would pay that much for a key when you can get an entire box of paper clips for two dollars.

But when I went to jiggle the lock, I realized that it was already open. Not enough so that anyone else would notice, but I frowned and put my paper clip back. Breaking into things is half the fun, after all.

"You cheated," was the first thing I said when I saw Angelo.

He turned and smiled at me, folding his copy of *The Guardian* newspaper. He had become greyer since the last time I had seen him, nearly a year ago during a stopover at DeGaulle in Paris. His eyes were a little bit crinklier, but he was as impeccably dressed as always. Dark suit, lavender tie, and pocket square.

Of *course* he had a pocket square. Some things never change.

"How am I supposed to practice my skills when you

44

leave the gate open?" I said, though I couldn't help but smile. "Nice pocket square."

"Thank you, my love," he said, then stood and hugged me. "Oh, you've gone and grown up."

"*Pfft*," I said. "I've been a grown-up since I was, like, four. Here," I added. "Double espressos."

"Oh, lovely, darling, it's perfect." He sat back down on the bench and patted the seat next to him. "Come, sit, discuss world affairs with me."

I plopped down. "The world is ending." I sighed. "Have you heard? It's terrible news."

"The world *is* ending," he said. "The *New York Post* reminds me every morning."

"You read that?"

"It's important to absorb the entire news spectrum." He sipped at his espresso. "Aaah, Irving Place. Delicious. So, you and your family are back in New York and the world is ending. What else is happening?"

I fixed my eyes on him. He raised an eyebrow. "This is serious," I told him. "You saw where you left your card, right? It was at a high school. I have to go to *high school*."

His mouth quivered just a bit.

"Don't laugh at me!" I cried.

"Not laughing, my love, just a slight inward chuckle." He dabbed at his mouth with his handkerchief. "It sounds like a perfect assignment for you. Think of all those lockers with locks."

I waved my hand. "Whatever. Master Locks are child's play." I fixed my eyes on him. "Angelo?"

"Yes, love?" He was still trying not to smile.

"It's terrible. *Terrible*. You have to get me out of it. You've been part of the Collective for a billion years—"

"I'm slightly younger than that, darling, but I appreciate the sentiment."

"—and you can tell them that it's crazy." I sipped my espresso and made sad puppy eyes at him over the rim of my paper cup.

Angelo looked at me and shook his head. "Well, first, I don't have quite the influence over the Collective that you think I do, so I'm afraid that you are going about this the wrong way. Now, sit. Drink your coffee. Look at the beautiful fall leaves. Breathe."

See what I mean? Yoda.

We sat in silence for a few minutes until I was almost done with my espresso. A bunch of kids my age were starting to stream past the park gates, completely oblivious to Angelo and me sitting mere feet away. Just hearing their laughter made my stomach feel hot, then cold.

"See those girls?" I said, motioning toward four girls giggling and walking past us. "I can't do that."

Angelo looked over his shoulder at them. "They look relatively harmless."

"Ha! That's because you're not a teenage girl. They're piranhas, Angelo. Really well-dressed piranhas with shiny hair, who wear their clothes inside out."

Angelo's eyes cut to me. "Was someone cruel to you today?"

"Well, no. But it could happen! I've seen it in the movies."

"Maggie, my love." Angelo smiled. "Have we finally

discovered something that scares you?" He gasped dramatically. "And they said it wasn't possible!"

"I'm not scared!" I scoffed. (I was lying, I was totally scared, but there was no way I was going to admit that to Angelo.) "*Please*. I was in Egypt when the government collapsed, okay? *That* was scary. This is just annoying and stupid. I'm annoyed that it's stupid."

I sat back and motioned to the girls, who were now screaming with laughter over someone's cell phone. "See, they're probably a group of friends, but one girl's like the ringleader"—I thought briefly of Roux—"and another's the weak-link follower, and then the other two basically work as crowd control and—"

Angelo put his hand on my arm. "Maggie," he said. "Your job has always been to be a spy. And now you're going to be a spy in a high school. That's all it is. No more, no less. Now explain the assignment to me."

I sat back and gave him the brief rundown about the Oliver family and their wayward father and son. "So basically, I have to befriend some guy." I rolled my eyes. "He's probably a douche."

Angelo cleared his throat.

"Sorry. He's probably a jerk." I sighed again. "He can't even steal a paperback *book*, Angelo. It's ridiculous. And I have to do homework and write term papers and it's going to be horrible."

Angelo patted my back consolingly. "Well, darling, all I have to say is that you are a wonderful spy, the daughter of wonderful spies, so I'm quite confident that you will make a perfectly adequate high school student."

"Thanks," I mumbled. "Tell me that part where I'm a wonderful spy again."

Angelo laughed and shook his head. "Maggie, you've been the same since the day I met you. Very smart and *very* dramatic."

I smiled despite myself. "Hey, thanks for the boots," I said, holding up one leg to show him my new footwear. "I knew you picked them out."

"My pleasure," he said. "I did some research on what girls your age wear. Which reminds me . . ." He reached into his valise and pulled out a plastic bag from Hudson News. "I brought you some reading material."

Teen Vogue and *Seventeen* magazines were inside, the cover girls beaming up at me. "Spice Up Your Uniform!" screamed one of the headlines. I wondered if they suggested wearing your uniform inside out.

I looked up at Angelo. "You bought these for me?"

He shrugged a little. "A bit of an awkward experience, to be sure, but yes. Consider it a welcome-to-New York gift."

"You knew I was going to high school, didn't you."

"Of course," he said. "I thought you might be ready for the challenge."

I put the magazines on my lap, feeling a little bad. All I had done since I had seen him was complain. "I'm sorry, Angelo. I'll be fine. I'll survive the cutthroat experience with minimal scarring. What's happening with you? How long are you here?"

"Oh, who knows," he said, using a tone that said he

definitely knew. "I'm enjoying my little life, my neighborhood, my new knives."

"Are you slicing and dicing food or people?"

"Food." He frowned down at me. "*Really,* Maggie."

"Just checking." I grinned. "Any cool assignments lately?"

"Oh, here and there," he said, maddeningly vague. "I enjoy a bit of retirement now and then."

"*Pfft,*" I scoffed at him. "Retirement? This from the man whose idea of fun is outrunning diamond smugglers in Botswana?"

He frowned. "Your parents weren't supposed to tell you about that."

"They didn't. I overheard."

He raised a disapproving eyebrow at me and sighed. "That's very uncouth, Maggie."

I just grinned. "Careful when you throw those rocks from your glass house," I teased him. "Seriously, Angelo. Why don't you go work for the Collective in London? You'd be good at it. You're all mysterious and calm."

Angelo shifted a little and looked over my head at the birdhouse. "Quite a ridiculous pagoda for birds," he murmured. "And I don't know, my dear. We shall see what happens."

I was about to ask more, but he cut me off with, "Now, darling, I have to be going, but don't worry, I'll be around as you need me." He stood up and straightened his suit jacket. "And you are going to be a lovely student. Just remember what we say—it's all make-believe."

"Make *them* believe," I replied. Angelo had been drilling that into my head for years. "Thanks for the magazines."

"And thank you for the espresso. A fair trade, I'm sure." He offered me his arm. "Walk an old man out?"

I rolled my eyes but took his arm anyway. "Back to the world of assumed identities and dark secrets," I said as we passed through the gates.

"Just like everyone else," he replied, then leaned over and kissed the top of my head. "Tell your wonderful parents hello." And just like that, he slipped his arm from mine and went around the corner, disappearing once again.

After Angelo left, I circled the park once to see if there were any new locks that I hadn't seen yet. They were still the same, though, simple and easy to access, and I knocked back the rest of my espresso, spilling a drop on my white shirt (of course), and headed home.

My mom called when I was two blocks away from the loft. At first I didn't even realize it was my phone that was ringing. It was a new disposable cell that had some crazy German-dance-rave ringtone, and by the time I finally got it out of my bag, I was mortified.

"Where are you?"

"I went to see a friend," I said. "A friend" is what we call Angelo over the phone. "He bought me magazines with teenage girls in them."

"How nice." She totally wasn't paying attention. "How was school?"

"Wow," I said, "how weird is *that* question coming out of your mouth?"

"It's definitely odd," she replied, "and you didn't answer it."

My jacket flapped a little in the breeze from the river, and I tried to button it with one hand. "Frustrating," I told her. "I didn't see him yet."

"Really? Why not?"

"Because there are a thousand people at that school!" I exploded. "And apparently he ditches a lot, so if you want me to meet him, then I guess I'm going to have to start smoking really bad weed in some back alley with all the other delinquents, or whatever it is that he does!" I sighed and shoved my hair out of my face. Stupid bangs. "This is difficult, okay? It requires a little precision. I'm safecracking a *person*. I gotta figure out the code before I'm in."

"Honey, we need to get this information as soon as possible—"

"I know!" I cried. "You think I don't know that? I'm very aware that this whole thing is on *me*, thank you very much."

"Margaret."

"Sorry," I said immediately. "Look, I can do this. I can do this better than anyone because I am a spy, okay? I am a *great* spy and—and something is licking me."

There was a definite wetness on my calf and I glanced down to see a huge, shaggy golden retriever pushing his nose against my leg, then giving me a big doggie grin. I had seen this dog somewhere before, and I looked from the dog to his leash to his very cute owner.

Oh, no, I suddenly realized, my heartbeat flying into overdrive. *Oh no, oh no, oh no.*

"So," Jesse Oliver said, "what's this about being a great spy?"

"Maggie?" my mother chirped on the other hand. "What exactly is licking you?"

"Bye," I said, then pressed the END button as fast as possible. Jesse was still standing there; his dog was lying down, still giving me the doggie smile. "Um, do you always eavesdrop?" I asked. "It's rude."

He shrugged. "Do you always talk on your phone while surrounded by strangers?"

Why did he have to be so fast with a retort? I tried to think even faster. "I'm not telling you what I do," I said.

He raised an eyebrow. "Is that because you're . . ." He leaned in for greater emphasis, and why, oh why, did he have to have such nice, soft-looking skin? ". . . a spy?"

"I was talking," I said huffily, "about a Halloween *costume*. Yes. A Halloween costume. That will be the best one ever. Yes." I had no idea what I was saying. Halloween was still a month away, and the last time I dressed up, I was four and trick-or-treated at exactly one house: Angelo's. (He gave me a full-size Snickers bar and a diary with a little lock and key. It was awesome.)

But that was then, this was now, and I had to get in the game.

"My friend Roux is having a Halloween party," I continued, like I hadn't just met Roux six hours ago. "Costumes are very important."

"Roux?" Jesse repeated. "She's having a party?"

"You know her?" I pretended to play dumb and twirled a lock of my hair for good measure.

"How many Rouxs do you think there are?"

"The one I know is the only one that matters." My hair was starting to get tangled around my finger and it was hurting. I let it go and it spiraled out into a snarl. *Wonderful.*

Jesse snorted, which was really not an attractive quality for him. "You'll probably be the only person at the party. So, you go to Harper?"

"Maybe," I replied. "Where do you go?"

"Harper." He extended his hand and his stupidly adorable golden retriever leaped toward him, like he was expecting a treat. "I'm Jesse. This is Max."

"Hi. Hi, Max," I added for good measure. Max appeared to have an out-of-control drooling problem, and I took a step back as he came toward me.

"What, you don't like dogs?" Jesse asked.

"I like dogs. I don't like saliva. Are you sure he's not going to dehydrate?"

"So you're new at Harper?"

"You ask a lot of questions," I pointed out.

"Well, you're answering them, so . . ." He shrugged.

"Yes, I'm new at Harper." *Pull. It. Together. Maggie.* "I'm a junior. I didn't see you around school today. Where do you ditch?"

Jesse gave me a real smile for the first time. "Here and there."

"Is it easy to get off campus?"

"Not really, no. You have to want it."

"Oh, I want it," I said, and then found myself blushing a little. "You'll have to show me sometime."

I was so, so, SO thankful that this conversation wasn't secretly being recorded. I think I would rather have been targeted by a sniper than have anyone overhear it.

"We'll see," Jesse replied, then tightened Max's leash around his hand. "C'mon, buddy, let's go. Bye, Spy Girl," he added as Max trotted past me, leaving a drool trail behind him. I watched them leave while mentally readjusting my to-do list.

Number one: make Roux my friend. Number two: convince her to throw a Halloween party. Number three: invite Jesse Oliver.

And somewhere in there, figure out how I became such a bumbling, ridiculous spy.

CHAPTER 4

The next morning, after tossing and turning for most of the night, I had a shiny new plan.

And like most of my plans, it involved deviousness, blatant lying, and coffee.

I started with the coffee first.

I had come up with the shiny new plan (SNP, because acronyms always sound more important) about three in the morning, after I realized that what I had said to my mom earlier was true: I was cracking a person, not a safe. Jesse Oliver didn't have a keypad attached to his forehead, and this "let's make googly eyes at each other" business was going to be a lot harder than I thought it would be. Let's just put it this way: I've never had a safe make googly eyes at me.

The first step: changing my class schedule.

The second step: making Roux my new BFF. (Acronyms, like I said.)

I strolled into the school's office at eight the next morning, large coffee in hand, still wearing my boring and itchy school uniform. (Unfortunately, my SNP didn't involve accessorizing. I'm a talented person, but some things are just out of my league.) Kids were filling the hallways, each person looking cooler than the next. Were teenagers always this loud? I was going to need to buy an economy-sized bottle of aspirin before this job was over.

"Hey!" someone yelled, and when I turned around, I saw Roux strolling toward me. "Seriously, not even a pin or something?"

"What?"

She waved her hand toward me. "Your uniform. Didn't we discuss this yesterday?"

"Oh." I glanced down at my plaid monstrosity. "Um, I thought that was more of a theoretical conversation."

Roux just stared at me. "Theoretical conversation? Are you for real?" She continued on before I could even answer. "Look, please, do it for me. My eyes, they burn when I look at this situation. Help *me* help *you*."

I've met a lot of people in my life, but this girl took the cake. "You realize that it's just a uniform, right?" I said. "It's not the be-all, end-all of who I am."

"Good thing," she replied. "Because if it was, it would be saying, 'I'm boring.'"

"Boring?" I cried before I could stop myself. "*Boring*? Are you kidding me?" I started to laugh. "Oh my God, you have no idea." *Boring people do not flee the Luxembourg government*, I wanted to add, but I kept my mouth shut.

Roux gave me the side eye as I tried to compose myself. "*Riiiiight*," she said. "Okay, I'm just going to back up slowly

56

and hustle myself to class while you figure out something to do about this."

"You do that," I told her, still giggling. "I'm sure I'll come up with a creative use for some safety pins and paper clips in the meantime."

"That's the spirit," Roux said. "Trust me, I'm trying to save you from social extinction." Then she turned and walked down the hall, so confident in her stride that people moved to get out of her way.

I could see that step 2 of SNP was going to need some revising. As was my uniform.

I shook it off, though, because I had bigger fish to fry. I needed to get my class schedule synced up with Jesse Oliver's, which meant I needed to get into the school's computer system.

This is always my favorite part of the job.

The administrative office smelled like old paper and burned coffee and looked like the kind of room where dreams go to die. There was a halfhearted GO HARPER! sign stretched across one wall, but it just looked ambivalent. It could have said, WE LOVE CHEESE! for all it seemed to care.

There was only one secretary in the office that morning, her desk empty save for a large box of Kleenex and a photo of her two kids. She was typing away furiously and didn't even look up when I stood right in front of her desk. "And how may I help you this morning?" she asked.

"Hi," I said. "I'm Maggie, I'm new here, and I think I have a problem with my class schedule."

"Do you now?" She didn't make it sound like a question, though.

I plopped down into the chair next to her desk, balancing my coffee in one hand as I began to rifle through my bag. "It's just that I'm in geometry, and my parents, they want me to, you know, reach my potential and try to maximize my abilities." I had no idea what I was saying, but it sounded good to me.

"Your class assignments are permanent unless—"

"Oh my God, are those your kids?" I changed topics like a seasoned pro. Which I was. "They're so cute!" And they *were* cute, in a sort of missing-teeth chipmunk way. "Twins?"

This time, the secretary actually smiled a little. "Yes," she said. "Six years old."

"What are their names?"

"Detroit and Dakota." She smiled a little more while I tried not to widen my eyes too much. Apparently I had got off easy with a name like Margaret. "They just started first grade yesterday and—"

"Oh my God, I am so sorry!" The coffee fell from my fingers and flooded over the box of Kleenex and the desk, dripping into the secretary's lap. I had made sure it was lukewarm beforehand, just in case of that. "Oh, no, let me help!"

She leaped up from her seat as the coffee continued to stream across the desk, flooding everything in its path. "It's all right," she said, trying to hold her soaked sweater away from her. "Just let me, um, get cleaned up here." She tried to wipe the coffee off her desk, which was useless. Believe me, I know how to make a real mess. "Oh, geez."

58

"I'm really sorry," I said, which wasn't a lie. "I'm such a butterfingers. Maybe too much caffeine this morning. I'll totally pay for the dry cleaning."

She nodded, already looking down the hall toward the restroom. "Why don't you come back later this afternoon?" she said. "We can talk about your schedule then and . . ."

"Great," I said, and made a mental note to send her an anonymous fruit basket. Detroit and Dakota would probably love it.

"I'm just going to go get cleaned up and . . . yeah." She didn't look thrilled with me, and I couldn't blame her. I hate when innocents are in the line of fire.

As soon as she disappeared into the restroom, I slid into her seat and immediately pulled up the log-in screen. Her user name was still there, but the password was empty.

Hello, kiddos.

I tried entering "DETROIT" but it didn't work. Then I tried "DAKOTA."

Bingo.

Sometimes it's so easy that it's not even fun.

My fingers moved fast, pulling up my and Jesse's class schedules. He had chem, French, calculus (which he was failing, I noted), English III, and AP US History. Also, despite the failing math grade, he was an A/B+ student. "He totally cheats," I whispered to myself.

I opened up my schedule next and immediately put myself into Jesse's French and calculus classes, dropping geometry for good. I thought about putting myself in AP English, as well, but come on. Like I have the time to read all those books and write the papers.

The secretary still hadn't come back yet (coffee can be such a bitch to get out of cotton, I knew from my own clumsy experience), so I took a risk and opened up Roux's class schedule. She had French, too, but I wasn't about to move her into our class. I wasn't going to spend an hour every day listening to Roux translate "Why is your uniform so boring?" or "What do you have against accessorizing?"

I logged out and slid myself away from the desk and out of the dusty office just as the bathroom door swung open. The secretary wasn't thrilled to see me in the hallway. "So sorry!" I said again. "So klutzy! I'm amazed I haven't spent half my life in traction!"

"You better get to class," she said. "You don't want to be late."

First period was calculus with Jesse. "No, I definitely don't," I said. "Good call."

CHAPTER 5

After my first week of high school, I was ready for it to be over.

I was exhausted from waking up at five forty-five every morning (while my parents got to sleep in, ugh), tired from trying to navigate crowded hallways filled with teenagers, and annoyed with the amount of homework I had. Did they assign so much just to keep us busy and off the dangerous streets of Manhattan? It felt like a conspiracy to me, and if I saw the words "Make sure to show your work" or "Why or why not?" written on assignments one more time, I was going to have a meltdown.

I had seen Jesse Oliver a few times in the hall, but I couldn't figure out how to talk to him. He was always nodding at people, and one time he even nodded at me (I can't lie, I was secretly thrilled), but by the time I figured out what to say to him, he had already walked away.

My parents, by contrast, were slowly going crazy at home. It was obvious that they weren't used to not running a job, so every day when I came home, they bombarded me with questions. Did you talk to Jesse today? Did you talk to other kids? What's the geographical layout of the school? Does anyone seem suspicious?

"Everyone seems suspicious," I answered that last one. "It's high school."

And at the start of the second week, I got an even bigger surprise.

"Parent-teacher conferences?" I said, looking at the piece of paper that had been distributed during first period. My parents had been assigned Wednesday afternoon at three o'clock. "Oh, no, this is not happening."

"Tell me about it," Roux said, coming up behind me. "It's so elementary school. But hey, when you pay thirty thousand dollars a year for your kid's education, I guess you want proof that people are earning their money."

"When are your parents coming?"

"Oh, they're not." Roux examined one of her perfect cuticles. "They're in London for the Frieze Art Fair. When are your parents coming? Do I get to meet them?"

Hell no was my first thought, but I kept it to myself. "Um, I'm not sure they can make it, either," I told her, deflecting the question.

"They should come. It's a really big deal. Like, whose parents care the most."

"So if they don't come . . ."

"People will talk about you just like they're going to talk about me."

I sighed. "Fantastic."

* * *

My parents, of course, were thrilled that they got to finally do *something*. "Here are the rules," I told them on Wednesday morning before I left for school. (They were up early that morning, those crazy overachievers). "You do not embarrass me."

"And?" my dad asked. "What else?"

"That's it. Consider that rule number one, two, and three." I gathered up my bag and my coffee. "And please, don't wear anything weird, okay? Just look like regular Soho parents. This is the most basic assignment ever. Just be yourselves."

But even I knew the truth: in high school, that was easier said than done.

By Wednesday afternoon at 2:45, I was a nervous wreck. "Did you have a triple espresso or something?" Roux said as we packed up at the final bell. "You look all wobbly."

"Don't tempt me," I replied.

"Here," she said, shaking a bottle in my direction.

"What is that?"

"Xanax, duh! Never leave home without it."

"Are you crazy?" I snapped at her, throwing a quick glance down the hallway to make sure no one saw us. "You could get us both suspended for having that here!"

"Oh, relax. I have a prescription."

"You do?"

"No, I lied. It's my mom's."

I shoved the bottle back in her bag. "Here. Go. Do something."

"I will. I have a massage appointment with Rosie the

Miracle Worker. It's not her official title, but it should be. She's way better than a parent-teacher conference."

"Well, enjoy your relaxing life," I said. "I'll be here, dying of embarrassment."

"Ta-ta," she said, wiggling her fingers at me. "You probably won't recognize me the next time we meet, I'll be so mellow."

"We can only pray," I replied.

But when my parents showed up at school, I realized that I should have gone with Roux.

"Um, excuse me," I said to them, "but what in the world are you *wearing*?"

My mom was wearing a Chanel suit and taller heels than I had ever seen her wear before, making her an inch or two taller than my dad. A double strand of pearls hugged her neck, and her makeup looked professionally done. She had a wig on, a blond bob that hid her black hair and looked completely natural. I smelled perfume, too, something strong.

"Too much?" my mom asked.

"Too much *perfume*," my dad told her, waving his hand and wrinkling his nose. He had a suit on and kept tugging at the collar, but his shoes were polished and his hair looked newly cut. They seemed to be the perfect Upper East Side parents I had never had.

"One problem," I said, then stopped myself. "Actually, there are multiple problems, but this is the main one. You look uptown and we live downtown."

"Downtown is the new uptown," my dad said. "Look, my socks match my tie!"

"He read that in the *Times* Style section." My mom rolled her eyes. "Maggie, fix your hair." She reached out to brush a lock of hair off my shoulder.

They may have looked different, but they were still my parents.

They were suitably impressed by the school building. "Wow, look at this masonry," my dad said. "What is this, prewar, do you think? Or maybe—?"

"It's old," I said, cutting him off. "That's what it is. And it's worth thirty-thousand dollars a year, apparently."

"Is that a community garden?" my mom said, peering out a window. "Do they do organic?"

"Sure," I said. I wasn't the only student hurrying their parents through the hallway, though. Several other kids were herding parents into classrooms and looking just as mortified as I felt. "All the organic you want."

My parents were due to meet with my French teacher, Monsieur McPhulty, whose name my dad had a hard time swallowing. "I'm pretty sure 'McPhulty' isn't in the original French," he had grumbled when I first told him, but when I introduced them, it was all "*Bonjour*" this and "*Merci!*" that.

"I didn't realize that Maggie had French-speaking parents," Monsieur McPhulty said, shooting a glance in my direction. "Her accent is, well, terrible."

Parent-teacher conferences, I decided, were the dumbest things ever.

I hung out in the hallway while they talked, dragging the toe of my boot back and forth across the floor. I could hear someone banging on a locker and I finally got annoyed and went to inspect the noise. I found Jesse Oliver trying to get his Master Lock open. He would try, then bang it against the locker in anger, and try again.

If this wasn't a sign from the heavens, I didn't know what was.

"Hi," I said. "Do you need help or is this just an extreme sport?"

"I'm fine," he muttered through clenched teeth. "This lock is just broken."

"Want me to try?"

"Be my guest," he said. "I hope you enjoy frustrating experiences."

"Oh, I live for them," I said, then starting spinning the dial around. "Are you here for your parent-teacher conference?"

"Yeah, my dad's supposed to be here soon."

Armand was going to be here! My heart started to beat a little faster and I glanced toward the closed door of my French classroom. There was no way that my parents and Armand could see each other, not if I had anything to say about it. They would probably try to usurp the whole mission, and I wasn't about to surrender my very first assignment. Not yet, anyway.

"Do you know what you're doing?" Jesse said after I started to spin the dial back and forth, trying to feel the catch of the wheel.

"I picked up this talent in middle school," I replied. "My locker was always busted. What's the combo?"

"24-37-2."

"Easy enough." I spun it a few times, then felt the wheel catch on a 3. "I think it's actually 24-37-3."

"No, it's not. The locker assignment said . . ."

I popped it open. "It's three," I said. "Trust me."

"Wow." He looked at the lock, then back at me. "That explains why I can never get it open."

"You're welcome," I said.

"Sorry. Thanks. Thank you, that was awesome."

I shrugged. "Like I said, easy enough." Down the hall, the double doors swung open and I saw a dark-haired man heading toward us. He had the same build as Jesse and looked to be about the same height.

I didn't need a dossier picture to know that it was Armand.

"Well, see you around," I told Jesse, starting to walk backward. "Good luck with the conference. Hope you're not failing calculus."

He looked at me oddly. "I *am* failing calculus. How did you—?"

But I was already around the corner, ducking behind another row of lockers. "Stupid!" I whispered to myself. Why didn't I just tell Jesse that I knew his entire school transcript? I had never tripped myself up like that before.

"Is Mom here?" I heard Jesse ask, and I pressed myself against the wall and tried to be as small as possible.

There was a pause before Armand said, "No," and an even longer pause before he said, "I'm sorry."

Where was Mrs. Oliver? As far as the dossier knew, they were still married. Was she out of town?

"It's cool," Jesse said, and I didn't have to see his face to know how disappointed he was. He was the aural equivalent of a kicked puppy.

"I'll e-mail her an update," Armand said. His voice was deep but not all villain-y. "I'm sure she'll appreciate it. I'll send it as soon as I get home."

"No, don't do that," Jesse said. "If she wanted to know, she'd be there."

"Son, I'm sure she—"

"Forget it. C'mon, you're late."

Armand sounded way nicer than I had imagined. I don't know why I had pictured some gruff guy sitting behind a computer and chomping on a cigar, but it was clear that he was trying to make Jesse feel better about his absent mom.

I was tempted to follow Jesse and find out more, but I heard the door to the French classroom open and I hustled over as fast as I could. My French is so bad that I couldn't tell what my parents or Monsieur McPhulty were discussing, but it sounded like they were long-lost friends by this point.

"Hey," I said brightly. "How'd it go? Am I expelled?"

"Hardly," my mom said.

"We should go," I said. "Right now. Thanks Mr.— I mean, Monsieur—McPhulty."

"En français, s'il vous plaît."

Oh, brother.

"Bonjour. I mean, *merci.* Shoot, I mean, *au revoir."* I was so eager to get my parents out of there before they accidentally ran into Armand that I would have had better luck speaking Swedish.

"What is wrong with you?" my dad whispered as soon

68

as we rounded the corner. "Did someone phone in a bomb threat?"

"Worse. Armand is here."

"Did he see you?" both of my parents asked at the same time.

"No, but it was close. C'mon, let's go."

"That garden," my mom said as we hurried out of the building, "really is just *darling*."

CHAPTER 6

It took me nearly an hour to find Roux after school the next day. I looked all over the campus, and when that didn't work, I hunted in the surrounding neighborhood, poking my head into every Starbucks, anti-Starbucks, and clothing store that I passed. I figured I would hear Roux before I could see her, since her mouth is bigger than her height, but after turning up Roux-less, I finally gave up and trudged back to my locker.

And there she was, standing in front of her locker, angrily grabbing books out and shoving old ones back in like they had said something personally offensive to her.

"Roux!" I called out when I saw her, but she didn't look up. "Roux, c'mon!"

"You don't have to shout," she said when I was close enough. "It's not like half the school is named Roux. I heard you the first time."

"Where have you been?" I asked her. "I looked all over for you. I had to eat lunch in the *library*."

"That's good for you. Builds character."

"Roux."

She sighed and slammed her locker shut. "Look, today has been the longest day ever and now I just want to go home and soak in my bathtub and watch reality television so I can feel better about myself. So please, tell me what you need so I can get it for you and then go about my business."

I paused. "You know what? You should take debate or something. I mean it, you're really eloq—"

"Did you just chase me down to suggest that I enroll myself in a class that teaches useless arguing?"

"Um, no." I stood a bit taller and put on my best smile. "We need to talk about Halloween."

Roux just sighed and brushed past me. "The devil's holiday. Don't eat unwrapped candy. Trick-or-treat with a buddy. There, I think we've covered everything."

I dashed to catch up with her and planted myself directly in her path. "I need your help."

"I gathered."

"I may or may not have told Jesse Oliver that I was going dressed as a spy for Halloween."

"Excellent. Try to figure out how you can show some cleavage in the costume." She started to walk away again, but I moved so she was trapped in the hallway. "Um, does this count as harassment?"

"Nope. Now please, help me. I need help. You always tell me that."

"Fine! Oh my God, you're relentless. I admire that, I have to admit. So what do you need? Night-vision goggles?"

"No, those are way too heavy to be useful," I said without thinking, but all my comment did was make Roux smile. A reluctant smile, but a smile just the same.

"Okay," she said. "So you need help with your costume."

I twisted my hands in front of me. "Kind of?"

"Kind of."

"I also need help with a party. Wait!" I said as she rolled her eyes and started to walk away. "Look, he overheard me talking about my costume and so now I have to have one, but it doesn't do me any good to wear it on Halloween night without going out. So I need a party."

"What, do you think I just carry parties around in my pocket?"

"Well . . ." I gave her my most charming, possible-BFF smile. "Maybe *you* could throw a party?"

"HA!" Her laugh sounded anything but amused. "Trust me, Mags, if I threw a party, the only people who'd be attending would be you, me, and the housekeeper. And she leaves every night at seven."

"Come on!" I pleaded with her, following her down the steps of school and into the front of the building. It was chilly in the shade, and I was glad for the peacoat that Angelo had bought for me. "You probably know how to throw a party better than anyone else."

When in doubt, go with flattery. A tried-and-true rule.

"That's true," Roux admitted. "I can throw a hell of a party. The only problem is that no one will come. I just told you."

"Well, aren't you popular?" I said.

Roux snorted.

"You have friends, right?"

Roux held her arms around and turned in a circle. "Yes, these are my friends. All of them. Can't you see them? Aren't they stunning?" She dropped her hands back down at her sides and glared at me. "I don't know which of your five senses doesn't work, but in case you haven't noticed, I don't have any friends."

"Well, okay, maybe not here at school, but . . ."

"No friends. Nowhere. Nada. No one's told you yet?"

"No one really talks to me," I admitted. "I don't have any friends either."

"Well, at least there's *hope* for your friendless life." She glanced down the street. "God, I need a cigarette."

"You smoke?" I gasped before I could help myself.

"Not anymore. I quit last year. The teeth bleaching was getting too expensive. You know."

"It's so bad for you," I said. "The smoking, I mean, not the teeth bleaching."

"Well, yeah, that too. Look, here's the deal. I'm just going to tell you because clearly someone has to, and it might as well be me." She took a deep breath and closed her eyes, as serious as I had ever seen her. "Last year, I slept with this girl Julia's boyfriend, and it really upset her because it was true love, et cetera, and I screwed it all up for her. Literally *and* figuratively. And for some reason, everyone else has taken her side."

"For *some* reason?" I repeated. "Roux, that's kind of a big deal."

She shrugged. "I don't know, it was . . . I didn't mean to, let's just say that."

"So everyone just stopped talking to you?"

She was looking guiltier by the minute. "Well, I had kind of not really been nice to a lot of people. Like, ever. At all. And it's a small school and karma's a bitch, as they say."

"Were you a Mean Girl?" I asked. "I saw the movie."

Roux paused for a long time before finally saying, "Yes. I was a bitch to people. I talked about girls, made up rumors, all of that. Ever since fifth grade."

"So now you're persona non grata," I said. "Wow. Social justice, like, *never* happens. I'm sorry!" I told her when she frowned and started to walk away. "I'm really sorry, it just slipped out."

"Yes, please, enjoy my karmic retribution." Roux didn't even turn around as she walked away. "Forget I said anything. Good luck with your party." She disappeared up the street and around the corner, lost in the midafternoon crowd.

Fifteen minutes later, as I was trudging toward Gramercy Park to think, my civilian phone rang. "Hello?"

"Hi."

"Hi?"

"It's Roux. Wow, answer your phone much?"

"Oh, hi!" I said. I hadn't had a friend call me on the phone since, well, ever, so this was kind of a big deal for me. "Sorry, I wasn't paying attention to the caller ID."

"Yes, I can tell. Look . . . I'm sorry for being all

awkward and walking away. I don't really talk to anyone about what happened . . . so, yeah. Sorry. Sometimes I'm weird."

I grinned. "S'okay. Sometimes I'm weird, too."

"I know." I could tell she was smiling when she said it, though. "Are you still at school?"

"No, I'm just heading home," I said as I kept walking farther away from home. "And I'm sorry, too. That was a really rude thing to say. True, but rude."

"Fair enough. Apology given and accepted. Now do you still want a party?"

"Of course." I ran my hand along the side of the grate along Gramercy Park South, my fingers making *thudthudthud* sounds along the iron bars. "Are you going to bite the bullet and throw one?"

"No. But I heard that Jesse Oliver is."

I came to a screeching halt. "Are you serious? How do you know?"

"I heard this girl talking about it after I walked away. She's a senior, she knows things. We used to be fr— anyway, he's having a Halloween party in two weeks. You're welcome."

I couldn't stop the stupid grin that was crawling up the sides of my face. "This couldn't be more perfect!" I squealed. "Is he having it at his house? When is it?"

"Yes, and Halloween night."

I gleefully punched the air, attracting absolutely no interest from any of the other pedestrians. "This is so perfect!" I told Roux, but she had no idea how perfect it was.

Make nicey-nice with Jesse Oliver? Check! Get into his house so I can scope out his father's office and see what his safe situation was? Check, check! Foil Dad Oliver's plan, save the world, and be promoted to *head spy of all time?* CHECK, CHECK, AND CHECK!

"Are you there?" Roux's voice crackled over the phone. "Maggie? I hope you didn't get hit by a bus."

"I'm here. No bus casualties." I straightened my coat and tried to brush my hair out of my face. "I'm cool. I'm just so happy!"

"Have you never been to a party before?"

"Um, you mean, like, ever?"

"I mean as a teenager. Oh no," she moaned when I hesitated, "you haven't."

"I'm a really fast learner!" I protested. "Just come with me."

"Uh-oh, you're breaking up!" she said, even though the reception was crystal clear. "What terrible timing! Don't you just hate the cell phone area near Central Park? Bye!"

I just smiled to myself and tucked my phone back in my pocket. Getting Roux to the party would be a piece of cake.

Did I say a piece of cake? I'd like to amend that statement. It was like an ant trying to haul a boulder up a hill. Twice. That's what it was like.

I begged, cajoled, and pleaded with her for a full week, but she refused to attend. "There's no way I'm dressing up as a social outcast for Halloween," was her answer every time I asked.

"But that was *last* year," I protested as we walked through school on Tuesday, three days before Halloween. "I'm serious, you know how people are. They forget about things."

"Oh, really?" Roux said, then turned and smiled at a brunette passing us. "Hey, Julia, what's up? How are things?"

"Slut," Julia responded, and kept walking.

Roux just looked back at me knowingly. "You were saying?"

"Roux . . ."

"Here's how it works," Roux said, not even slowing her pace. "Once you fall, you fall. You're like that ring thing in the lava. You're not coming back."

"The ring thing?"

"With the short guys."

"Oh, you mean *The Lord of the Rings*."

"Yeah, that. I don't get to climb the social ladder anymore. Maybe if I move to Poughkeepsie, then I'll have another shot at glory, but for now, I'm not going anywhere. I'm dirt. And dirt," she concluded just before she ducked into her English class, "isn't exactly welcome at parties."

"I don't know what I'm going to do," I told Angelo on Wednesday as we drank hot chocolate in front of the New York Public Library. (He had summoned me there with a quick pencil sketch of two lions reading books.) "I've tried everything."

"Flattery?"

"Duh." I poked at the marshmallows in my rapidly

cooling cup. "Why don't we ever meet somewhere warm? Why can't we meet at the movies?"

Angelo raised an eyebrow. "I was unaware that you enjoyed films."

"I can learn if it means I'm warm."

"You are a fast learner, I'm sure you'd be quite proficient in French—"

"Quit the flattery. You've heard my accent."

Angelo smiled and adjusted his scarf a little. "Well noticed. So your friend Roux—charming name, by the way—"

"Ha. Wait till you meet her before thinking that."

"—refuses to go along with you to this Halloween party. And you're upset. Can you go by yourself?"

I guess my face gave it away because Angelo kept talking. "Obviously not. Well, then, I'm sure you'll figure it out."

"That's it?"

Angelo merely shrugged. "I don't know this Roux as well as you do. I can only tell you what I would do if I had to convince you to do something."

I waited but he didn't say anything. "And?" I prompted. "Throw me a rope here."

"I would tell you that you couldn't do it." He was getting a bit of a hot chocolate mustache, which looked hilarious on him. "What if I told you that you wouldn't be able to crack a safe? What would you do?"

"Learn how to crack it, then crack it," I admitted. "As fast as I could."

"Well, then, there you have it. Roux and you sound very similar. Let me know how it works out."

"We sound similar? Really?"

"Very much so, yes. Witty, talented, and in need of a friend." He patted the top of my head and neatly balanced his empty cup on top of an already overflowing trash can. "Let me know if you need any costume ideas." He gestured to his pinstripe navy suit. "I can be quite dapper."

"So are penguins!" I yelled as he disappeared around the corner, but I wasn't sure if he heard me. It was probably for the best if he didn't.

CHAPTER 7

On Thursday morning, I waited for Roux to find me. I'm not a patient person, as you can imagine. I hate waiting. My dad always says that I would be terrible on a stakeout and could probably never work for the FBI. I replied that I couldn't work for the FBI because of that whole Luxembourg thing, much less my lack of patience.

Anyway, waiting. I hate it.

And waiting for Roux was even worse. If my reverse psychology plan didn't work, then I'd be stuck going to Jesse Oliver's party by myself, and it'd be nearly impossible to snoop around if I didn't have a sidekick to distract everyone else while I dug through personal files and whatnot. By the time third period rolled around and I still hadn't seen Roux, I was convinced that she was out sick, or worse, was trapped under something heavy in her apartment. When I didn't see her by fourth period, I was sure that she had contracted and succumbed to smallpox, all within a twenty-four-hour period.

When I finally saw Roux in the courtyard at lunch, I ran over to her and gave her the biggest hug imaginable. "I'm so glad you're alive!" I gasped.

"*Mmmmpphow.*"

"What?" I took a step back.

Roux looked annoyed. "Why are you hugging me?"

"Oh. Sorry." I let go of her and hastily straightened the lapels on her school uniform. She seemed, in a word, displeased. "Sorry, I just didn't see you and I was worried that maybe you were sick or something."

"I am. I was just crushed to death." She smoothed her hair, then shook it out again. "My ribs hurt."

"Sorry," I said again. "Do you need an Ace bandage?"

"Like a hole in the head. What's up?"

I sighed deeply, just like I had practiced in the mirror the night before. "I just wanted to apologize to you."

She frowned. "For what?"

I sighed again and drew a line on the ground with my toe, just like I had seen Roux do when she was so contrite the other day. "Oh, you know, just bugging you about the party. I know it makes you uncomfortable and you probably don't want to go to parties anymore."

"Well, it's not that I don't want to go—"

"And you've probably got better things to do than show me around my first party. I'm sure I can get the hang of things from the other girls there."

She raised an eyebrow. "The other girls? Sweetie, you'll be innocent chum in the shark-infested waters. Remember what I said about dirt? The only thing worse is a person who goes to a party *alone*." She made it sound like being alone was on par with having a bedbug infestation.

"Whatever. I'll survive. Everyone has to go to their first party sometime, right? I'll be making memories that'll last a lifetime." Now I was completely improvising and starting to sound like a bad Hallmark commercial. "Gotta build up that party callus, after all."

"Did you just call it a party *callus*?" Roux looked toward the sky. "Give me strength, you're going to be socially murdered."

"I've survived worse!" I said brightly. "At least we can be social outcasts together!"

"Okay," Roux interrupted me. "I cannot in good faith, or in any sort of faith, let this happen." She put her hand on my arm and sighed. "You owe me *so* big."

"So, does that mean you'll go with me?"

She closed her eyes for a few seconds before answering, "Yes. You're practically a lion cub all alone in the African grasslands. You'll be eaten alive by wild hyenas and—"

"Okay, can we just cool it with all the *Lion King* metaphors about how I'll be murdered?"

"They're actually similes."

"Whatever. So, you'll come with me?"

"Yes. Against all of my better judgment, yes."

"*Yay!*" I leaped into the air, then started to hug her again, but Roux stepped away and put her hand out.

"Whoa, chief," she said. "I'm still bruised from the last time you hugged me."

"Sorry, sorry. I just get excited. This is going to be so much fun! Our first party together!"

"Waaaaaait a minute." Roux crossed her arms and gave me a look. "Did I just get reverse psychology'd into going to this Halloween crapfest?"

"You promised you'd go!"

"I *did* get reverse psychology'd!" she shouted. "I'm such a moron, oh my God!"

"It'll be fun," I promised.

"I'm going to kill you." She glared at me. "And that is *not* a metaphor."

"Simile," I reminded her. "So what's your costume going to be?"

"Someone who's plotting to murder her best friend."

We both stopped short.

"Wait," I said. "I'm your best friend? Really?"

"Well, there aren't exactly a lot of candidates," she admitted. "So don't get all excited."

I could feel the stupid smile already stretching across my face. "I totally accept," I told her. "Maybe we can wear matching costumes, bestie!"

But Roux was already starting to gather her bag and walk across the quad. "You owe me!" she repeated as she walked away. "A lot!"

"Yes, I do," I said. "A lot."

CHAPTER 8

I had the Halloween party lined up for next Friday. I had Roux agreeing to go with me to the party, which was sort of like an early Christmas miracle, and with any luck, she'd cause enough of a ruckus that I could get into Daddy Oliver's office and start snooping around. Things were looking good. I felt good.

And then I realized that I needed a costume. A spy costume.

Here's the thing about dressing as a spy: an authentic spy costume doesn't exist. Yeah, it looks cool in the movies, but when we're working, we dress like everyone else. I mean, can you imagine? You're just walking down the street and you see a guy creeping around wearing a trench coat, hat, and night-vision goggles. C'mon. Chances are you're looking at either a conspiracy theorist or a terrible accessorizer, not a spy.

Basically, I had no idea what to wear. The last time I dressed up for Halloween, I was a four-year-old ghost, and all you need for that costume is a sheet, a pair of scissors, and Band-Aids for your knees after tripping over the sheet every six feet. (Totally not bitter, though. Scarred, but not bitter.)

On Friday morning before school, I did some searching online for spy Halloween costumes, if only to get some ideas about what I was supposed to wear. The first costume that popped up involved way more latex than looked comfortable, and the second costume came with a push-up bra and garters. Another website suggested that I wear a sleek ballgown or better, a belly-dancing outfit.

Two minutes later, I was still laughing hysterically. "What's so funny?" my dad yelled from the kitchen.

"Nothing!" I yelled back as I started deleting my browser history. "Do people really wear these things?" I asked the computer. "How are you supposed to run in these outfits? It's like how Wonder Woman always saves the day in hot pants and a bustier. Give me a freaking break." The computer, of course, didn't have a response, so I kept searching. "Stupid Halloween," I muttered.

I thought about my costume all day, even consulting Roux in the hallway before her French class. "So what are you wearing tonight?" I asked her as she shoved books into her locker and pulled out new ones.

"You're looking at it," she said. "I'm going as an outcast. I told you."

"No, seriously."

"No, seriously. What are *you* wearing? Do you want to borrow my costume from last year? I was a cheerleader."

I couldn't picture Roux cheering for anything. "Does it involve a crazy push-up bra or something?"

"Of course. Why else would you wear a cheerleader costume if your boobs aren't going to look good?" She glanced into the classroom to see if anyone was in there yet. They weren't, of course. We were all standing just outside, waiting for the final bell. I learned on my first day that only the nerdiest of nerds went into class before the bell.

"Oh, dear Jesus," Roux said, turning back to me, "please tell me you're not going as, like, a pioneer girl or an extra from *Little House on the Prairie*."

"No, no, I'm allergic to calico." She didn't get the joke, so I moved on. "Anyway, I already told Jesse Oliver—"

"Why do you always say that? I know who you're talking about if you just say 'Jesse.'"

"I don't know, it's weird! I can't help it. Anyway, I told Jesse Ol— I told him that I was going as a spy."

"Oooh, sexy." Roux wiggled her eyebrows at me. "A catsuit for sure."

"It's entirely too impractical," I replied without thinking.

"What?"

"It's entirely too uncomfortable. So now I don't know what to wear."

"Well, sister friend, you're on your own. Get a fedora or a trench coat—a sexy trench coat—or something like that. Best of luck." She patted me on the shoulder and strolled down the hall to class while I stood there and tried to figure out what a sexy trench coat would even look like.

Finally, that night, I managed to pull together a costume.

I put on black jeans and a black turtleneck, then found a Burberry trench coat in the back of my closet that could only have come from Angelo. I wasn't sure if it was sexy, but the label would probably count for something. I added a pair of binoculars around my neck and some dark sunglasses, then added a fedora that I found at a thrift shop on Crosby Street.

It wasn't a belly-dancing costume, but it was better than nothing.

My parents were in the kitchen when I came out, blueprints of floor plans opened on the table in front of them. "Oh, good, you're here," my mom said. "This is the Olivers' house. Here, look."

I glanced down at the mess of lines and numbers. Even on paper, the house looked huge, four stories with wide staircases linking them together. "Wowsa," I said. "Nice digs. How come we never get to stay in places like this? I want a mansion next time we move."

My parents ignored me. "We think this is his bedroom here," my dad said, pointing toward a space on the fourth floor. "There's a cutout in the wall—are you looking? You're not looking."

"I'm looking, I'm looking. Cutout at the end of the hall in the room on the left. Got it." My fedora was starting to make my head itch.

My mom was tracing an exit path with her finger. "There's a balcony off the second floor. If you get stuck, go out here and signal for Angelo."

"What?" I cried. "No! No way! I don't need a chaperone! I've never had one before!"

"Yes, but this is your first party and there's no adult supervision and—"

"No, no, no, *no*. And frankly, I'm insulted." I crossed my arms over my chest, but the trench coat was a bit tight so I dropped them back down to my sides. "If I get stuck, I'll do what I always do, which is get myself unstuck. Remember when we were in Buenos Aires and that one guy broke into the hotel room? I got out of that situation just fine."

"Yes, and it took ten years off my life." My mother sighed. She doesn't like to talk about Buenos Aires. Things got a little wonky during that assignment. Mixed signals and such. Occupational hazard; it happens.

"I'll be fine. The worst that can happen is that someone gets drunk and pukes on me. Which would be *terrible*," I added, "but not dangerous."

"Well, Armand is in Los Angeles on business—"

"Lucky duck," I said. "When do we get to go back to LA?"

"Maggie, honey, please focus," my dad said. "Armand's in Los Angeles, but there are probably a few housekeepers, butlers—"

"Do you think they have a butler named Jeeves?"

"Maggie."

"Sorry, okay, focusing." I tend to get a rush of adrenaline before going into an assignment, and now that there was my first official high school party on top of everything else, it sort of felt like my veins and arteries were exploding.

"Do you see this?" my mother said, pointing to what looked like a long hallway. "This is an elevator." She looked up and glared at me. "You do not use it. You do not even think about getting into it."

"Fine, fine, okay. No elevators. I'm a Luddite tonight."

My dad was about to say something else, but then he stopped and frowned. "What's your costume supposed to be?"

"Is that a Burberry trench coat?" my mom asked. "I told Angelo, no designer labels."

"Yes, and I'm going as a spy. It's a long story, but don't worry, I've got it covered."

Both of my parents' faces went blank. "A spy?" my dad said.

"Yes. Is that okay?" Maybe I should have checked first.

My mom was the first one to burst out laughing. "Is that how people think spies dress?" she howled. "Oh my goodness, this is hysterical!"

"The fedora!" my dad cried, collapsing in laughter next to her. "Are those binoculars? Tell me you're not wearing night-vision goggles, too!"

"Stop! My sides hurt!" My mom was laughing so hard that tears gathered in the corners of her eyes.

"I hope you realize how damaging this is for a teenager's self-esteem." I glared at them. "But no, go ahead and laugh at me. It's cool."

"I'm sorry, sweetheart," my mom said, now wiping her eyes. "You look adorable."

In a world of push-up bras, garter belts, and potential belly-dancing costumes, "adorable" wasn't exactly what I was going for. "So do I look like a spy or not?"

"You look like someone who has never been a spy, trying to dress as a spy." My dad's face was red, a sure sign that he was trying not to laugh any more than he already had. He's terrible at hiding his emotions. That's why he always does the behind-the-scenes work.

"Well, good, that's what I wanted." I belted my trench coat, then made sure that people could still see my binoculars.

"You're like a cuter version of Kojak," my dad told me.

"Who-jack?"

He just shook his head. "You have no appreciation for the classics."

"Can I go now, please? Roux's meeting me on the corner and I'm going to be late."

"What time is the party?"

"Roux said that parties just sort of start. There's no time." I left out the part where I asked Roux if I should RSVP to the party for both of us or for just me, and she stared at me for a full minute before asking if I had been raised in a barn.

"And where's the safe again?" My mom straightened my hat and I pushed it back.

"Fourth-floor bedroom. Have a little faith in my memory skills."

"Fine. Love you."

"Love you, too. And tell Angelo to stay away!"

Roux and I had agreed to meet on the corner at eight thirty, and the streets were already full of people in costumes. I knew there was a parade over in the West Village, but it seemed like the parade was everywhere in the city. I even passed another trench-coated and fedora'd "spy," and he tipped his hat to me as we passed each other.

Roux was in front of the Dean & Deluca on Broadway, wearing sparkly devil horns and looking a little wobbly. She seemed small surrounded by the hustle and bustle of the street, but when she saw me, she lit up and gave me the biggest smile that I've ever seen her give.

"I'm the devil!" she cried. "Look! Horns! Like a bull!" She mimed trying to stampede me.

Oh no.

"Are you drunk?" I whispered. "Seriously?"

"I'm *happy*," she said. "Drunks are sloppy. I'm *happy*. And why are you whispering? Hey, are those binoculars?" She grabbed them from around my neck and looked through the larger lens. "Whoooa, you're so far away! Hi, Maggie!" She waved in front of my face as I grabbed them back from her.

"Are you crazy?" I snapped. "You could get arrested for public drunkenness."

"On Halloween in New York? C'mon. And there is no way that I was going to this party sober. If I'm lucky, I won't remember *anything*." She wobbled in her platform heels, which sent her devil horns a bit askew.

"Just stand here." I propped her up against the wall and left her ogling the Dean & Deluca cheese display in the window while I recalculated. Sober Roux would already be enough work, but drunk Roux? I would have to keep my eye on her the entire night, which meant that I couldn't get into the office and look for the safe.

"If I ever have a daughter, I'm going to name her Brie." Roux sounded dreamy about it.

If I didn't act fast, then this was going to be worse than the hotel room in Buenos Aires.

"Okay, look at me," I said, then grabbed Roux by the shoulders so we could make eye contact. "Here's the deal. You're going to sober up right now."

She started giggling. "It doesn't work that way, silly!"

She had a point.

"Listen. We're going to get you some coffee and some water. We're going to Poland Spring you back to sobriety, and then? We are *going* to the party."

Her eyes sort of looked like whirligigs. "Can we get some cheese, too?"

Thirty minutes, two bottles of water, a double espresso, and a wedge of Brie later, we were standing in front of Jesse Oliver's townhouse on Warren Street. "I might have to puke up all these cheesy calories later," she said as she continued to eat the cheese with her fingers. "Kidding," she said quickly when I narrowed my eyes at her. "Upper East Side humor."

"Not funny," I told her. I had been nervous before, sure, but never like this. Not only did I have to sneak into an office, find a safe, and figure out how to break into it, but I also had to make sure that Roux didn't end up with alcohol poisoning and that Jesse Oliver never noticed I was snooping through his dad's stuff.

"Mmm, cheese," Roux slurred next to me.

What could possibly go wrong?

CHAPTER 9

I need to stop here to explain something: Jesse Oliver didn't just live in a loft. He didn't even live in a brownstone or anything else.

No, Jesse Oliver and his family lived in *a house that was on top of a six-story building.*

"Someone dropped a house on Jesse's house," I told Roux, trying to look up so I could see more of it. Even from six stories down, the house seemed white and massive.

"Oh, yeah, that," Roux said, then held out her hand toward me. "Want some Brie?"

"I'm good to go on dairy, thanks." I looked skyward again. "Who lives up there, the Wicked Witch of the West?"

Roux wrinkled her nose at me. "What?"

"You know, when the house dropped from the sky, goes boom on the witch . . ."

"Are you sure you're not drunk, too? Anyway, whatever. Jesse lives there."

"Seriously?"

She hiccupped a little. "Yep."

"Wow. Okay, then." I straightened my fedora for the eighty-fifth time, then turned to Roux. "Are you ready?"

"Of course not. Why do you think I got drunk?"

I was about to respond to her when I saw a familiar figure in the bookshop on the ground floor of Jesse's building. "Oh, you have *got* to be kidding me," I muttered, then shoved Roux toward the front door. "Wait for me inside," I told her. "My phone's buzzing, I have to answer it."

"But—"

"I'll be there in a sec."

"When did you get so bossy?" I heard her ask just as the door closed behind her.

I mimed taking my phone out of my pocket and answering it, but as soon as Roux was out of sight, I stormed into the bookstore and found Angelo in the rare-edition section of the store. It wasn't hard to spot him: he was the only man in a ten-block radius wearing a three-piece suit. Everyone else must have thought he was in costume, but I knew that for Angelo, a three-piece suit was casual Friday wear.

"Do you *mind*?" I asked him.

He turned with a smile on his face and a book in his hand. "Don't you just adore bookstores?" he asked me. "The smell of old paper and new ideas thrills me every time."

"That's great. Are you spying on me?" I asked him. "Really? Have you sunk *that* low?"

He was trying to hide an even bigger smile, I could tell. "How ironic that you asked me if *I'm* spying on *you*."

I waved to cut him off. "You know what I mean. Come on, Angelo, it's a party, not an assassination. I can handle this."

"Your friend appears to be having quite a time already." Now he wasn't even hiding his smile.

"Okay, yes, Roux's three sheets to the wind, but it doesn't matter. I'll shove her in a coat closet if I have to. I'm sixteen, I'm going to a party, and I'm going to do my job. It happens."

Angelo, of course, feigned innocence. "I don't know what you're talking about, my love. I was just perusing the first editions—have you read Agatha Christie? Oh, you must, I insist. Intrigue, our favorite thing—when you interrupted my browsing."

Sometimes Angelo is so calm that it sends my blood pressure through the roof.

"Just . . . please stay away, okay?" I asked him. "The only people in the house are drunk teenagers and a butler named Jeeves."

"Really?"

"Possibly. It's like the kindergarten version of assignments."

Angelo raised a knowing eyebrow and shrugged. "Let's come to an agreement. You go to your party, I browse at my leisure?"

"Agreed." I started to flounce out of the store, but turned around halfway and went back to him. "Hey. Thanks for not listening to my mom and getting me this coat."

He merely winked and went back to his book.

By the time I caught up with Roux in the lobby of the building, she was more sober . . . and more impatient. "Sorry, parents," I said, patting my phone in my pocket. "They get nervous."

"Gee, how hard your life must be."

Yes, Roux was definitely sobering up.

There was a private elevator that led directly into the front lobby of the Olivers' apartment, and when the doors opened up, I almost fell over at the view. Every wall seemed to be made of glass, showing a near 360-degree panorama of the Manhattan skyline outside, and in addition to that, there seemed to be a lot of people in the room as well. It was quite possible that every Manhattan teenager was attending the Halloween party.

"Oh, Christ, everyone's here," Roux said under her breath, and I had to lean in to hear her. "Word must have got out," she explained.

I was starting to feel warm, way too warm in my turtleneck, hat, and trench coat. And that was exactly the problem: only a few people were in costume.

Time to reassess.

I took off the hat and immediately crushed it up in my hand, then pulled off my coat and hung it in the front closet because I planned on forgetting it later. I might need an excuse to get back into the Oliver house and coming back for my coat was plausible, and I wasn't going to leave it crumpled up on a couch so someone could spill beer on it. Burberry plaid, hello.

Roux gave me the eye when she saw my turtleneck and

jeans. "I thought you said you weren't wearing a catsuit," she said.

"It's a turtleneck," I told her. "Totally different animal."

She gave me a knowing look, but all she said was, "I wonder where Jesse is." She seemed to be getting more tense as she led me into the kitchen, which was probably one of the largest kitchens I had ever seen. There was no food, but a ton of wine bottles and alcohol littering the marble countertops. "Seriously?" I said. "Not even carrots and dip or something?"

"What?" Roux yelled. She had to, the music was loud and pounding. I suspected it was the kind of music that sounded better when drunk.

"Is there food?" I yelled back.

"Looks like a liquid diet tonight," Roux said with an exaggerated wink, then immediately grabbed a bottle of red off the countertop and took a swig, not even waiting for a glass. The label was French and I assumed that it was as expensive as everything in the house seemed to be. "Uh, do you want a glass?" I asked her. "Maybe a Dixie cup?"

"Nope!" she said, wiping her mouth a little. "Tastes better when it's direct from the source!"

We wandered out of the kitchen to come face-to-face with a huge stainless steel staircase. It spiralled upward through three more floors and just looking at it gave me vertigo. I wish I hadn't promised not to use the elevator. Just as I was about to say something to Roux, a kid dressed as a ninja suddenly came leaping toward the stairs, and even though I couldn't see his face, it was obvious that he was drunk.

Sure enough, he tried to jump over the railing, but he lost his footing and sort of dangled for a second, before falling several feet to the marble floor. It was so noisy that only a few people noticed, but Roux saw and she shook her head in disgust. "Ugh," she said as he peeled himself off the floor in a daze. "Worst. Ninja. *Ever.*"

She wandered off with her wine bottle, and I really wanted to follow her just to make sure she didn't end up crumpled in a bathtub somewhere, but I had a job to do. Roux was a big girl, she would just have to take care of herself.

It didn't stop me from feeling a little guilty, though, as I left her behind.

As I wandered into the center of the house, I recognized a few faces from school, but hardly anyone even acknowledged me, which was awesome. The fewer people who remembered seeing me there, the better. Still, it was hard to move through the crowd and I found myself throwing a few inconspicuous elbows just so I could clear a path through the human sea.

After elbowing Batman out of the way and fending off the inappropriate advances of Spider-Man ("No, I don't want to be caught in your human web, gross"), I made it back over to the huge stainless-steel staircase and started to climb. Halfway up, I heard a crash and prayed that Roux wasn't bleeding from an arterial wound somewhere in the foyer. What had I been thinking, making her come with me? She was a disaster, so drunk that she looked like a broken marionette. I had never had such a liability before, and I swore that as soon as this job was over, I was never going to have another friend ever ag—

"Do you always talk to yourself?"

Jesse was standing at the landing of the stairs, smiling down at me. "Let me guess," he said. "Multiple personality disorder."

"Excuse me?"

"Your costume."

I knew I should have taken the elevator.

"I'm a spy," I told him, wondering if I could shove him down the stairs and make it look like a tragic accident. "No multiple personalities yet," I added, and then wondered if having twelve different passports totally refuted that statement.

"Oh, that's *riiiiiight*," Jesse said, leaning against the silver banister. "Spy girl. I remember you. How's it going?"

"Just ducky," I said. "Halloweening it up, you know." I glanced past him and saw that the rooms upstairs were fairly calm, as compared to the near-riot of people downstairs.

"Did you just make Halloween a verb?"

"Poetic license," I shot back, even though the thought of Jesse discussing verbs was enough to make me hate him a little less. "What are you supposed to be?"

He stood back a little and showed me his tuxedo, his tumbler half-filled with ice and what looked like scotch, the toy gun tucked underneath his jacket. "I'm James Bond," he said.

This was all becoming a little too meta for me, but I guess Jesse took my surprise for disdain. "Sorry, that was really cheesy." He grinned, and I was totally not admiring his smile and his nice dimples and, my God, it was really warm in this house.

"It's okay," I told him. "Hey, is there a bathroom up here?"

He pointed vaguely over his shoulder. "There's a few up there, but they're all taken by people making out." He wiggled his eyebrows at me before cracking himself up. "Sorry, that was really cheesy, too. Did you just get here?"

"Um, yeah." My opinion of Jesse seemed to be changing every three seconds. He knows about verbs? He has a nice smile? He doesn't take himself too seriously? Our dossiers really needed to start including this kind of information. "I came with a friend."

"Oh yeah? Who's your friend?"

"Roux?" I said it like a question on purpose, just in case Roux did something that made us all end up in court. I wasn't going to jail for that drunk muppet, that was for sure.

"Roux? Are you serious? She's here?" Jesse looked down the stairs. "Holy shit, she's brave."

"Yeah, well, she's a big girl." I climbed the stairs so that Jesse and I were both on the landing.

"Is she drunk?"

"I'll give you one guess."

Jesse sighed a little. "I better go lock the wine cellar. Last Halloween she drank an entire bottle of '72 Bordeaux.

I thought my dad's head was going to explode. He takes his wine seriously."

It sounded like Roux and Armand had something in common, but I filed the information away for safekeeping. I wasn't above drugging someone's glass of Pinot Noir to get access to his files.

"Yeah, you go lock that wine thing," I said, patting him on the shoulder. "I'm gonna wait in line for the bathroom. Say hi to Q for me."

"Wait, so you're not even going to tell me your name?"

"You're the secret agent," I told him. "Figure it out."

I climbed the stairs until I couldn't go any higher, finally reaching locked double doors. "Why, hello," I said softly, then found the bobby pin that I had stashed in my hair for such an occasion. I straightened the pin and slid it into the lock, then wiggled it around. Usually when I pick a lock, it can cause a racket, but the music was a perfect distraction. I probably could have used dynamite to blow open the doors and no one would have noticed, that's how loud it was.

I felt the lock click into place a minute later and the French doors opened to reveal plush carpeting and dark wood walls. I crept in and shut the doors behind me before calling, "Hello? Is there a bathroom here?" I knew that my parents had placed Armand in Los Angeles, but there could easily be a wife or a mistress or a boyfriend or, I don't know, Max, that crazy friendly golden retriever, lurking somewhere upstairs. I wasn't taking any chances.

The coast was clear, though, and I locked the doors

behind me before pulling leather gloves out of my pocket and putting them on. "Game on," I whispered, then got to work.

The entire upstairs was a master suite, I soon realized, including a huge bathroom with a Jacuzzi tub and a skylight in the massive closet that revealed a clear, empty sky overhead. The Icelandic nights had been so light, and I still wasn't used to New York's darker heavens. It was nice to see the moon again.

I could feel the party pulsing under my feet as I prowled the huge walk-in closet. I was pretty sure that the closet was the size of our temporary loft in Soho and easily twice the size of our house in Reykjavík. Surely big enough for a safe, right?

Wrong.

The cutout that my parents had showed me on the blueprints turned out to be nonexistent in the actual house. I started shoving clothes aside, moving shoes and feeling the walls, checking the edges of the carpet to see if it would pull up and reveal a floor safe. Nothing. My heart was starting to pound in time with the music and I wished I wasn't wearing a turtleneck. How was I supposed to get anything done when I was being strangled by my own clothes?

"Shit, shit, *shit*," I whispered to myself as I felt the wall behind a tie rack. Jesse already knew I was at the party. What if he was wondering where I was? Time was always of the essence, but especially when people were looking for you. *Especially* then.

A few minutes later, I realized that the closet was a waste of time. There was nothing in there, no safe, nothing but socks and ties and men's shoes, all of which looked really uncomfortable. I moved back into the bedroom, looking behind artwork that was probably worth several million dollars, dropping to my knees to glance around a dresser that was too heavy to move.

Nothing.

Five minutes later, I left the room frustrated and empty-handed. I hate when I can't find the damn safe. I *hate* it. It's my job, the one thing I know how to do, and when it's not there, it's like *I'm* not there.

The party was still raging, though, and it seemed to have only got more crowded. Roux was nowhere in sight and I only saw the top of Jesse's curly head as it disappeared around a corner. Everyone else was a stranger, and I had a rare moment of self-pity when I thought that I should have just stayed home and read a book instead. Angelo could rappel himself into the house later.

I was just trying to figure out which window I could open that would make it easier for Angelo when I heard the fight. I didn't know it was a fight at the time, though. I just thought it was one girl screaming a lot. And then I heard the name "Roux" and immediately followed the noise into the library.

The library.

Oh my God, I'm an idiot, I thought. And apparently my parents were useless at reading blueprints. Libraries had shelves, empty books, plenty of room for hidden safes galore!

I canceled my mental image of Angelo ziplining in through the window.

The fight, however, was still going. Roux was backed against one row of books, half-ready to tip over, looking angry and sad at the same time. "You know what you did!" another girl screamed at her. I recognized her as Julia, the jilted girlfriend whose ex-boyfriend had slept with Roux.

Hoo boy.

"He didn't even like you anymore!" Roux said, her words slurring together. "He liked me! He was gonna break up with you!"

"Lying bitch!" Julia yelled back, and oh my God, I was at a high school party and there was alcohol and an actual girl fight. When did my life turn into a movie?

Everyone watching took a collective breath when Julia busted out the word "bitch." Apparently that's a fighting word in Manhattan private schools. Roux's red sequined horns were askew on top of her head, but she seemed to be breathing fire, just like a bull, just like she had said when I first met up with her that night.

"Ask him!" Roux shouted, and pointed toward one of the dopiest-looking guys I had ever seen in my life. His eyes were red-rimmed and he had a smile that seemed to suggest he had been stoned for the past six years. He was still wearing his school uniform, and I would bet a hundred bucks that he was one of those teenagers who went trick-or-treating as "a teenager."

They were fighting over *this* clown? Now I had seen everything.

"Jake?" Julia said, crossing her arms and looking over at Stoner Boy. "Is it true? Who did you like better, babe?"

Babe? *They were still together?* Jake cheated on Julia and she took him back? If this were a TV show, I would have been recording every single episode on my DVR. And judging from the crowd in the room, I wasn't the only one who felt that way.

(And Jake and Julia? Really? It was so matchy-matchy that I wanted to gag.)

Jake looked like a deer that had just woken up to find a hunter's gun pointing at him. "Uh," he said, and Roux managed to roll her eyes a little at his denseness. But then she bit her lip and looked at Jake, and it was suddenly so obvious.

Roux was still in love with him.

Julia looked ready to turn Jake inside out using only her menacing stare, so he answered quickly. "You, babe." He smiled at her. "Jules, I *told* you, Roux didn't mean anything. She was a mistake. She meant *nothing*."

I looked at Roux when he said that and immediately wished I hadn't. Roux looked like she had been slapped, her mouth twitching before it smoothed back to her normal, neutral expression. "There you go, Julia," she said. "He's all yours."

"Damn right," Julia replied, then threw her arms around Jake's neck as the crowd started to disperse. Roux stayed standing next to one of the bookcases, but her knuckles were white against the mahogany wood.

"Roux," I started to say when I was close to her.

"What?" She sighed. "Just . . . what."

I had no idea what I was going to say, but before I could even think of something, Roux interrupted me. "He's an asshole," she said.

"Yes," I said. Agreeing seemed to be easiest.

"A really big asshole."

"Absolutely."

"I hope he gets hit by a giant truck and they can't even peel him off the street because he's so flat." Her words were slurring again, but I think that's what she said.

"And then flattened again by a steamroller," I said, then added "flattened a *lot*" for good measure.

Roux was starting to sink down against the wall, and she pulled a plaster head of some ancient Greek god down with her. "I'm just going to stay here and sulk with my new Roman friend," she said.

"I think he's Greek."

"God, Maggie, *really*? You want to play 'Guess the Ancestry' right now?"

"Sorry," I said. "Sorry, I'm a jerk. But not as big a jerk as Jake."

"Yeah." Roux sniffled. "You can't spell 'jerk' without 'Jake,' righ—? Oh, wait. Yes, you can. Never mind."

She was quite a sight, red horns slipping closer to her forehead as she cuddled the Greek (no way was that thing Roman) head close to her. I sat down next to her, unsure of what to do or say. I had never been in love before, and I had never, ever seen a fight over a guy before. What were the rules here? Were we supposed to eat chocolate now? Maybe

Jesse's mom had some contraband Hershey bars stashed in her nightstand. I couldn't find a safe, but I could damn well track down some Halloween candy.

"He used to be really nice." Roux sighed. "He said a lot of things. . . ." She trailed off, her eyes filling with tears.

"Oh, no! Please don't cry!" I told her. "Roux, c'mon, you said it yourself. He's an asshole."

"I'm going to be alone for the rest of my life!"

"You're not even seventeen!"

"That just makes it worse!" She wiped her nose on her sleeve and sniffled again. "The only guy who will ever love me is Caesar here."

"Well . . ." I tried to find something to say. "At least he died nobly."

Roux looked at me and for a minute I thought she was going to start yelling again, but then she giggled. "You are so weird!"

"Says the demon girl who's snuggling with Caesar's head!" I protested, but I was giggling, too. "This party sucks."

"It so sucks," Roux said, agreeing. "They always do, though. Getting ready for the party is the best part of the party. It's all downhill after." Her gaze drifted from Caesar toward the bookshelves. "That picture sucks, too. It's ugly."

"Totally," I said. It was a framed picture in the middle of two bookcases, a sailboat on choppy seas, an obvious Winslow Homer knockoff. Even the frame looked cheap, and I was pretty sure that Armand Oliver didn't do anything cheap.

"I need more wine," Roux announced next to me, wiping the leftover tears from her face. "Right now. Garçon!"

"Um, are you sure?"

She just waved away my concerns as she struggled to her feet, Caesar bouncing to the ground when she dropped him. "I'm fine," she said. "Don't be a worrywart PTA mom, okay? It's not cool. Be cool. Where's that happy wine land from last year?"

Wait a minute.

Why did Caesar's head just bounce? That thing was made of plaster, right? Plaster should shatter or at least just fall, not bounce.

"Found it!" Roux cried, and apparently Jesse hadn't locked the wine storage yet because Roux disappeared down the hall, followed by several other people. I didn't have time to chase her, though, because I realized that I had found the safe.

I scrambled to my feet and grabbed the bust off the ground. It was surprisingly light in my hands, plastic instead of plaster, and I found the nearly invisible hinge at the back of his head. When I opened it up, I saw the key sitting inside.

I had to hand it to Armand, he knew how to make a job challenging.

I fished it out and put Caesar back on his pedestal, then hurried over to that ugly sailboat painting. I was right, Armand didn't do anything cheap. And this wasn't a cheap picture, it was a secret safe.

There was no one in the library, but I moved fast and

quick, just like I had been trained. I lifted the picture off the wall and sure enough, it was one of those safes hidden behind a painting. They're notoriously easy to open, even without the key. All it needs is a four-digit code, and most people don't get creative enough.

But it didn't matter. I had the key.

The back of the painting came shooting out when I turned the key in the lock, revealing shelves that looked like they belonged in a medicine cabinet. There was a flash drive on the bottom shelf and I grabbed it.

"Where's that Bordeaux?" I heard Roux yelling, but she sounded far away. *She's fine*, I told myself as I hid the flash drive in the front pocket of my jeans. The party was still raging just outside the library, and I knew that anyone could come walking in at any minute, see me standing there with a painting and a broken plastic head, and ask what I was doing.

Ten seconds later, the safe was back on the wall and Caesar was back on his pedestal. I had done it. I had the files. I could leave.

"There you are," Jesse said when he saw me come out of the library. "What are you, a bookworm?"

"That was last year's costume," I said. I was feeling magnanimous toward him, now that I had incriminating evidence that would probably ruin his dad's big story and possibly his dad's big magazine, too. I wondered if they would lose their apartment, or if Jesse would have to leave school. Would he end up homeless?

My elation at finding the safe was starting to ebb. I

wasn't used to seeing the people involved in the case. Usually it was just me, some combination locks, and maybe a few fancy keys if the safe was doubly secured. But now I was looking at Jesse and he seemed kind of drunk and pretty happy and all I could think was, *I am so, so sorry.*

"I like books," I told him now, glancing at the safe to make sure that it was hung straight on the wall. "Are some of these yours?"

"Nah, my dad's. Some are my mom's, though." He pointed to an old-looking title up on the top shelf. "First edition of *The Great Gatsby*. That was . . . That's her favorite."

"Why is that everyone's favorite?" I said. "Has *nobody* read *Tender Is the Night*? It's so annoying."

And then I realized that I had just insulted Jesse's mother's taste.

"Not that *Gatsby* is bad." I backtracked. "I mean, it's fine. I mean . . ."

Jesse was watching me with a little half smile that was becoming less annoying by the minute. "Do you want something to drink?"

Believe it or not, I've had wine before. I may have been raised in the insular world of international spies, but in Europe, they're cool with kids having wine. Still, there's a huge difference between your mother giving you the eagle eye while you sip half a glass of champagne, and a cute boy—I mean, a guy I was assigned to—offering you something in a red plastic cup at a Halloween party.

And I mean, c'mon, I'm supposed to blend in, right?

Right.

"I'll have what you're having."

He raised an eyebrow. "You want apple juice?"

"That's not scotch?"

He tipped his glass toward me so I could see into it. "Can you keep the secret?"

I just smiled. "I'll do my best," I said.

CHAPTER 10

Half an hour later, I knew a lot about Jesse.

He hated *Gatsby*, too, but not as much as he hated *The Catcher in the Rye*. He hadn't had a drink since his dad got sober last year. His favorite color was blue, and his dog, Max, the same one that had tried to lick me to death, was sleeping upstairs in his bedroom, blissfully oblivious to the racket that was happening around us.

"Then why did you throw this party?" I said. We were sitting on the massive steel staircase, shifting every time people walked around us. "I mean, if you don't drink and your dog doesn't like crowds."

He shrugged. "I dunno. People expect it. And when people expect you to do something . . ."

"You do it," I finished, understanding all too well what he meant. "Does anyone else know that you're totally sober right now?"

"Just you," he said, then clinked his glass against my plastic cup. "And besides, I thought if I threw a party, you might show up."

I immediately choked on my water and Jesse whacked me on the back. "You okay?"

"Ow. That's not very helpful," I sputtered.

"Sorry."

"It's okay." I wiped my mouth with my sleeve. (Somewhere, Angelo was clutching his heart and wincing.) "Okay, help me understand this. You threw a party?"

"Obviously."

I made a face at him. "You threw a party that you wanted me to attend?"

"Another secret out of the bag."

"And you didn't even bother to *invite* me? Are guys always like this?"

"Um. Kind of?"

I threw my hands into the air. "This is why the world's a mess!" I yelled. "Because no one can just say what they want to say!"

"I think that's a John Mayer song," Jesse pointed out.

"It is not. And don't change the subject. Why didn't you just invite me?"

Jesse looked around the room, probably praying that Roux would storm through it, doing her best whirling dervish impression, and get him off the hook. "Well, I mean, it's not like *anyone* was invited. People just sort of show up."

"But what if I didn't show up? What if I stayed home and handed out candy or played Angry Birds instead?"

"You like Angry Birds? What's your score?"

"Stop changing the subject!"

Jesse just started to laugh, though. "Were you an

interrogator in a past life? Calm down, everything worked out. You're here, I'm here, it's all good."

I took a deep breath and leaned against the (really uncomfortable, oh my God, who designed this place?) stair railing. "It's not going to be all good for Roux tomorrow," I pointed out, "but wait. Why didn't you say anything?"

Jesse shrugged and ran his hand through his hair in a way that was not adorable or charming. At all. "Well, um, you're kind of intimidating?"

I was definitely intimidating, but not for any reason that Jesse Oliver would or should know about. "What do you mean?"

"Well, in class you're always taking notes . . . and frowning?"

"Are you asking me or telling me?"

"See?" Jesse protested. "You're really argumentative, too."

(Is it weird that hearing him use a polysyllabic word gave me butterflies? Yes, that's weird. Forget I said anything.)

"But it's kind of cute," he continued. "You always get this little wrinkle when you're taking notes." He scrunched up his forehead in what was apparently an imitation of my notetaking face.

The butterflies had quickly turned into a teeming mass of electric eels, and I felt the heat creep into my cheeks. This was the first job I had ever had that made me blush. I didn't even know I *could* blush! "Oh, um, okay. Thank you?"

"Are you asking me or telling me?" Jesse cracked up even as I swatted at his hair. "Hey, watch the 'do!"

"Don't make fun of me!" I cried. "No one's ever called me cute before! I don't know what I'm supposed to say."

He kept smirking in his smirky way. "Do you always know what to say?"

I did.

And that was the problem.

But before I could say anything, right or wrong, I heard a commotion coming from the media room. Roux had got her hands on a red Rhone blend and had retreated there to watch a movie by herself.

And judging from the noise, apparently the movie had ended.

"Does Roux always drink like this?" I asked Jesse. "Or is it just a holiday thing?"

"It's a party thing. Ever since we were twelve."

"*Twelve*? Does she still have a liver?"

"Well, to be fair, she hasn't really been at any parties lately. You know, the whole . . ." He waved his hand toward the library where the huge confrontation had taken place between Roux and Julia.

"Yeah, she told me all about that. I think she feels really bad about it."

Jesse glanced at me. "I think she's glad to have a friend again."

I nodded. "Can I ask you a question?"

"Shoot."

"Bang."

"You are *such* a dork."

"Am not. But it's about Roux and Julia and that dude."

Jesse snorted. "You mean Loser Jake?"

"*Thank* you!" I said. "The whole time they were arguing over him, I was just, like, '*Really?*'"

"He's a tool. He cheats on Julia practically every week. But Roux used to be her best friend, so I guess that got everyone all upset."

"So why does Julia stay with him?"

"Who knows?"

"Ridiculous," I said. "So damn ridiculous."

The commotion in the media room was getting louder, and I was pretty sure I could hear someone singing "Tomorrow" from the musical *Annie*, someone who sounded a lot like a drunk Roux.

I looked over at Jesse. "Please don't tell me . . ."

"Oh, yes."

"Oh, no."

"Who doesn't love karaoke?" he asked.

"I'll give you twenty bucks if you go shoot her with a tranquilizer dart."

"I'll do it for ten," he said. "Holiday sale."

By the time we got the media room, there was a circle of people around Roux, who was clearly having a grand old time with the family karaoke machine. (And nowhere in the research did it say that Armand Oliver enjoyed a nice round of karaoke, by the way. That would have been good to know.)

"Maggie!" Roux cried when she saw me. "This song is such a *metaphor* for *life*!"

Jesse nudged me. "Don't you wanna go do orphan backup?" He grinned.

"After you, Daddy Warbucks." Then I turned to Roux. "Roux, honey, this isn't pretty."

"I *knoooow*," she said. She had the microphone in one hand and the empty wine bottle in the other. "But the sun, Maggie? The sun is going to come out! Tomorrow!" She pointed the wine bottle at me. "And do you know what kind of life it is?"

"A hard-knock one," I answered. "Too easy."

"Does she take requests?" Jesse asked, then ducked out of my reach.

"That's exactly it!" Roux said. "Oh my God, where has this song been all my life?" She pressed a button and started the song again.

To be fair, even though she was drunk and barely able to stand, Roux didn't have a bad voice. Her singing voice was actually beautiful, and she managed to hit every note even while slurring the lyrics. "This song is annoying," Jesse muttered. "We get it, the sun is going to come out. *Jesus*."

Once again, the spy had to save the day. I walked over to the machine, found the plug, and yanked it out of the socket. Roux got some scattered applause, and she gave them a wobbly curtsy. "I'm here all week!" she announced. "Residency!"

"Roux?" I said. "Let's go home."

She looked like one of those geckos you see on Animal Planet, the ones whose eyes go in completely different directions. "Is there more wine?" she asked.

"Not for you," I said, then let her put her arm around my neck. "You're done for tonight."

"Okay. It's important to pace yourself. Where are we going?"

"Home."

"My home or your home?"

"Your home."

"But you don't even know where that is!" She giggled.

I looked over at Jesse. If he thought my wrinkled-notetaking face was cute, then he was going to love my puppy-eyes face.

"Oh, no," he said. "Nuh-uh. No way. You're on your own."

"I can't carry her by myself!" I protested. "Please? You said yourself that it's good she has a friend."

"There are, like, a hundred people here! In my house! How am I going to get them out?"

"Easy," I told him, then poked my head around the corner. "Oh, shit, the cops are here!" I yelled.

And voilà, it was a teenage stampede out the door.

Jesse looked at me. "You are very lucky," he said, "that you're so cute."

I helped him carry Roux down the stairs and to the front door, even as the electric eels continued to thrash around in my stomach.

The cab driver who pulled to the curb took one look at Roux and shook his head. "Got change for a hundred?" Jesse asked him, flashing the bill before herding me and Roux into the cab.

"I charge a fifty-dollar, cash-only cleaning fee if anyone pukes in the back," the driver said, pocketing the cash even before Jesse had shut the door behind him.

"A bargain at twice the price," I told him, but he didn't

seem amused. Jesse laughed, though, then shoved Roux toward me when she started to loll toward him.

"Maggie?" she said.

"Yeah?"

She opened her eyes and smiled at me. "I think Jesse Oliver likes you."

Jesse groaned and Roux turned to look at him. "Oh my God!" she cried. "You're here, too?"

CHAPTER 11

The cab driver let us out across the street from Roux's building, and it took both Jesse and me to get Roux back to the house, mostly because she couldn't make up her mind about whether she wanted to walk next to Jesse or me. First it was me, then she decided I was too short, so she walked next to Jesse. Then she decided that he was too tall ("You're crowding me!"), so she made us stand next to each other so she could walk between us. "I can't be on the end!" she said, giggling. Then she waved the wine bottle as if it were a baton and sent Jesse and me scrambling for safety. An empty wine bottle is still really heavy, after all, and I wasn't born into a family of international espionage experts just so I could get clocked by a drunk high school girl with bad coordination.

Roux's apartment was across the street from Central Park. It took us thirteen minutes (Jesse timed it on his phone) to get her across the street to her building. That should give you an idea of what that experience was like.

The doorman eyed the three of us suspiciously as Jesse and I dragged Roux through the ornate lobby. "Harold!" she crowed when she saw him. "It's me! Wait, wait, wait!"

Jesse and I came to a halt as Roux started digging around in her purse. Some lip gloss clattered to the floor, along with a MetroCard and what looked like a movie-ticket stub. I hoped Roux wasn't going to the movies by herself. That would just be sad.

"Here!" she cried, finally producing a five-dollar bill. "For the swear jar!"

Jesse and I looked at each other, but Harold just produced an old glass jar that was filled with bills. "You have a swear jar with your doorman?" Jesse asked, incredulous.

Roux hung on a little tighter to my arm, wobbling on her heels. "Let's just say that some neighbors and I had a little run-in three months ago."

"And by run-in, you mean . . . ?"

(Harold was now reading his newspaper like we weren't even there.)

Roux grinned, the happiest drunk on the block. "I told this one tenant that he should—how can I put this?—have sexual relations with himself. And that did *not* go over well."

"Wow," Jesse said. "This might be a New York first."

"So now I'm working on being a better person, which means I don't get to drop f-bombs anymore. And I'm putting Harold's grandkids through college!"

Harold just tucked the glass jar back under the desk, muttering something about rich kids. I'm not sure what he said, though. It was hard to hear over Roux yelling, "Bye, Harold!"

I dug through Roux's purse and found her keys while Jesse propped her up against the elevator wall, using his arm and hip to keep her upright. "Ow," she kept saying, but she didn't move, so we ignored her. The front door lock looked pretty basic—just a normal deadbolt—but Jesse and Roux were right there and there was no way I could open the lock without them noticing. Or Jesse noticing, at least. I was pretty sure that Roux couldn't focus her eyes.

I finally found the keys and opened the front door while Jesse moved Roux inside. Everything was dark and drawn. It was sort of creepy to enter this huge apartment and not see a single adult, but Roux didn't seem too put off by it, so I guessed it was normal for her.

"Okay, kid," Jesse said to her as he steered her toward the stairs. "Here's the plan. You're going to drink some water and sleep it off and start fresh tomorrow."

"I love water." She sighed. "I love Maggie, too. Jesse!"

"Yeah, Roux?" His voice was muffled as Roux flung her arm around his neck, whacking him with her oversized coat sleeve.

"You like Maggie, too, right? She's hot. Don't you think Maggie's hot?"

"Roux, I will murder you," I muttered. "Well, *I* won't, but I *know* people. They can do it without making a mess."

"Hot like *burning*," Roux continued, ignoring my death threats as she put one foot on the stairs. Then she stopped. "Whoa, spinning stairs. Terrible idea."

Jesse looked at me over Roux's head. "She's so trashed," he whispered.

"*So* trashed," I said.

"You'd think she'd build up a tolerance at some point."

"Hey, I have tolerance," Roux said before lurching violently and nearly knocking Jesse and I back down the stairs. "I don't hate *anyone*."

"Of course you don't," Jesse said as I caught Roux by the shoulders and pushed her forward.

"People hate *me*," she replied as we kept nudging her up the stairs. "But I have only love in my heart for those assholes. Ugh, swear jar! I owe Harold five more dollars now. Remind me tomorrow! Where's my room? I need to puke."

I looked at Jesse. Jesse looked at me. Roux's suite seemed to be a very long hallway away, and she looked six shades of queasy. "Can I puke here?" Roux asked as she neared a potted plant that sat at the top of the stairs. "How about this? It's a plant. Hi, plant!"

"Oh, boy," Jesse said under his breath.

"Okay, Operation: Save the Plant and Move Faster is now in effect," I announced, and the two of us got Roux down the hall in record time.

"Hold it for about thirty seconds, okay, buddy?" Jesse said. "Or I'll never forgive you."

"Yeah, you're my buddy, Jesse." Roux grinned. "My good buddy. You were and then you weren't but now you are." She shifted her glazed eyes to me. "It's because you're hot, Maggie," she whispered conspiratorially.

"Oh my God, shut *up*," I hissed at her. "If you have

even a *molecule* of sobriety in your body right now, you will stop talking."

Roux just laughed and stumbled through her doorway. She would have fallen right into a pile of shoes if Jesse and I didn't catch her. "You're turning an interesting shade of green, Roux, you know that?" Jesse grimaced as he turned her around.

We steered Roux into her massive bathroom. Bottles and beauty products littered the granite countertop, and a hair dryer dangled precariously from an outlet. "Okay," I told her. "Anchors away."

And right on cue, Roux pitched toward the toilet and puked up Jesse's parents' very expensive French wine.

CHAPTER 12

I took care of things after that, since although guys like to gross each other out, when girls do gross things, guys apparently turn into delicate Puritans. *Whatever.*

Anyway, I cleaned Roux up, gave her water and an aspirin, and Jesse and I got her facedown on her bed before tiptoeing out of the room. "Do you think we should stay?" I whispered.

"No, she's fine," he replied. "She's been way more trashed before. This was like middle-school drunk."

"See," I said, "that doesn't make me feel any better."

"Trust me," he said. "It's not dangerous until she starts speaking with a Russian accent."

"A Russian accent?" I wondered if Roux could teach me how to do that.

"Yeah, it's bizarre. No one gets it."

We went through several more gilded rooms in Roux's house, sneaking past floor-length windows as we crept toward the massive mahogany front door. "This apartment," I murmured, "is ri-donk-ulous."

"I didn't know people actually said the word 'ri-donk-ulous,'" Jesse replied.

"I didn't know people actually thought about the word 'ri-donk-ulous,'" I retorted.

Jesse grinned and gave me a shove. "You started it."

"Seriously, though, this apartment is crazy, but yours? Is bonkers."

"That's one word for it."

I decided to risk it and say something very nerdy. "Are Roux's parents home? Like, is there a responsible adult on the premises?"

"Nah, they travel a lot," Jesse said. "Her nanny used to show up at all the school events, but, you know, then we grew up. No one has nannies anymore. And besides, her parents are still married. Roux won the lottery."

I thought about my family as we went down in the elevator and strolled past the doorman. I hadn't spent a night away from my parents in my entire life. They were always home when I came home, and I was pretty sure that even if they *weren't* spies, they'd be able to tell if I stumbled home wasted. And then I thought about Roux in her echoing, empty apartment and felt kind of sad for her. Growing up with spies, I always had someone to count on.

I wondered if maybe Roux was counting on *me*.

Jesse and I walked down Eighty-Second Street toward Central Park, me shivering in my turtleneck and jeans. "Spies don't wear a coat?" he asked me.

"*What?*" I gasped. "What are you talking about?"

He raised an eyebrow. "Your costume."

"Oh." *And that concludes this week's heart attack.* "I think I left mine at your place. If anyone took it, I'm going to be pissed."

"Here," he said, and started to shrug out of his tuxedo jacket. "My good deed of the day."

"Thanks," I said. It smelled a little musty, but it also smelled like Jesse. *Focus,* I thought to myself. *Go in for the kill.*

"So," I said as we passed the banners outside the Metropolitan Museum of Art, "I couldn't help but notice that you didn't have a chance with the magical karaoke machine."

Okay, not my strongest kill shot, but I was new to this sort of conversation. You know, alone. With a boy. *Alone.*

"Neither did you," he said.

I laughed and tucked my hair behind my ears. It had come unpinned somewhere around hour four of the party, when Roux had been busy showing me her favorite wine. For the third time. "Well, I only karaoke to 'Bootylicious' but you didn't have it."

"Want to do it right here?"

I looked up at him. "Are you insane?"

"C'mon, it's just this bodega." Jesse waved his arm to indicate the small store on the corner. "Your audience is small."

"I was kidding!" I cried. "I don't even sing in the shower, much less in public!" I had spent my entire life trying to blend in with the people around me, and I was fairly certain

127

that singing like Beyoncé on a Manhattan street corner would ruin that whole effect.

Jesse was starting to hum and shake his own booty, though, wiggling his eyebrows at me. "You know you want to," he sang.

Time for a distraction.

"You know what I *do* want?" I replied. "Ice cream."

"What?"

"Ice cream," I told him. "To quote Kanye, 'Me likey.'"

"Ice cream," Jesse repeated.

"Cherry Garcia."

Jesse glanced down at me. "That is a *brilliant* idea."

A few minutes later, Jesse emerged from the store with a paper sack, two plastic spoons, and a small plastic package that he tossed at me. "Here," he said. "Don't get excited, it's not a real ruby."

I put the cherry-flavored Ring Pop on my left hand and hugged it close. "I'll never take it off," I promised.

"C'mon," he said, nodding down the street. "Let's find a stoop."

Which was how we came to sit on the front stoop of some brownstone at one in the morning, passing the pint of ice cream back and forth. The autumn air was even chillier now, but Jesse's jacket was surprisingly warm and the ice cream tasted so good that I didn't even mind how cold it was.

"You know what would be cool?" I said as I passed the ice cream back to him.

"If that ring *was* real so we could auction it at Sotheby's

128

and split the profits? Sixty-forty, of course, since I *did* buy it for you."

I giggled. The candy looked ridiculously huge on my hand, but I didn't want to take it off. "Nope. Try again."

"If Radiohead played at my next birthday party?"

"Haven't they already done that?"

Jesse passed the pint back to me. "No. Selfish bastards."

"Shame. But what I was going to say was that it'd be cool if we could keep hanging out like this." I dug into the ice cream, then glanced at Jesse. "Are you eating all the cherries out of this?"

"No. And yeah, that'd be cool." He was *totally* stealing all the cherries, that liar.

"Yeah?" My heart was sort of pounding, but I told myself that it was just the sugar and leftover adrenaline from the party earlier than night.

"Yeah." He looked up at me and grinned. "Maybe we could skip the part where we carry Roux's drunk ass upstairs, though."

"Maybe we can do something easier next time," I replied. "Like scale the Empire State Building one-handed."

Jesse bumped me with his shoulder. "You first, Spy Girl." He laughed. "You look geared up for it."

"Ooh, don't call me that," I said before I could stop myself.

"What? Spy Girl?"

"Yeah." I glanced around us, but the people walking by were all in a hurry to get home. No one cared about our conversation. "It's just a costume. And I have a name, you know."

"I know," he said. "Maggie."

No one had ever said my name like that before, like it was quiet and special and unique, the only real name that I had, the one hardly anyone knew.

"I just . . ." I tried to explain without actually explaining. "I like my name. I like when you say my name." Then I passed him back the ice cream. "It's melting. You should eat more of it."

"I'm good," he said, and he took the ice cream and set it on the step without breaking eye contact with me. "Maggie."

My heart was turning into a hummingbird, crashing against my ribcage every time he said my name. I've been nervous and scared and even petrified before, but I had never felt like this. "Well, you don't want to wear my name out," I teased him, moving back ever so slightly and reaching for the ice cream. "You sure you don't want more? Because I'm starving."

I was so not hungry.

"Wait, you just told me to call you by your real name, then when I say it, you get all weird and uncomfortable." His eyes were boring into me, like he could see every phony birth certificate, every illegal passport. "You don't like your name?"

"No, I like my name a lot," I lied. "Margaret's a very . . . *classic* name. I just . . . I feel like we keep talking about me. And Roux. Let's talk about you."

He paused and ran a hand through his hair, which only served to make it curlier. "So what about me? What, did you google me or something?"

Jesse seemed annoyed now, looking everywhere except at me. I had thought that I couldn't handle him looking at me anymore, but now that he wasn't, I wanted his gaze back where it had been.

"I didn't google you," I lied. "I just—"

"So you googled my dad probably. Every other girl has."

The condensation from the ice cream was starting to run off the carton and onto my fingers. "Who's your dad?" I asked, hating the way the lie felt in my mouth, dirty, like ash. "Why would I google him?"

Jesse took a deep sigh and his shoulders sagged forward. His hair fell back over his forehead, and I found myself wanting to brush it away, to touch his skin with my fingertips. "Sorry," he said. "I get a lot of girls trying to use me to get to my dad. For internships, college letters of recommendation, party invites, all that. And it's been a really shitty year. Especially this summer."

"What happened this summer?"

He laughed a little, only it wasn't a funny laugh, more like an exhalation of breath. "I haven't told anyone yet. You can't tell anyone, either, 'cause it could really screw things up for my dad."

My heart was starting to race again. Was it because Jesse was about to say something about the magazine article? Or was it because he was sitting so close to me that our hipbones touched? "Okay," I said. "I know how to keep a secret."

"My mom left in June."

"Oh. I'm sorry."

"Yeah. She and my dad never really got along. They were either fighting or not talking. But then I guess everything came to a head and she left right before school ended in June."

"Do you know where she went?" I asked. The street was quiet now, a temporary lull caused by red lights and the late night, and I lowered my voice to match the hum of the distant traffic.

"I think Connecticut. We have a house out in Westport. Or maybe she's in Europe. I'm not sure. She said she'd call"—he shrugged—"but she doesn't. When she left, she said she just needed time alone for a while. And my dad doesn't want anyone finding out because he's already under a lot of pressure with work and, you know, if a blogger finds out or someone at the *New York Post* . . ." Jesse's voice trailed off and his eyes looked glassy, like a doll's. "He thinks rumors could spread and hurt business."

I sat next to him and thought of my summer days spent watching Icelandic TV and endlessly spinning locks on the safes' dials, watching the neighbor boy and wishing I knew what to say to him. I wondered if Jesse had felt the same way, lonely for someone to talk to, penned in by things beyond his control. "Do you miss her?" I asked.

Jesse was quiet for a long time. "I miss the idea of her," he said at last. "It's like when people leave, you can't change anything or make it better. Maybe you can't do that when they're still there, either, but at least you think that you can maybe try one day.

"You know what I did?" he said, then continued before

I could even answer. "I'm an idiot. I stole this book from the bookstore and then got caught."

I froze. I couldn't help it. "Really?"

"Yeah. I practically waved it in the security guards' faces as we left, so it wasn't really hard to catch me. I just thought . . ." He trailed off for a minute and then let out a deep sigh. "I thought that maybe if I got caught, it'd get in the papers and blogs, and my mom would read my name and think of me."

My heart was somewhere in my throat, pressing down so hard that it made me hurt. "That's kind of the saddest thing I've ever heard," I murmured.

"If by 'sad,' you mean 'pathetic,' then yeah, it is." He smiled, only it wasn't much of a smile. "Anyway. That was my lame attempt at teenage rebellion. Woo. All I got was grounded and a paragraph on Page Six."

"That's very *Gossip Girl*," I told him, trying to make him smile again. It sort of worked. He had a crooked smile that was starting to look less crooked by the minute. "And I'm sorry about your mom. And the bookstore."

"Yeah, well." He shrugged. "What are you going to do?"

"I know what you mean, though," I told him. "About people leaving."

Jesse looked up. "Did your mom bail, too?"

"No, no, not at all." The idea of my mom suddenly waking up and leaving one day was impossible to comprehend. "I just meant that I know what it's like to leave. Or to be left."

"Yeah?"

I nodded and stirred the melted ice cream. "We move a lot for my dad's job."

"What does he do?"

"He works for universities. He speaks a lot of languages, but jobs are sometimes sort of tricky to get, so we move a lot." I had told this lie so many times that once in a while I even found myself believing it. "But, you know, that means leaving friends, family, homes, and it's never the same again."

Jesse nodded as he took the ice cream back from me. "This is really gross now," he said, smiling a little. "It's sugar soup."

"Yeah, nice try," I said. "Changing the subject."

He shrugged. "Guilty."

We sat together for a few minutes without saying anything. It was nice. Sometimes New York is a lot quieter than you think it can be.

"I haven't told anyone about my mom," Jesse finally said, his eyes focused somewhere toward the Chrysler Building. "So, you know, please don't . . ."

"I won't tell anyone," I promised. "Here, pinky swear."

He turned his head to look at me. "Pinky swear?" he said. "What are you, six years old?"

"It's a time-honored oath!" I countered. "Pinkies out, c'mon."

He rolled his eyes but did so anyway. His skin was a little cool. *Does this count as holding hands with a boy?* I suddenly thought. *Oh my God, I'm holding hands with a boy. A cute boy. It's not like he's someone's cousin who's supposed to be a pity date.*

"Are we sworn now?" he said, his eyes crinkled at the corners.

"Yes," I said, and tugged on his finger for good measure. "It's also possible that we're now considered married in the country of New Guinea."

We both cracked up at the same time. "Kidding!" I giggled. "Kidding! At least I think I am. Who knows?"

"Let's Wikipedia that when we get home," Jesse suggested, but he was still laughing. "Are you always this goofy?"

"I—I don't know," I answered. I didn't know. I had never hung out with other teenagers before. I hadn't even had a friend my own age since the third grade. "I guess I can be *kinda* goofy. Maybe it's one of my hidden talents."

"One of? What other hidden talents do you have?"

"Well, I can't tell you or they wouldn't be"—I lowered my voice dramatically—"*hidden*. But I have a few skills."

And suddenly I realized that Jesse and I were *really* close together. More specifically, our mouths were really close together.

"Oh," I said. "Um, hi."

"Hi," he whispered back. "This okay?"

"Well, we're already married in New Guinea," I whispered back. "This is just the natural progression of—"

And then he kissed me.

Not that I had any experience with this sort of thing, but Jesse was a really good kisser, and I suddenly wondered if I was holding up my end of the deal, so to speak. I tried desperately to think of all the movies I had seen where people make out, but my brain was in meltdown mode and so I just went with it.

135

Best. Assignment. Ever.

"You're shaking," he said when we pulled apart after a minute or an hour or a year. I'm not sure how long we were together. However long it was, it wasn't enough.

"Oh, yeah, um, sorry." I put my hand on his arm to steady myself. "Ice cream. Sugar rush. You know." *Also the fact that you just kissed me.*

"I'm sorry I was an asshole to you when we met," he murmured, pushing my hair out of my face.

"It's okay. I was an asshole, too. Sometimes I'm bossy."

"*Really?* I had no idea!"

"Shut up!" I cried, swatting at his arm. "I can't help it, it's my nature."

"Luckily you're a good kisser."

My head swam and if I weren't already sitting down, I would have had to sit down. "I am?" I asked. "I mean, I am! Duh."

"Waaaaaait," Jesse suddenly said, leaning back a little and staring at me. "Am I your first kiss?"

Whoops.

"Define first," I said.

"I think it defines itself."

"Then no. Because Brian McConnell was pretty handsy back in preschool."

"Okay, fine. Your first kiss after you turned twelve."

I screwed my eyes shut in embarrassment. "Yes," I admitted. But when I opened my eyes again, Jesse was still staring at me. "Okay, you can stop doing that now," I told him.

"I like looking at you," he replied. "I like kissing you, too."

"You do?"

He nodded and leaned in again.

We pulled apart after another few minutes. "You know what?" I whispered. My arms were looped around his neck so I could rest my forehead against his. Sometimes it amazes me, all the things that can happen in a single evening.

"What?"

"Second kisses are even better than first kisses."

"Wait until you get to the third one."

I was about to find out when Jesse's phone suddenly started buzzing, jolting both of us back onto the step. "Shit," he whispered, glancing at the screen. "It's my dad. I'm late. Shit."

I looked at the clock on his phone: 2:02. "Wow," I said. "It's tomorrow."

"Yeah, guess so." He tapped out a message to his dad before tucking the phone away. "C'mon, let's get a cab."

I held his hand as we walked to the corner. "God, your fingers are freezing," I told him. "Do you want your coat back?"

"Nope." He held out his free arm and a cab slipped up to the curb, Celine Dion blasting from the radio. "After you," Jesse said. "Celine insists. Loudly."

The cab's heater was running full blast, making it feel like we were stuck in a moving hair dryer, and I scooted across the cracked pleather seat to make room for Jesse.

"Just so you kids know," the cab driver announced over his shoulder, "I charge a—"

"Fifty-dollar cleaning fee, yes, we know," Jesse interrupted him.

"Good thing Roux's not here," I said as we lurched away from the curb.

"For many reasons, yes."

I was sort of tempted to kiss him again, but I was afraid the cab driver had a ten-dollar surcharge for making out, so I settled for continuing to hold Jesse's hand. "You know what I like about cabs?" I murmured as I leaned against his shoulder. "They move fast."

Jesse laughed a little. "What, do you normally travel by horse and wagon?"

"No, I mean that usually in New York, you walk everywhere, right? But when you're in a cab, it's like flying."

"Unless there's gridlock. Plus the subway moves way faster."

"True. But then we wouldn't get to be serenaded by Celine."

"And that would be tragic."

The cab driver suddenly braked, sending both Jesse and me into the plastic divider that separated the backseat from the front. "We also wouldn't get facial contusions if we were on the subway," Jesse muttered as he settled himself back in his seat.

"It's part of the experience," I reassured him. "There should be a Dramamine dispenser back here."

By the time the cab pulled up in front of my apartment,

we were both white-knuckling the door handles. "Is this where you live?" he asked, peering up at my building through the window. "I live just around the corner. Crazy."

"Yeah, totally random," I said, then climbed out of the cab before my face could give away how nonrandom it was. The air outside was crisp and cold, but it felt icy against my flushed cheeks, and it was just starting to hit me: not only had I kissed a boy, but I had been lying to him the entire time.

Jesse paid the driver and followed me up to the front door. "This is fine," I said, rushing my words. "I can make it from here, I'm good."

"I had fun," he said. "Keep that ring safe."

I smiled and glanced down at my Ring Pop, which was still ridiculous. "I'll treasure it forever," I promised. "Cross my heart."

He smiled and leaned in again, kissing me so hard that it left me a little breathless. "I'm really glad I met you," he whispered. "Seriously."

"Me, too," I whispered back. "More seriously."

"Have a good night. Happy Halloween."

"Halloween's over," I reminded him. "It's November first now."

"Ah, you're right. Guess you're not a spy anymore."

I smiled at him, but my heart felt like someone was squeezing the blood out of it. "Right," I said. "Good night."

Inside the elevator, I took a huge deep breath and leaned against the wall. "Oh my God," I whispered to myself. "You just made out with a guy. Oh my God, oh my God, oh my God." Three months ago, I couldn't even make eye contact with the neighbor boy, and now I was making out with a guy? Talk about overachieving.

I entered the code to our front door and opened it carefully. My parents were probably sleeping and I didn't want to—

"Where have you been?"

Both my mom and my dad were standing in the kitchen, arms folded, staring at me. I hadn't seen them look that angry since . . . well, *ever*.

"Oh, hi," I said. "I can explain."

CHAPTER 13

Do you have any idea how worried we were?!"

The confrontation had moved from the front door into the kitchen, where I could see remnants of my dad's stress eating habit: a crust of toast and a smear of jelly on a plate next to his open laptop. Not a good sign.

"Look, I'm sorry, but what do you want?" I said. "You signed me up for this, so this is what I have to do. I have to go to Halloween parties and spend time with people! It's my job!"

"It's two thirty in the morning!" my mom cried. "In Manhattan! Do you know all the things that could have happened to you?"

I looked at my parents like they were speaking Korean. (And to be fair, my dad can speak Korean, so it wasn't outside the realm of possibility.) "Wait, so let me get this straight," I said to them. "We moved here so I could make friends and get information from Jesse Oliver, right? So why are you so mad when I've spent my entire evening doing exactly that?"

"Because it's *two thirty in the morning*!" my dad shrieked. In English.

"We need to set up some ground rules," my mom added. She was starting to pace, and Pacing Mom was the equivalent of Stress-Eating Dad. "This cannot happen again. We were worried out of our minds."

"Did it occur to you," my dad chimed in, "to call us?"

Of course it hadn't. I had been hauling a very drunk Roux around Upper Manhattan and kissing Jesse. I didn't even think about my phone. "I agree with Mom," I said. "We need some ground rules. And rule number one: you need to trust me to do my job!"

"You could have been kidnapped!"

"Or worse!"

"Oh my God!" I said for the thirtieth time that night. "Okay, you know what? You guys need to decide whether you want me to do this or not."

That stopped them in their tracks.

"I mean it," I continued. "Because I can either do this job and hang out with this guy and make friends with people and *get the information that I was assigned to get*, or I can quit and someone else can do it."

I had no intention of quitting, though. This was the first solo assignment I had ever had, and the perks included making out with cute guys. I was going to try to hang on to this for the rest of my natural life.

My mom finally spoke. "We need to compromise. A curfew."

"Excellent," my dad said. "Ten o'clock at night."

My eyes almost fell out of my head. "Ten o'clock?"

142

I screeched. "In New York? Are you trying to sabotage me?"

"Margaret." My mother's tone of voice was warning enough. Sabotage was not a thing we joked about in our household, but I didn't feel like backing down.

"I'm serious!" I sent my own message right back. "This is the first time in my entire life that I get to hang out with people my own age, and you're trying to stop it!"

"We're not trying to *sabotage* you," my dad insisted. "We're trying to make sure you're safe. We need to know where you are because there are dangerous people out there, and I'm not talking about regular-city dangerous people, either. There are people that want to be able to do what you do." He paused for a few seconds. "They would do anything to get your talent."

The air hung heavy between us. I knew this, of course. I had always known it. You don't grow up like this and *not* know it. "It's just . . . it's nice to pretend to be normal," I told them. "You guys already had your teenage years before you joined the Collective. I didn't get to do that."

My parents exchanged glances. "Being a normal teenager means having rules and boundaries," my mom said.

"But I'm *not* normal," I shot back. "That's the problem."

My dad sighed and leaned against the countertop. "Let's just go to bed," he said. "It's late, we're all tired. We can figure this out tomorrow."

The idea of waking up and having this conversation all over again was exhausting, but I didn't say that. "Oh, by the way," I said instead. "I had a really fun time tonight. Thanks for asking."

CHAPTER 14

I barely slept that night, thinking about my parents and Jesse and Jesse and my parents some more. I wasn't sure how my evening had gone from sublime to shitty so quickly, but it had. My parents and I had never fought like that before. No one had ever kissed me before. It was an odd night of first-time experiences, let's just say.

I finally dozed off right when the sun was a pinkish hue in the gray sky, and when I woke up again, rain smacked against my window and Angelo's card was propped up next to my bedside lamp. I squinted at it, trying to focus my eyes on a pencil sketch of a garden atrium, a tiered fountain in the middle surrounded by Greek columns. It was the garden court at the Frick Museum on the Upper East Side. Angelo used to take me there on rainy days. I was being summoned.

My phone started buzzing and I scrambled for it. Was it Jesse? Was he calling me? I was too busy turning my phone around and around in my hands to look at it. Was Jesse doing the same thing? Was he debating whether or not to call me? Should I just wait until Monday morning at school to talk to him?

Roux's number flashed on the screen.

"Pray tell," she croaked when I answered, "why are there feathers everywhere?"

"Hi to you, too," I said. "How are you feeling?"

"*Eeuuuuurgh*." She made a sound that didn't sound human. "Seriously. Feathers. Why?"

"No clue."

"I think I dreamed that I was the Black Swan. Oh my God, I need *coffeeeeeeee*. If I don't have coffee, I will shrivel up and die just like one of those little roly-poly bugs." She paused. "There's a feather in my mouth. *Blechhh*."

"Roux," I said, trying to bring her back to the present. "I need to talk to you."

"Is this an intervention?"

"What? No. God, no." I didn't have that kind of time, for starters. "I just have some questions."

"Okay. Come over now. Bring coffee for your good friend Roux."

"I can't right now, I have to . . ." I hesitated, not wanting to mention Angelo. "I have to run some errands for my mom."

"In the rain? Child abuse."

I rolled my eyes and rested my forehead against the window. The next time I had to infiltrate a bunch of high schoolers, I was not picking the recently exiled mean-girl drama queen for a friend. I would head straight to the library and find the nerdish bookworm instead. "It is *not* abuse," I told her. "Go shower. Do something productive. Gather up all the feathers and make a pigeon sculpture."

"Pigeons are gross. I wish every pigeon would fly away and take a squirrel with it."

"Such a charming visual. Look, I'll be there soon, okay?" Angelo would have to wait for an hour or so. It was all right, though, I knew he loved hanging out at the Frick.

"Okay. Call when you're on your way. Bring coffee!"

My parents were in the kitchen when I finally emerged from my bedroom, showered, dressed, and grumpy from caffeine withdrawal. "Was Angelo here?" I asked, holding up his business card. "Because this happened."

"He said to meet him whenever you could," my mom said, clicking away on her laptop without looking up at me. I could tell she was still pissed. "Take an umbrella if you're going. It's raining out."

I bit back my sarcastic response and reached for the coffeepot. "I don't know when I'll be back," I said. "I might have to go see Roux." *And Jesse*, I thought. Just thinking about him made me nervous, which was weird because I *never* get nervous. My dad used to call me "Steely McGee" because my hands wouldn't shake, even when I opened the most difficult combo locks, but now when I thought about Jesse, it felt like my stomach was filled with liquid gold, warm and burning.

And to be honest, I wasn't sure what I was supposed to do now that we had made out. Should I text? Was I supposed to send a thank-you note or something? Did Jesse even want to see me again? I needed Roux's advice, and I knew she'd have no problem giving it to me.

"—car," my dad said, and I realized he had been talking. "What, sorry?"

"We've got a town car now," he said. "New rule starting this morning. It'll take you wherever you want to go."

I raised an eyebrow. "So, we're not going to talk about last night and instead you got me a chauffeured car?"

My mom put up her hands. "Hey, not our call. This was all Colton's idea. You know that."

I did know that, but I was still annoyed. I sort of wanted to apologize for being so angry the night before, but I also didn't know what to say or how to say it. My parents and I had always been a team, but now it felt like me versus them, and I didn't know how to play the game.

"Better go," my dad said. "The umbrella's broken, by the way. I found out the hard way this morning."

Great.

My Hunter rain boots clomped on the floor as I headed toward the front door, but my mom stopped me with her arm. "Here," she said. "Take an apple. You didn't eat breakfast." Then she brushed an invisible piece of lint off my red plaid coat and kissed my temple. "Don't worry," she said. "We'll figure it out."

I bit my lip and gave her a quick hug. "Don't stare at the computer screen too long," I told her as I left. "You kids these days, you'll ruin your vision."

Things may not have been perfect, but at least they were a little better when I left.

The anonymous black car took me uptown on the worst route ever, in the slowest traffic imaginable, made slower by the rain, but we finally made it to the Upper East Side. Roux's apartment building seemed even more austere in the daytime than it did on Halloween night, which was saying something. For starters, it had gargoyles—full-on "I will eat your face, you urban heathen" gargoyles—that leered down at me as I waited for Harold the doorman to let me in to the marble lobby. (Did he ever *not* work?)

"Oh, it's *you*," he said when he saw me. "Delightful." He seemed anything but delighted.

"Yeah, because it was a blast for me to carry my drunk friend home," I retorted. "Thanks for helping, by the way. You're a peach."

He waved me away and I pressed the PH button to take me up to Roux's apartment, where the scene was no less pretty. Every shade was still drawn and there had been some sort of smoothie accident in the kitchen that left the blender oozing onto the granite countertop. My mother would have had a coronary if she had seen the mess.

I, however, had no problem walking away from it and going upstairs to find Roux. I found her, all right, sprawled on her bed in a room so dark that I had to feel along the wall for a light switch.

"You went back to sleep?" I demanded.

"Go 'way, Pollyanna."

"You look ridiculous with that sleep mask on. C'mon, rise and shine."

Roux sat up, her blond hair a huge tangle around her

head, and raised her sleep mask to reveal one bleary eye. "Do you have provisions?"

"Pro-what-ins?"

"Bagels. Coffee." When I admitted I forgot, she sighed and flopped back onto the bed. "As a New Yorker, you are useless."

"As a friend, though, I'm pretty damn useful, especially the part where I made sure you got home safe last night."

"Fair enough. We'll order in."

Ten minutes later, she had got out of bed, brushed her teeth, and sent a messenger to pick up breakfast from Absolute Bagels, while I scrolled through the channels on her massive flat-screen television. I stopped at a romantic comedy and muted it so I could talk to Roux at the same time. "Your doorman's a jerk!" I called to her. "Seriously!"

"More talky, less yelly." She winced as she came back into the room.

"Sorry. Your doorman's a jerk."

"I know. Don't you just love him? I love him. He *gets* me." Roux glanced down at the huge pile of clothes that were on her floor. "Clothes are hard." She sighed. "It's Sunday. Pajamas are allowed all day, right?"

"Sure. Hey, what happened downstairs?"

"Where?"

"In the kitchen. It looks like someone had a fight with the blender and there were no winners."

"Huh. Not sure. Maybe I tried to make a smoothie last night." She shrugged and flopped down beside me on the bed. "I love this movie," she said. "It's so unrealistic, but I love it. I'm such a sap. I'm a pine tree filled with sap."

"You're ridiculous," I told her. "You need your own reality show."

"Don't think I haven't tried!"

"Imagine my surprise," I replied. We watched the movie in silence for a few minutes. It was the most calm I had ever seen Roux, her mouth moving along with the words. I wondered how many days she had spent in her room watching movies while her parents were halfway across the world. It seemed fun but not really, like being the only person in an amusement park. No one wants to go on rides all by herself.

After our coffee and bagels arrived ("Harold, you're a curmudgeon and a beast!" Roux yelled into the intercom when the doorman rang. "Kisses!"), we sprawled on the couch in Roux's living room. It reminded me of a museum where everything seemed expensive and sort of cold. I was sure that the furniture had been picked out by a designer who had probably never met Roux's family.

"Oh my God, bagel, I love you! Get in my mouth." Roux sighed happily as she devoured her cinnamon raisin bagel. I watched her, sipping my coffee and trying to get comfortable on the hard-backed sofa. "So. You were saying?" she asked finally.

"I was?"

"You needed to discuss something. Step into my office, we're open for business."

I picked up a bagel and twirled it around my finger. "I need to talk to you about Jesse."

Roux froze. "Did you do it?"

"Do what?"

She gave me a look that, oddly enough, reminded me of Angelo's "we are not amused" face.

"Oh my God, no!" I cried. "We didn't have sex! We just kissed!"

"You kissed Jesse?" Roux screeched, then winced. "Ow, ow, my head."

"We *made out*," I clarified. "Like, multiple kisses. Plural."

"I get it, yes, thank you." Roux sat up so that she was on her knees. "Was it good?"

"It was . . ." How was I supposed to describe it? It felt like adequate words hadn't been invented yet. "It was amazing."

Roux shook her head. "It's always you quiet girls, I swear. We think you're hanging out in the library, but really, you're just banging your way through the guys."

"I only kissed him!" I told her, throwing a pillow in her direction and making her duck. "I don't think that makes me the poster child for promiscuity!"

Roux just wiggled her eyebrows. "Okay, so tell me," she said. "Everything. I like heavily detailed stories. Leave nothing out or I'll *know*."

So I gave her the entire saga: how he gave me his jacket, the front stoop, the Ring Pop, and the ice cream kisses. I even told her how soft his curly hair was and how he had told me some really intimate things. When Roux pressed for even more details, though, I shut her down. I had promised Jesse that I wouldn't tell anyone his secrets, and I planned on keeping that promise for as long as I could.

"So," I continued. "What do I do now?"

"That's easy. Keep making out with him. Why are you here and not with him?"

"No, I mean, what do I do now? Like, do I call him? Do I text? Do I send flowers or a thank-you note?"

"Uh, Maggie? Jesse is not your grandmother, okay? Whatever you do, do *not* send him a thank-you note."

"Okay, but then what do I do? The clock is ticking here. What if he's already making out with someone else?" I was only kidding about that last part, but when I said it, the idea made my stomach drop. "Oh my God, do you think he's making out with someone else right now?"

Roux waved the idea away. "Nah, Jesse's not like that. He doesn't dabble. He commits. In fact, I've heard he's actually a little clingy, like moss. Or a monkey with attachment issues."

"Roux. Please focus."

"Okay. We need a plan." She set her coffee down and folded her hands. "Has he texted you yet?"

"No. Is that bad?"

"He's probably still sleeping."

"Okay." I reached for my phone, then paused. "Should I text him? What should I say?"

"What do you want to say?"

"That I . . ." I had no idea. "I'm terrible at this!" I cried, tossing my phone onto the couch. "I don't even know what to say! Why can't they teach *this* in high school? I'm good at so many things, why can't I be good at this, too?"

"We all shine in our own special star way," Roux assured me.

"No, I should know how to do this!" I protested. I got up off the couch and started to pace across the dark hardwood floors. "I mean, I've done some really difficult things before! Like, *really* difficult! And now all I have to do is text someone and it's like my thumbs are broken." I held up my hands in front of Roux and shook them. "Look, broken thumbs!"

Roux gave me the side eye. "Do you need something?" she asked. "Because my mom's got a stash of pills in every color of the rainbow."

"No, I'm fine," I said.

"Really? Because your eyes look like they're spinning counterclockwise."

"I'M FINE!" I took a deep breath. "I'm fine. I just feel like I'm screwing up a lot of things here." Talk about understatement.

"Here's what we're going to do," Roux announced. She looked much better than she had when I first arrived, and I realized with a start that she must have been really lonely before I arrived in town. This girl-talk thing was right up her alley. "You're going to text him and say something about the ring or the ice cream. Visual cues, if you get what I'm saying."

I held my phone in front of me. "Just like, *Thanks for the ice cream*?"

"No. That's lame. Try something like—"

But she was interrupted when my phone started to ring. It was Jesse's number.

"It's him!" I screamed. "Oh my God, what do I do? Do I answer?"

Roux jumped up on the couch, screaming along with me. "Answer it! No wait, don't, don't!"

"Why not? It's still ringing!"

"Voice mail! Voice mail!" Roux was so excited that she spilled her coffee all over the couch.

"WHY?"

"Trust me!"

"AAAHHH!"

Roux did a victory dance that looked a lot like the Funky Chicken that my dad sometimes did to embarrass me or cheer me up. "He called you first! He wants to talk to you!"

"And now he probably thinks I'm lost in Siberia or something because I didn't answer it!"

"Lost in Siberia?"

"It's a lot more possible than you might think," I informed her.

"Whatever. You don't want him to think that you're just around whenever he calls."

"But I'm totally around! I was even holding the phone!"

"No, let him wait. Let him think you're busy with other things. Guys love the chase."

"Okay, seriously? This is the twenty-first century. That's ridiculous."

Roux shrugged. "You came here for my advice and sweet company. Now you have both."

I looked at my phone. No voice mail. "He didn't leave a message. He hates me. He's going to ask for his ring back."

"*Never* return the ring. These are gems I'm giving you here!" Roux flopped back down on the couch next to the coffee stain, not even bothering to try and clean it up. "Call him back in two hours, after you run those errands for your mom."

"The errands? Oh, right, right." In all of the excitement, I had forgotten that I was supposed to be meeting with Angelo. "Are you sure?"

"Look, I realize that you met me after I achieved social martyr status, but trust me. I still have the touch. This kind of gift doesn't just disappear." She finally dabbed at the stain with a napkin, then gave up and tossed it on the hardwood floor.

"Do you not have a housekeeper?" I finally asked. "Or at least some stain remover under the sink?"

Roux just shrugged. "Inez doesn't work on Sundays. She has a family." She looked a little lonely when she said that, and I realized that if it weren't for me coming over this morning, Roux probably wouldn't have talked to anyone all day. I wished that I could invite her over to dinner, or at least maybe tea with Angelo, but there was no way. I had already mixed enough business with pleasure this weekend.

"—when you call him back," Roux was saying, and I forced myself back into the conversation, "just act cool. Answer questions, don't ask them."

"I can do that," I told her, and it was true. If there was one thing I could do, it was draw information out of people without giving up too much of myself. Finally, being a spy was paying off in at least one romantic area.

Roux looked unconvinced. "Really?" she asked through another mouthful of bagel. "I find this hard to believe."

"Have faith," I told her, then started to get up off the couch. "I gotta go meet—run those errands."

"But you didn't even finish your bagel."

I felt terrible, but I couldn't keep Angelo waiting, either. "Yeah, my parents are really pissed that I came home so late last night." Roux's face fell even further. "No, I mean, they're not mad at you or anything."

"No, it's just cool, you know, that they're worried." Roux drew a small pattern with her toe on the coffee-dripped floor. "It's cool, I get it."

"I'll call you immediately after I talk to Jesse," I said. "Go shower and do homework or something."

She rolled her eyes but followed me to the front door. "I'm staying in bed all day and eating french fries," she told me. "I have to build up some strength so I can Cyrano you through this Jesse fling."

"*Thing*," I corrected her. "It's a thing, not a fling."

"Whatever. Go errand run." She waved me away. "And tell Harold that I'm going to make his life miserable if he doesn't smile at you every time you come over."

I had no plans to tell Harold anything, but I just said, "Okay," and let myself out the front door. "Don't do anything I wouldn't do!" Roux yelled behind me and even after the door shut, I could hear her giggling.

CHAPTER 15

The car glided up to the front of the museum on Seventieth Street, and I climbed out before the driver could open the back door. No point in both of us getting soaked. There was hardly anyone in the front hallway, save for a tall, grayhaired man with his hands clasped behind his back, casually standing next to the admissions table like he had done it every day for his entire life.

Which, knowing Angelo, he probably had.

"Fancy meeting you here," I said when I was close to him.

He glanced down at me and smiled. "You look like a drowned rat."

"Drowned rats have broken umbrellas," I replied. "I read it in a fortune cookie once."

"Ah, of course." He took out his wallet, even though the sign said it was "pay what you can" Sunday, and pulled out a hundred-dollar bill. "Will this cover the young lady and myself?" he asked the girl behind the admissions desk.

"Y-yes," she stammered. "Um, yes, of course."

"Lovely. It's always nice to support the arts." Angelo took our tickets and then led me through the front of the museum into the courtyard, where a large marble fountain gurgled and bubbled. It was a little humid in the room, and dozens of white orchids grew up from the ground. "Hothouse much?" I asked as I sank down on one of the marble benches.

"Isn't it beautiful?" Angelo asked. "The renovations were well worth it. It's so important to stay up to date and modern."

"So says the man with the Olivetti typewriter," I teased him, grinning when he smiled down at me. "Here," I added, and passed him the flash drive. "I found this in a safe at the Oliver house. I'm not sure what's on it, but it was pretty well hidden."

"Stay modern, but remember the classics," he amended. I'll remind you that I also have a laptop. And well done, you. The Collective and I will have a look as soon as possible." Then he paused before saying, "So I hear there's a bit of discord between you and your parents."

I sighed and looked toward Angel, the bronze Angel statue on one side of the courtyard. It was pointing directly at me, almost accusing. *You kissed a boy!* it would probably say if it could talk. *You're supposed to be working. For shame!*

"Here's the thing about my parents," I said. "They want me to do this job, right? *They* want me to do a great job. *I* want to do a great job. The entire free *world* wants me to do a great job. But when I actually *do* my job, they freak out. I can't win."

Angelo nodded a little and adjusted his cufflinks, both engraved with calligraphied *A*s. "The thing is, my love, you are their daughter first and a spy second."

"It usually feels like the opposite, though. Like, last night was the first time that I ever hung out with kids my own age. And it was fun. It was awesome. There was a Halloween party, but I was still doing my job and it was like—"

"Living in California three years ago ruined your grammar," Angelo interrupted with a sigh.

"—so cool," I continued. "But Angelo, that shouldn't have been the first party I've ever gone to. There should have been a lot more. My parents can't decide now that they want me to be normal when they've spent my entire life making sure I'm anything but."

"Yes, I agree." Angelo nodded. "You raise an excellent point."

"Really?"

"Certainly." He watched as two tourists made their way through the garden, pointing at the fountain along the way. "Do you see them?"

"Do you know them? Are they assassins?"

"No, they are most likely not assassins. I have never met them before. But they seem to be perfectly lovely and normal people, yes?"

"Yes," I admitted.

"Some people, they have ordinary lives. They go to

school, get married, raise children, whatever they wish. Nothing very exciting will happen, just the beautiful mundanity of life. But you, Maggie, you can have an extraordinary life because you have an extraordinary gift." He looked down at me, his icy blue eyes still as warm as they have always been. "You have a talent that many people would love to possess. Would you give it all up to have a normal life?"

"Sometimes, maybe," I murmured. "I don't know. I just wish my parents would trust me to do my job."

Angelo took a deep breath and looked up at the skylight. "Do you remember," he said slowly, "when you came to my house dressed up for Halloween?"

"Of course," I said. "You gave me a candy bar and a diary. Angelo, that was over ten years ago. Why—?"

"And what were you dressed as?"

"A ghost. I wanted to take off my costume, but they said I had to keep it on until we got to your apartment."

"Yes. Because that was the night you were almost kidnapped."

I stared at Angelo, my mouth open. "What are you *talking* about?"

"Word had got out about how talented you were with locks, that you were a prodigy. A new member of the Collective was so excited by this that he couldn't keep it to himself, and, well, I suppose he thought that he could use your gifts for his own nefarious purposes."

"And by 'nefarious' you mean . . . ?"

Angelo shrugged. "In this business, there is always

danger. And there is always money to be made. He could have trained you himself, had you open bank vaults for the wrong people, crack safes that were never meant to be opened." His voice trailed off, and I knew Angelo was thinking about even worse fates for me.

"Do you know who it was?" I asked.

"He was a new recruit," Angelo explained. His eyes were fixed on the Angel statue, not even looking at me. "Oscar Young. He had only been with us a few months before the kidnapping attempt. His plan was to grab you on the east side of Gramercy Park."

"Well, what happened to him?" I peeked over my shoulder, suddenly very aware of my surroundings, but Angelo just patted my hand.

"Not to worry, my love, he died. His body washed up in South America a few months later." But Angelo's mouth was tight, and the crease between his eyes was deeper than ever.

I swallowed hard. "Um, Angelo? Did you—?"

"Oh, no, no, darling. I didn't kill him. I would have, but somebody beat me to it." He glanced down at me and gave me a small smile. "Unfortunately."

"So then what? Did my parents get a ton of extra security? Did you put a microchip in me?" I felt the back of my neck. "You microchipped me, didn't you."

Angelo's smile widened. "Of course not. And yes, security increased for all of us for a few months. Colton was . . . poor Colton, he was beside himself. He was the one who had brought Oscar Young into the Collective, had sworn that Oscar was one of the best in the business. Colton was absolutely gutted when he found out about the kidnapping attempt."

I tried to imagine Colton Hooper being anything except smooth and unruffled. I couldn't do it.

"He apologized and swore to your parents that he would always look out for your personal safety. He effectively assigned himself to your family. I still remember his words exactly. He said, 'I suppose Oscar Young was no knight in shining armor.'" Angelo shook his head. "An understatement if ever I heard one."

My head felt too small to hold all this new information. "So Oscar Young is dead?" I asked.

Angelo's face became gentle. "Oh, love, I've scared you, haven't I."

"No, I'm not scared," I told him, and I wasn't. "I'm angry, though. I want to dropkick Oscar Young off a tall building and then give Colton a hug."

Angelo laughed. "Well, your first wish is nearly as impossible as your second," he told me. "How does your generation say? Colton Hooper does not do hugs."

"So you've met him?"

"A few times, yes. Right after the kidnapping attempt. I don't think I'll ever forget the look of devastation on his face."

Something in me burned bright when Angelo said that. I had an entire network of people supporting me, protecting me, looking out for me. Including, I realized with a guilty jolt, my parents.

"I bet my parents freaked out."

"Yes, they did. In fact, you were the only one who remained unruffled. You were just excited to dress up as a ghost." Angelo looked down at me. "I suspect that this incident is the reason your parents were a bit upset when you didn't come home last night. Especially since this happened in New York."

"Yeah, you think?" I said. "If they had just told me, though! I mean, it was ten years ago. I can handle that news."

"I can also tell you that your parents were not thrilled about accepting the assignment here," Angelo continued. "They didn't want to put you in such a central role." He paused before adding, "I think they have been surprised to discover that you've grown up before their eyes."

I thought about the night before, about the party and dragging Roux to her bedroom and kissing Jesse on the cold stoop, about all the ways I had grown up that my parents hadn't even begun to realize. "Well, I did," I said. "I grew up. That's usually what happens to kids."

"So they say." Angelo grinned down at me. "I'm telling you this not to frighten you, of course. I just think you should know the truth about how valuable your talents are, as well as how strongly we all want to protect you."

"But they can't protect me from everything. Even if I were just an average kid, they couldn't."

"No, they cannot, that's true. Nor can I. You have to have the good judgment to protect yourself."

I wondered if this was starting to steer toward the

safe-sex speech, so I quickly steered it far, far away. "Maybe I could just dress up as a ghost again."

Angelo smiled and patted my knee. "A subtle response, to be sure."

"Well, I learn from the best." I grinned back.

"Touché." Angelo straightened his cufflinks again. "So what else does the day hold for you? Studies, I assume?"

"Ha, yeah, no. I just saw my friend Roux and she's sort of exhausting. I think I need a nap."

"Ah yes, little Miss *Je Ne Sais Quoi*. And what about Jesse Oliver? Are you enjoying his friendship, too?"

I blushed. I couldn't help it. "Yes," I said. "I enjoy his friendship." That seemed to be the safest non-lie answer. "But don't worry, I know what I'm doing."

Angelo arched an eyebrow at me and didn't say a word.

"I do!" I protested. "I've got this one in the bag. Trust me."

"I have always trusted you," Angelo said. "Never forget that." He glanced up at the tourists who were walking back through the garden. "There are many untrustworthy people," he replied, and in his voice I heard a brief second of worry that had never been there before, "but you, darling, are not one of them."

I thought about kissing Jesse the night before and didn't say anything.

"Now, you seem to be in need of an umbrella before you go. Take mine."

"But what about you?" I asked as he pressed it into my hand. It was heavy, made of oak and canvas, the base

164

inscribed with the same *A* that was on Angelo's cufflinks and business cards. It wasn't the kind of umbrella that you could buy for five dollars from a vendor at the subway entrance, that was for sure.

"A little rain shower is good for an old man like me," he said as we walked toward the exit. "It keeps me young." The car was waiting at the curb, just as I had left it, and Angelo hustled me into the backseat. "Talk to your parents," he said before shutting the door. "They're looking out for your best interests, just as I am."

"Okay, I will," I promised. "Get home safe! Stay dry!"

But he had already shut the door and was strolling up Seventieth Street. I looked out the back window as the driver pulled out into traffic, but Angelo had already turned the corner and melted into the soaked crowd, like the rain had washed him away.

CHAPTER 16

Back in the car, I dialed Jesse's number.

"Hi," he said, picking up before the second ring. "I'm glad you called me back."

"Of course I did. You have my coat."

There was a pause. "Oh," he finally said. "Oh, I thought . . ."

"I'm kidding!" I said. "Oh my God, I'm kidding! I mean, I'm not kidding about the fact that you have my coat, that part was true. But I would have called you anyway."

"Well, do you want to come over and pick it up?"

I thought fast. Armand was probably in the house and I couldn't risk running into him. "Why don't we meet somewhere?" I said. "Have you had coffee yet?"

He just laughed. "Why don't we meet at Grey Dog on Mulberry? Does that work? They have good coffee. You like coffee?"

"I like it like breathing."

"Good answer. Thirty minutes?"

I glanced outside at the rain. "Sure, that's fine. Don't forget your umbrella."

"Okay, thanks, Mom."

"It's raining! I'm trying to help you out!" But we were both giggling. "Fine, get wet. See if I care."

"Twenty-nine minutes. Don't be late."

I stuck my tongue out at the phone as I hung up. "So annoying," I muttered, but I was smiling as I said it.

"Two minutes to spare!" I said as I leaped out of the car, dodging between the now-calmer raindrops. "I'm early! What do I win?"

Jesse looked up at his phone and tapped it. "Oh, no no no," he said. "My phone says it's been thirty minutes. You're exactly on time."

"Let me see that," I said, but he held it out of reach over my head. "Your phone is biased and a liar. It looks shifty."

"How dare you," Jesse said, and when I went to grab for it again, I stumbled over my boots and half tripped, half tumbled into him. "Whoa, easy there."

"It's the rain," I said. "I'm slipping on everything." That wasn't true, but I needed to say something to make up for the fact that I was starting to blush. "And hi."

"Hi," he said, smiling down at me. "Nice to see you again."

"A pleasure, I'm sure." I hung on to his sleeve while righting myself, and when I was steady, he handed me my coat. "I made sure that Max didn't shed all over it," he said. "You're welcome."

"Thanks. And tell Max thanks, too." Jesse held it for me while I slipped my arms into the sleeves, then helped me pull my hair out from under the collar. "Good as new!" I said. "Where's the coffee?"

"Are your eyes dilated?"

"I just really like coffee."

"Do you think you may have a problem with caffeine addiction?"

"I only have a problem with caffeine when there *isn't* any caffeine." The line was already forming out the door and I craned to see how far away the cash register was.

"Look at you!" Jesse laughed. "You're twitching!"

"Maybe we should get in line."

"Maybe we should get you to a methadone clinic," he replied, but let me drag him into line, anyway.

We left the coffee shop twenty minutes later, sweet coffee in hand, as I gave my driver the signal to stay where he was. "I couldn't help but notice that you weren't wearing your ring," Jesse said.

I yelped and quickly moved to cover my hand. "It's being resized at the jeweler's!"

"I don't want to make it weird or anything!" he said, even though we were both laughing by now. "I just couldn't help but notice!"

"It was sending me into diabetic shock just by wearing it!" I cried. "I didn't do it for me, I did it for *us*!"

He playfully shoved me, then grabbed my elbow and saved me from plowing into a bunch of women with handheld shopping carts. "Sorry," I said to them. "It's the caffeine, makes me all wobbly."

They looked unamused, and Jesse and I turned the corner, heading toward absolutely nowhere. "So . . . ," I said, wiping some stray coffee off the lid with my thumb.

"Sooooo . . . ," Jesse said.

"So that happened."

"What did?"

"We kissed."

"We did? I'm kidding!" he said when he saw my face. "You looked like you were about to cry! I'm only kidding, I swear."

"I wasn't going to cry; I was going to murder you." *Note to self: Hide emotions better.*

"Oh, well, that's more like it. And yes, we kissed." He shot a sidelong glance at me. "Are we still cool with that or . . . ?"

"Oh, we're cool. We're very cool. No worries there, my friend. We are A-OOOOOO-KAY." *Shut up, Maggie. Just stop talking right now. Right this very second. I mean it.*

"So, we're not going into some weird friends zone?"

"What? No! I mean, unless you want to. Do you want to?"

"No. Do you?"

"No. Okay, wait." I reached out and grabbed his arm, pulling us under an awning and out of the way of the rest of the pedestrians. "Why are you being weird?"

"I'm not being weird. I just wanted to make sure that you were cool with everything."

"I don't know how I can say this any more clearly: I'm really glad you kissed me last night."

"Yeah, but then you didn't call me back right away this morning and I was just worried . . ."

"You were worried because it took me fifteen minutes to call you back?"

"Um, maybe?" Jesse smiled, but his eyes were nervous and he kept running his hand through his hair, making it curlier with every swipe. It was kind of adorable, but he seemed agonized.

"Can I ask you a question?" I said. "A quick one?"

"Of course."

"Which girl screwed you over?"

His eyes widened even as his shoulders relaxed. "So Roux told you."

"Roux didn't tell me anything, amazingly enough."

"Wow, that's cool of her."

"*Names.* I want names."

"Claire Thomason." He took another deep breath. "Last year, right around Christmas. Messed me up pretty bad."

So not only was his mom MIA, but he had been emotionally crippled by an ex-girlfriend. Leave it to me to be assigned to the most wounded bird in all of Manhattan. "Tell you what," I said, looping my arm through his. "Let's walk and talk about Claire."

And that's what we did for a good hour, winding our way up and down the streets of Nolita in downtown Manhattan. He had dated Claire for six months and was head over heels for her, but she always gave him mixed signals, wouldn't return his calls, and so on. "It was like we'd make out all night on Saturday and then on Sunday, nothing. No phone call, text, IM, nothing."

"Which is why you're trying to put me in the friend zone," I said. "I'm not a therapist, but I think you might be transferring your feelings for Claire onto me." I *definitely* wasn't a therapist, just a kid who had spent way too many summers watching *Oprah* and *Dr. Phil* reruns.

"I know," he said, rubbing his hand over his face and making a growly sound that was more cute than threatening. "You girls are confusing."

"Well, guys are confusing, too. Look at Roux and her pothead Romeo. That looks like it was a huge disaster. Everyone sort of screws everything up all the time. It doesn't mean they're not trying their best."

"Are you saying Claire was trying her best?" Jesse looked dubious.

"No, I'm saying that we should try *our* best. And that means talking about things like Claire and being honest with each other." Even as I was saying the words, I could feel the lump forming in my throat. Here I was, talking about honesty while lying through my teeth. "Or, at least, as honest as we know how to be."

He glanced down at me. "I don't think I've ever had a conversation like this with a girl in my life."

"Well, if we're going to be honest, then I should tell you that I'm just trying to get you to kiss me again."

"Really?"

"I'm losing patience, too."

He bent down and kissed me. Softer this time, not like

last night. "Thanks," he whispered against my mouth. "I mean it."

"Of course," I whispered back, then kissed him again. "So, Claire," I said after we separated a few minutes later. "Tell me about her. What does she look like? Where does she live? Does she have any fears? Phobias? Is she afraid of death?"

Jesse looped his arm around my neck and kissed the top of my head. "Sometimes you scare me." He grinned. "It's kind of hot."

CHAPTER 17

On Monday morning, I woke up earlier than normal, which put my nerves on edge. And by the time I showered, dressed, and made my way into the kitchen, I realized that I was right to be edgy: both my parents were seated at the table. So was Angelo.

I hesitated in the doorway. "Let me guess," I said. "You didn't get together this early in the morning because there's good news."

My mom gestured toward an empty seat at the table. "Here, come sit down. We need to talk."

This day was already off with a bang, I could tell.

After I poured myself some coffee and settled myself at the table across from them, Angelo threaded his fingers together, then rested his chin on top of them. "That flash drive," he began, "definitely had some things on it."

"Well, I hope so," I said, then took a sip of coffee and immediately burned my tongue. "Ow!"

"Maggie," my dad said. "You need to focus right now."

"I *am* focused. I'm focused on the searing pain, ow."

Angelo passed me an iPad. "This is what we found once we hacked the password."

I took the tablet, almost scared of what I would see, but when I looked at the first images, I realized that they were baby photos of Jesse. Dressed up for Halloween as Batman; grinning on what looked like the first day of school; posed with a bat over his shoulder in a Little League uniform.

My first thought? *Oh shit, these aren't the documents.*

My second thought? *How cute was Jesse when he was a little kid!*

"This?" I said. "This is what was on there?"

My mom, dad, and Angelo all nodded silently. I could hear everything they weren't saying: *You messed up. The information is still out there. The article will be run and our family will be exposed.*

"Well, I mean, it was hidden! It was in a *hidden* safe with a *hidden* key, and do you know what I went through to find it? It wasn't easy! There was a party and a *ninja* and then this karao—!"

"Maggie." My dad interrupted me again, but I interrupted him right back.

"Look," I said. "You trained me to open safes. You didn't train me to know what was in the safes before I opened them. I saw a safe, I opened it, there was a flash drive, and here we are."

"We need to find the information," my mother said. "If you don't think you can do this, then—"

"But I thought I *did* do it!" I protested. But I knew I sounded childish, exactly what a spy isn't supposed to be. Even I was annoyed with myself.

You know how sometimes you realize you're doing or saying the wrong thing, but you just can't stop yourself? You can literally hear the words coming out of your mouth and you just want to shove them back in because the real you, the *good* you, would never want to be this way, but you just keep going?

Yeah. That was me. Because instead of agreeing to try harder, be better, I got whiny.

"Is this a trial?" I asked.

"It's not a trial," my mom said. "It's just—"

"Because it sure looks like a trial. I mean, you're all lined up here and *looking* at me. The only thing missing is that clackety-clackety person. You know, the one where . . ." I mimed typing away on a tiny keyboard. "What do they call that?"

"Clackety-clackety person?" my dad said.

"Are you biting your nails again?" my mom asked.

"Stenographer," Angelo answered.

"Stenographer, yes!" I said. "And yes, I'm also biting my nails again because that's what I do when I'm stressed. My cuticles are just going to have to ride it out until this *trial* is done."

Angelo laughed, though not unkindly. "I assure you, darling, this is not a trial. And if it were, we would be a very flawed jury, don't you agree?"

It was a hard point to argue.

"Look," I said. "None of you have ever made a mistake on a case before? Ever?"

"The point is not the mistake," my mom reassured me. "And I know it looks like we're ganging up on you, but that's just the way we're all sitting at the table. We need to get a round table." She was trying to make me smile, but I didn't take the bait, and that only made me feel worse.

"The point," she continued, "is that this magazine article is probably going to name names. *Our* names. *Your* name."

"I know," I said, but hearing it out loud gave me a weird shiver down my back. "I'm trying. It's not easy going to high school and trying to find time-sensitive documents, okay? It's really hard. I'm probably going to fail my French quiz today."

"*Comme si on pouvait apprendre le français à l'école*," Angelo muttered, and now I was *really* sure I was going to fail my French quiz because I had no idea what he was saying.

"*Ridicule, non?*" my father started to stay, but my mom cut him off.

"We don't have time to debate the merits of classroom education," my mom told them. "Can we focus, please?"

"Yes," I said. "Can we please focus on how I'm the worst spy in the world and I'm probably going to end up working the graveyard shift as a cashier at 7-Eleven?"

"See?" Angelo grinned. "You are very dramatic. The first sign of being a wonderful spy. Look at Emma Peel, James Bond. They were never subtle." He patted my hand, which made me feel better.

"Okay." I sighed. "I can find these documents. I will find them. I thought I did, but apparently that was just a dress rehearsal. I'll get them, I promise."

"It's not a matter of saying," my dad told me. "It's a matter of doing."

"Then I'll do it," I said. "I can. I will. I know how important this is and I won't screw it up." I didn't mention that I had already made out with the target's son. That probably wouldn't have helped anyone's confidence in me.

Least of all myself.

"I'll get the documents," I insisted when no one said anything. "Trust me, okay? I've got this."

I had no idea what I was doing.

CHAPTER 18

The day just got suckier.

It was raining out, which means the school hallways were humid and dank. My hair felt like a too-big hat on my head, and I had been splashed by a cab on Jane Street, which meant that everything below my waist was now soaked in gutter water. I was cold, miserable, the worst spy in the world, and now my bangs were so big that they could probably be used as a cell phone tower for all of lower Manhattan.

I had never missed Iceland more in my life. I would rather have been in *Luxembourg* than where I was at that moment, that's how cranky I felt.

And to make matters worse, I couldn't seem to open my locker. The lock was stuck.

"I hate my life!" I wailed, then started to bang my forehead against the metal.

"Oh, please. Self-pity is so last year."

Roux. The ray of toxic sunlight that I had been missing.

"Do you mind explaining to me why you're trying to make yourself look like the Phantom of the Opera?"

I didn't even know where to begin. How was I supposed to do this job when I couldn't even be honest with the people who could possibly help me? So I settled on the most honest answer.

"I burned my tongue," I told her.

"Huh." Roux sipped her latte. "That's the sign of a bad day to come. We should err on the safe side and ditch."

I stopped banging my head (which, despite what they show in movies, really hurts) and turned to face her. "I can't ditch, I have a French quiz."

"'Can't' should never be a word in anyone's vocabulary. It implies negativity."

"You don't get it!" I told her. "I have responsibilities, okay? I cannot miss French class today. Can't, cannot, will not, whatever word works for you. It isn't happening."

Roux just grinned. "Finally, a little feistiness! I've taught you well! And you don't have to pretend with me, I know you just want to see Jesse."

I did want to see Jesse, that was true, but at the same time, I kind of didn't. I knew I had screwed up by kissing him, and if Angelo or my parents ever found out, they'd probably banish me to the Arctic Circle to make snow cones for the rest of my life. Every time I saw him, I was reminded of how unprofessional I had been.

And yet at the same time, I couldn't *wait* to see him again.

I wondered if James Bond ever had this problem with any of his lady friends.

"You can see Jesse anytime," Roux said. "Hell, he's probably ditching, too!"

I sighed and tried again to get into my locker.

"Tell you what," she continued, "let's split the difference and go to Sant Ambroeus for coffee. It's French, right?"

"I think it's Italian."

"Whatever, it's all under the European umbrella. So let's go."

"Shouldn't you be worried about ditching too much?" I asked her, gritting my teeth and wondering if I could stab my locker with something sharp. "Don't you have to get into college?"

Roux twirled a bit of her hair around her finger. "Oh, that," she said, like we were talking about a forgotten errand or something. "College is so self-important. Everyone runs around and gives themselves an aneurysm about getting into wherever and then they get there and drop out after a semester. I'm not playing that game."

I stopped and looked at her. "Your parents are just going to donate money, aren't they."

"Duh. Plus, not to brag, but I am *amazing* at standardized tests. Filling in bubbles with a number 2 pencil is sort of a specialty of mine. So, do you want to go to Sant Ambroeus now or—?"

"Roux!" I finally screamed. I couldn't take it anymore, the nonstop chattering, the worry-free life, the fact that her biggest problem was that some loser pothead didn't like her anymore. "Do you *ever* back down? Because you are relentless. You're like a semi with no brakes on a patch of black ice! Just stop!"

Roux was silent for a few seconds before she said, "Well, that's, like, three similes all in one."

Her voice was the quietest I had ever heard, and I realized that I had hurt her feelings. Great, friendship was another thing that I sucked at. Add it to the list.

"I'm sorry," I said. "I just . . . I had a fight with my parents this morning because I said I would do this thing and I thought I did it, but they don't think I did and they're not listening to me and it's just a mess and . . . ugh, I hate this stupid locker!"

Roux reached over and slammed it with her fist. It popped open.

She just shrugged when I gaped at her. "I saw it in a movie once," she said. "I didn't think it would actually work. Do you still hate me now?"

"No, I don't hate you," I said. "I didn't hate you and I don't now. I'm just having a terrible day, as you can probably tell."

"I can tell. So what, your parents want you to do stuff? Like chores?"

I was pretty sure that chores were a foreign concept to Roux. "Sort of," I said. "It's complicated."

"Yeah, what isn't?" she said. "Y'know, you can always come stay with me if your parents are being lame. You can have your own room and your own butler."

"Really?"

"No. At least not the butler part." She smiled at me. "But you can borrow Harold."

I rolled my eyes but grinned back at her anyway. "No way. Harold hates me."

"Harold *loves* you. Don't let that skinny, bony old-man exterior fool you. He's a softie. A softie with an attitude problem, but a softie nonetheless. Hey! You should come over tonight! We can watch movies."

"I can't," I told her. "I'm sorry, it's just everything with my parents right now . . . I should probably lie low for a while."

"Or maybe I could come over to your place?"

There was something in her voice that I couldn't quite identify. Jealousy? Envy? Maybe even hope? From everything I had seen and everything Jesse had said, I knew that her parents were rarely home, and knowing that Roux could never meet my family only made me feel worse.

"Not today. Between school and tests and college stuff"—I didn't know what "college stuff" even meant, but I could make something up if I had to—"my parents just want me to focus." (That was putting it mildly.) "I'm sorry."

The hurt look on her face lasted for only a second before it smoothed back into Roux's casually arranged coolness. "That's fine," she said. "Harold loves watching *Manhattan* with me." The bell went off over our heads. "Damn, I have to go to history. I failed the quiz last week and my parents weren't home to sign off on it. Hello, detention, my old friend."

"You need a signature?"

"If you fail, yeah. I mean, it's good they're not home because now they don't know that I failed, but yeah."

"Why don't you just forge it?"

"I've done it so many times that they've figured it out."

I set my books on top of the lockers and gestured to her. "Here, let me try. Do you have a copy of your parents' signatures?"

Roux flipped through her textbook and produced a half-folded piece of paper. "Here, I failed this one two weeks ago."

"Why do you keep failing?"

"Because I don't study."

I just sighed and took the old quiz. It was her mom's signature, loopy and wide, almost like Disney handwriting, not too difficult. "You didn't see me do this," I told her, then proceeded to do a near-perfect signature on Roux's test. The Y could have had a bit more of a curlicue, but a high school history teacher wasn't going to notice.

Roux looked at my work, then up at me. "Is there anything you *can't* do?" she cried.

"Not really, no."

"Can I buy you a delicious off-campus snack to say thank you?"

"Roux."

"So sue me for trying. I'm persistent, you know. I'm a runaway black truck semi covered in ice, or whatever you said."

"You're crazy." I laughed. "Have fun."

"You know it. Tell Jesse Oliver I said *bonjour*." She wiggled her eyebrows at me and I shoved her shoulder, both of us giggling as we went our separate ways.

CHAPTER 19

The French quiz turned out to be a bigger nightmare than I could have ever imagined. For starters, Jesse ended up sitting directly across from me, and although I have been trained to do many things in my life, clearly flirting was not one of them. I managed to spend the entire class blushing and averting my gaze and wanting to look at him but *not* wanting him to catch me looking, but then wanting *him* to look at *me*. The whole thing was so exhausting that I needed a nap afterward.

Oh, and also? The quiz was an oral exam. So not only was I a stammering mess every time the teacher picked me to answer a question, but I get sort of self-conscious about speaking French in public because I'm always afraid that I'll sound insane, like the chef in *The Little Mermaid* movie. You'd think that the gene pool would have done me a solid and let me inherit at least some of my dad's linguistic genius, but no. All I got was tongue-tied and embarrassed.

Jesse, of course, did great and spoke French like he had

been speaking it since birth. *Maybe* he *should be the spy*, I thought as I waited for the bell to ring and release me from my misery. *He could be all dashing and suave and I could sit home with my old textbook and conjugate verbs.*

(Okay, my self-pity was starting to go off the rails, I admit it.)

He waited for me after the bell, packing up his bag twice before I realized that he wasn't going to leave without me acknowledging him. "So are you ignoring me, or are you playing hard to get?" he asked when it was just the two of us left in the classroom. "I always get the two confused."

Why did he have to be funny? And smart? This would have been so much easier if he were some himbo with the personality of a dirt clod.

"I'm not ignoring you," I said.

"Denial is the first step to acceptance."

"That's the dumbest thing I've ever heard."

"Ah, so you're playing hard to get. Did Roux tell you to do that? Because that's the dumbest thing *I've* ever heard."

I slung my bag onto my shoulder and looked at him. vHis eyes were (God help me, I swore I would never use this word) *twinkling*, but there was fear behind them. He had told me a lot about himself, his family, his sadness, probably more than he had ever told anyone else before.

We both had a lot riding on this relationship.

"Look," I said. "I like you. Like, *like* like you. Like, a *lot*."

185

"That's a lot of 'likes.'"

"Yes, it is." Angelo was right about the West Coast ruining my grammar. "But don't you feel like it's happening kind of fast? Shouldn't we just slow down a little?" *Slow down long enough so I can ruin your dad's magazine empire and save my family's professional and personal lives without breaking your heart at the same time.*

"Slow down? We've already made out. Oh my God, wait. I'm a bad kisser." He feigned shock, putting his hand over his heart. "Is that was this is about? What, too much tongue? Not enough tongue? Did I do that thing where I get overeager and almost knock your teeth out? 'Cause I do that sometimes. Sorry."

I smiled despite myself. "You're so weird."

"I'll take weird if it means I'm a good kisser."

"Yes, you're a great kisser. I don't have a ton of experience in that area, as you know—"

"I'm flattered."

"But, yes, you're a great kisser. Gold star for you."

He sat down on the edge of the desk, his hair curling into his eyes and making me want to reach out and brush it back. "So what's the deal then?"

"I told you, I just think we should slow down. I mean, we haven't even had a real date yet and I—"

"Ohhhh." Jesse nodded to himself. "That's what this is. I get it."

"What?"

"First date. Girls like dates. I'm such an idiot, I should have thought of that."

186

This was backfiring spectacularly.

"Maggie." He got up and came over to stand next to me, taking my hand in his. "Would you like to go on a date with me?"

At that point, I would have run away to Zimbabwe and raised herds of elephants with him.

"Yes," I admitted. "Do you want to go on a date with *me*?"

"Are you kidding? I'm going to show you how it's done. I'm going to date you like you've never been dated before."

"Oh, yeah?" I said, not able to stop a smile from escaping. "You think you got what it takes?"

"We're talking fireworks, okay? Literal fireworks. None of this 'let's eat ice cream in the freezing cold while we sit on a dirty stoop' shit. I'm pulling out all the stops. Call me LL Cool Jess."

"You are ridiculous!" I cried, shoving his shoulder even as he grabbed my hand again. "Are you serious about the fireworks?"

"Well, first things first. You haven't said if you want to go out with me or not."

Bad idea, my inner voice said. *Bad, bad, baaaaad—*

"Of course," I told him. "I would love to."

"Then fireworks it is!" He leaned forward and kissed me before I could say anything, and I immediately sat back down on the desk, wrapping my hand around his neck to pull him closer.

"Monsieur! Mademoiselle!"

We flew apart to see Monsieur McPhulty glaring at us.

"Are you both aware of the school rules? No public displays of affection during school hours?"

"*Je suis désolé*," Jesse said, even as he held on to my hand. His hands were cold and rough but surprisingly soft at the same time. "You know how it is, Monsieur McPhulty."

"French *is* one of the romance languages, after all," I pointed out.

It was worth getting detention just to hear Jesse's laugh.

CHAPTER 20

Both my parents were waiting for me by the time I got home on Monday afternoon. "Where have you been?" my mom said. "You're late. School gets out at three."

"Wow, calm down," I said, dropping my bag down on a chair. "I had detention. I would have called but they take your phones. It's really draconian."

"I don't think 'draconian' means what you think it means," my dad said just as my mom said, "Detention? What did you do?"

Clearly I wasn't going to say that I had made out with Jesse Oliver, son of the prime target in a major espionage case, in the middle of our French classroom. (Which would kind of make it "french kissing," but I digress.) "Um, nothing?"

My mother just shook her head. "Your lying skills are terrible."

"You raised a moral spy, what can I say? Is there any food? I'm *starving*. I could eat my body weight in peanut butter."

"Let's save that experiment for another day," my dad said, but he pulled out the bread and the peanut butter anyway.

"And I was talking during class," I told my mom. "That's why I got detention. They have rules about that, apparently. Is that chunky or creamy? Chunky makes me gag."

My dad just rolled his eyes. "So dramatic."

"Ha! That's nothing! You should meet my friend Roux. Oh my God, she redefines drama. She—what?"

Both of my parents were looking at me. "Friend?" my dad said.

"You made friends?" my mom asked me. It sounded like someone was throttling her while she was talking.

"Well, yeah, I kind of have to make friends with people if I'm going to do this job." I stuck the spoon directly into the (smooth, thankfully) peanut butter. "What, do you think I went to that Halloween party by myself?"

My parents exchanged the longest glance in the history of the world. "Honey," my dad said, "you know you can't really be friends with them. It's 'friends' in quotation marks, right?"

The thing was, I *did* know that. Somewhere in the deep, shameful part of my heart, I knew that I wouldn't always be friends with Roux, or even together with Jesse. It wasn't in the job description, and I had watched my own parents pack up and move so many times that I had lost track. None of this was a surprise.

But that was before I had made friends.

"I know," I told them. "But what else am I supposed to call Roux? My faux-friend? That'll sound great."

"Roo?" my dad asked. "Like Kang—?"

"She doesn't like that," I interrupted him. "Seriously. She'll cut you."

"Ah, wonderful."

"Her name is French. And besides, she doesn't have any other friends. I'm, like, her social life raft. Frightening, I know, but true."

"Please don't talk with your mouth full," my mom said. "Especially when you're eating peanut butter."

I hopped down off the stool and gathered up my bag and the jar of peanut butter. "Fine. I have to study, anyway. Calculus quiz tomorrow. It should be easy but the teacher likes to throw curve balls and I hate when that happens. So annoying." I was babbling, I knew it. "Anyhoo, you know where to find me and my one true friend, the peanut butter jar. We'll be hitting the books."

I could practically feel my parents' stares as I hurried off to my room, and who could blame them? I sounded like a peanut-butter-obsessed loonster. But I just turned on some music that Roux had sent me and immediately called her up. "Hi," I said. "It's me. Can you talk?"

"No, I'm sorry, I'm busy learning how to knit. Yes, of course I can talk! Are you crazy? You're the only person who ever calls me, anyway. My social life has been worn down to the nub."

Seriously, my parents wouldn't believe that Roux was real, even if they met her.

"Okay, anyway," I said, "do you promise not to freak out?"

"No."

"Roux, c'mon."

"Well, clearly you're about to tell me something that's worth freaking out about. So no, I cannot promise that. I have to freak out about things, I'm your friend."

Just hearing her use the word made me feel guilty. I hated that. "So Jesse Oliver asked me out on a date."

And true to her word, Roux proceeded to freak out.

"Get out of here!" she squealed after screaming directly into her phone and causing temporary deafness in my ear. "He did? Even though you two already sucked face?"

"Ew."

"That is so romantic, I'm gonna die. And then you'll have to revive me so I can come over and help you get ready. Are you going to get your hair blown out? I would if I were you. I mean, yes, the natural look is all well and good, but Jesse Oliver asked you out on a date, so this is no time to mess around. Even though you already sucked face."

"Can you please stop referring to it as . . . as *that*?" I said. "Really, it sounds awful. Like two floppy mackerels going at it."

"Okay, sorry. I'm just so excited for you! Did you tell your parents? What did they say?"

"They're . . ." I searched around for the right words and came up with the wrong ones instead. "They're not home yet. I'll tell them later."

"Do you think they're going to make him be all chivalrous

and come over to pick you up? Oh, I hope he brings flowers. Not roses, though. Blech. So cheap looking. Are you allergic to pollen? If you are, then I'll tell him so—"

"Roux?" I said. "Pump the brakes."

"Sorry." I could still hear her giggling happily, though. "Sorry, I just get excited. I should take a pill."

"Yes, you should," I said, before realizing that Roux probably *would* take a pill. "Actually, no, don't take a pill. Just answer me one question."

"For you? Two."

I glanced out my window at the sea of rooftops and fire escapes and cloudy skies. "What exactly am I supposed to wear on a first date?"

There was a pause before she answered, "You are *so* lucky that we're friends."

CHAPTER 21

On Thursday, the day before my date with Jesse, I got a note in my locker that wasn't really a note, just a careful ink drawing of a wide waterfall surrounded by café tables and trees, all sketched on heavy cardstock. I knew an invitation to meet Angelo at Paley Park when I saw one, so I made my way up to Fifty-Third Street after school, thanks to the always-present-and-always-creepy town car that the Collective was making me use.

(How did Angelo manage to get the note in my locker, you might ask? The answer is that I have absolutely no idea. I don't know how Angelo does 90 percent of the things in life, but I do know that it's best not to ask too many questions about it.)

All of midtown was in chaos, thanks to the autumn tourists and the parade that was happening on Seventh Avenue, and traffic was a nightmare because of it. After twenty minutes of going only three blocks, I couldn't take it anymore. "I'm good," I told the driver. "Just let me out here."

"It's my assignment to get you to your location," he replied, and his voice was a monotone, kind of how the robots will probably sound when they take over the planet.

"Um, thanks, pal, but another twenty minutes of hearing those cymbals is going to give me a migraine." I gathered up my bag and climbed out just as the cymbal section was passing by, which was a terrible decision on my part.

By the time I made it to Paley Park, I was half-deaf and all cranky. Angelo was sitting in one of the wire mesh chairs, as neat and prim as one could be while a parade raged just a block away. "We meet again." He smiled when he saw me, but the smile faded as I plopped down into the chair next to him. "Oh, dear. Bad day?"

"Bad everything," I said. "Why is there a parade? Why is there *always* a parade? And why do there *always* have to be cymbals in that parade?"

Angelo merely pushed his tea toward me. "Thanks, Angelo," I said. It's hard to be angry and frustrated when people do nice things for you, and I knew that sacrificing his tea was a big deal for Angelo. "I'm sorry, I'll de-crank in a minute."

He merely nodded and waited while I sipped. The waterfall was really beautiful, especially against the backdrop of the yellow-leaved trees, and despite the crowds on the streets, only a few people had taken refuge in the hidden patio. The sound of the water drowned out the parade, and after three sips, I was already feeling better.

"Thanks," I said again. "Really. I'm back to being me.

What's up? Nice drawing, by the way. You should do something with that. Put together a book."

"How do you know I haven't?" Angelo replied.

"Touché."

"And there's nothing important going on, my love. I just wanted to see how *you* were doing. There seems to be a lot of responsibility on your shoulders."

"You think?" I said. "I'm fine."

Angelo raised an eyebrow. "Ah, yes. Fine. A lovely sounding word that means absolutely nothing."

I pressed my knees together and covered them with my hands. I was wearing tights but they did nothing to keep the November chill away. I wondered what us private-school girls were supposed to do in January and February.

"Yes, I'm fine," I said. "All systems go."

I didn't even believe myself, though, and Angelo wasn't buying it either.

"Well, if you say so," he said. "Shall I get you an espresso?" He motioned to the cart that was at the patio entrance. "It's not the best the city has to offer, but I know how you feel about dodging cymbals."

I thought for a minute. There was something about sitting outside in the cold that didn't make me want coffee or hot chocolate or tea. In fact, there was only one food I was craving.

"Could I have some ice cream?" I asked.

Five minutes later, I was spooning up chocolate ice cream with the flat little wooden paddle spoon that always felt like it was about to give me a splinter in my lip. "So,"

Angelo started again. "You say that you're fine, but you're eating ice cream on one of the coldest days of the year."

"So?"

"And you seem a bit upset about parades."

"Well, I think that's a normal reaction."

"For you?"

I sighed and sat back in my uncomfortable chair. The waterfall was loud, I realized, almost too loud. "Did you get me here for a reason?" I asked him. "Because it's sort of deafening. Like, so maybe no one could overhear us if we were talking about important things?"

Angelo merely smiled. "One could assume that, yes."

"*Should* one assume that?"

"Let me put it this way." Angelo leaned forward and folded his hands in his lap before making direct eye contact with me. "If one should have something that he or she would like to say, this would be an excellent time to do just that. But I make no demands. I just offer an ear."

And of course I burst into tears.

"Everything is all messed up!" I cried. "I'm doing it all wrong, my parents think I'm screwing up, and there's this crazy amount of pressure and these school uniforms are terrible and sexist, too!" I used my chocolate ice cream-smeared napkin to wipe my eyes. "And I think I made a big mistake, too. Like, *really* big. The size of the solar system big."

Angelo unfolded his handkerchief from his pocket and passed it to me. "Thank you." I sniffled. It had a large *A* stitched into one corner, which was so Angelo. I wouldn't be surprised if he had ninety-nine more of them in a drawer

197

at home. "It's just been really hard and I don't know if I can do it."

"Why don't you start at the beginning?" he suggested. "It just so happens that I have quite a bit of time on my hands this afternoon."

"Is that so?" I asked.

"It happens to be so." He grinned.

So under the cover of a man-made waterfall in one of the most bustling parts of Manhattan, I told Angelo everything. Making friends with Roux, taking care of Roux at the party when she was too drunk to blink, barely being able to find the safe, and then how Jesse and I took Roux home.

"Angelo? I did something really bad."

"Is anyone dead?"

"What? Of course not. Not because of me, anyway."

"Then it cannot possibly be as bad as you think."

I paused before mumbling, "I kissed Jesse Oliver. And not because I wanted to get information from him. Because I wanted to kiss him."

Angelo pursed his lips before sitting back and nodding. He looked pissed, and disappointing Angelo was the worst feeling in the world. "I'm so sorry!" I said, the tears coming all over again. "I didn't mean to, it just happened! I think I like him, but I'm lying to him and to Roux, too. And now I've been lying to you and to my parents! I'm a lying liar who lies!"

"Maggie, Maggie." Angelo put his hand on my knee. "No, no, my darling. I'm not mad or upset. It would be quite hypocritical of me to be upset with you."

"W-what?" I stammered. "Why would you be a hypocr—? Oh my God!" I slammed my hand over my mouth. "Did you once kiss an assignment, too? Did you fall in love?"

"It was a very long time ago," Angelo admitted, and I put my other hand over my mouth when he said that. I was pretty sure that if my eyes got any wider, they would have fallen out of their sockets. "Many, many years ago," he continued. "Before you, even. An ancient era. But yes. He was my assignment and he was quite lovely, and well." He shrugged. "I suppose you can guess what happened next."

"Did you make out on a stoop on the Upper East Side while eating ice cream on Halloween night?" I asked.

"Not quite. We kissed in Paris while watching a film noir festival."

"Wow. Wow. Okay, so what happened? Did you break up after you got the info? What did you do? Did you keep any journals during this time, by any chance? Because I could really use a manual."

Angelo laughed. "We had a lovely time together for a while, but then we came to a fork in the road, and we both chose a different path. A bit of sadness at the time, but no regrets. We still have coffee whenever I'm in Paris."

"Did you get the information you needed from him?"

"I did, yes. And no, he didn't know I was a spy, either. He still doesn't. He thinks I'm an art dealer." Angelo smiled and I realized that the smile wasn't for me, but for the Parisian man across the ocean. "My point is, though, it happens to the very best of us. We can train everything but our hearts."

"That's a little cheesy, Angelo."

"I agree. But do you see? Love makes fools out of us all."

"Well, it gets worse," I told him. "I'm going on a date with Jesse tomorrow night. Like, a *date* date. I can probably get more information about his dad but . . ."

"But that isn't why you said yes to the date," Angelo guessed, and I nodded.

"I just . . . he's nice and he's cute and funny and it doesn't seem fair to punish him for whatever his stupid dad is doing. And he's even nice to Roux and no one's *ever* nice to her." I was starting to cry again. Apparently liking someone can make you really emotional. "And I know that as soon as this is over, we'll go on another assignment and I'll have to leave. I just didn't think it would be this hard. It's like I keep telling my parents, locks aren't like people."

Angelo let me cry for a few seconds before carefully putting both of his hands over mine. "Maggie," he murmured. "There's something that neither your parents nor I have said to you yet, and for that, I apologize. We should have told you this earlier."

"Am I adopted?"

"No, no, darling. We never told you how hard it would be to do this assignment. There is always a choice, but I'm afraid we never prepared you to make it."

I looked up at him, still clutching his handkerchief in my fist. "But the Collective . . ."

200

"They will always find a new person to take a job. I know you said yes because you wanted to prove yourself, but as I said, there is always a choice."

I nodded. "I know that," I told him, and I did, but it was still nice to hear him say it. "I just wanted to show you guys that I could do it."

"I know you can," Angelo assured me. "You have always been the same capable girl who learned how to pick my front door lock when she was three years old." He smiled at me, forcing me to smile back a little. "And now you know that this is what it's like. All the training in the world can't prepare you for a secret life. And there is absolutely nothing wrong with wanting to be honest with people."

"I'm trying to be as honest as I can be," I said. "I haven't actually lied to Jesse about anything. I just haven't told him the whole truth. My parents, though. I haven't even told them about the date yet. They're going to murder me when they find out."

"Don't worry about your parents," Angelo said. "I have faith in them just as I have faith in you. You leave them to me."

"Thanks," I said. "I mean it, really. I don't have anyone else to talk to about all this."

"I know, my love," he said. "And you are very welcome."

"Sorry about your handkerchief, too." It was now a teary, snotty mess balled up in my fist. "I guess I was a little upset."

Angelo waved the thought away. "I have a drawerful at home." (I knew it.) "It won't even be missed."

"Okay." I wiped my nose again. "Do you want more tea? My treat."

"No, I think we should probably walk." Angelo stood up and I realized that the park was suddenly being overrun with tourists. "Come along, take an old man home."

I took his arm as we joined the chaos out on Fifty-Third Street. "What would I do without you, Angelo?" I sighed.

"You'll never know." He smiled, then patted my hand as we turned the corner.

CHAPTER 22

H ey," Jesse said to me on Friday afternoon at school. "Don't forget, tonight is the night! Are you ready? Any last-minute concerns?"

I pretended to think. "No horse-drawn carriages. They freak me out. What if the horse is tired and doesn't want to walk? Or what if it wants to run? The horror!" I leaned closer to him. "*The horror.*"

Jesse laughed and put his hands on my shoulders. "No horses, okay. Noted. I'll just scratch 'rodeo' off the list of activities, while I'm at it."

"Good call," I said. "So what time should I meet you?"

"Meet? You don't want me to come over, meet the parents, shake the hands, kiss the babies?"

There was, of course, absolutely no way ever that Jesse could meet my parents. How awkward would that introduction be? "Oh, hey, meet the two people who are partially responsible for the downfall of your family empire? Do you want anything to drink?" No, clearly that would not be happening.

"They've got a thing tonight," I said.

"A thing?" Jesse repeated.

"A . . ." My mom was right, I was a terrible liar. "A benefit auction. A silent one. For children. Who have diseases. Bad ones. The diseases, not the kids." Yep, gotta work on those lying skills.

"A silent benefit for good kids who have bad diseases," Jesse repeated. "Got it, okay. Can I tell you something?"

"Anything."

"I just think you don't want me to meet your parents."

"Oh, I do!" I told him, and that was no lie. "You don't even know how much I wish you could. I *really* wish you could because I think they'd like you a lot. But . . . they're just not home tonight. It's you and me. And my dad will still break your neck if I don't come home by curfew, by the way." I had no idea what my curfew was, or if I even had one, but I thought it sounded more believable that way.

"Well, if he does, maybe then they could have a silent auction for me?" Jesse grinned, leaning forward, and I kissed him, risking yet another detention.

Worth it.

"You're antsy tonight," my mom said as she stirred the chili on the stove, but just the thought of eating made my stomach flip. "What's up? Friday night jitters?"

"I'm fine," I said, then remembered what Angelo had said about the word "fine." "I'm just thinking about everything that I have to do next week. Take another French quiz, find the Oliver documents, get the Oliver documents, get a pedicure. It's a lot on my plate."

My mom chuckled and I knew she thought I was joking around, which was great. Gotta butter the parents up, after all. If I had learned anything from watching hours of television, it was that parents are gullible. And yes, mine were spies and probably had a combined IQ score somewhere in the four digits, but I was their kid. All that intelligence had to distill down into something, right?

"Hey," I said. "Remember that girl Roux I was telling you about? Well, she's having some people over tonight and Jesse Oliver is going to be one of them, so I thought I should go."

"Okay," my dad said, where he was trying to solve the day's crossword puzzle. The Friday puzzle was never good to him. I glanced over his shoulder.

"Forty-nine Down is 'asinine,'" I told him. "Trust me. I know it is."

My dad frowned. "No, it's not."

"Are we looking at the same puzzle here? Because the puzzle I'm looking at—"

"Is mine," he finished. "Can you please corral your nosy daughter?" he asked my mom as I started to inspect the rest of the puzzle. "Let's all just stick to our respective talents, shall we?"

"You should probably do it in pencil," my mom replied. "In case you mess up."

"He wouldn't mess up if he put 'asinine' for Forty-nine Down," I said. "Do they even *make* pencils anymore?"

"Of course they make pencils!" My mom sounded almost offended at the idea. "What about standardized tests? And grocery lists?"

But my dad and I had tuned her out. "Look!" I said. "It's seven letters and the third one is an *I*!"

"Hey, when are you leaving again?" my dad asked. "Soon, right? Like, right now?"

"Ha, nice try. I still have to get ready." I had to get a lot ready, that was for sure. "I think I'm—"

And then someone knocked at the front door.

All three of us froze, my dad's pen poised over the crossword and my mom stuck between the refrigerator and the stove. "Um," I said. "Did someone order food?"

My dad made it over to the video surveillance monitor in what seemed like less than two steps. "It's a short person," he said. "Maggie, she looks like someone you would know."

Oh no oh no oh no.

"Roux!" I gasped when I opened the door. "What are you doing here?"

"Sorry I'm late!" she said, flouncing into the room. "I know, we've gotta do, like, three hours of prep in about half an hour, but don't worry, I've been training for an emergency like this. Oh, hi!"

My parents probably would have looked less horrified if there were a group of rogue assassins in the room. "Hi?" my mom said. "Um, Maggie—?"

"I'm Scarlet," Roux said, reaching forward to shake my mom's hand. "Everyone call me Roux, though. Except my grandma, but she lives in Arkansas, so who cares? Hi!" Now she was pumping my dad's arm up and down.

The jig was up.

"Is this the Roux that you were supposed to go see tonight?" my mom muttered under her breath.

"How did you know where I lived?" was the only thing I could think to ask her.

"I saw you go inside the building last week," Roux said, setting down her bag and starting to unwind her scarf. "And then I just took the elevator up."

So apparently the security in this building was complete crap. Great. I'll sleep like a baby knowing that.

"But what are you—?"

"Getting you ready for your date. Duh." Roux started to rummage through her bag. "I went to Sephora today. Thank me later."

"Your what?" my parents said at the same time.

I took a huge, gigantic, deep breath. Roux glanced up from her scrounging. "Oh," she said, eyeing my parents. "Oops."

"Yes," I said. "Oops."

"You have a date?" my mom asked. "With a boy?"

"No, with a tortoise," I said. "Yes, of course with a boy! With a boy *named Jesse Oliver.*"

"Ah," my dad said. "You have a date. With Jesse Oliver." I could almost see the aneurysm bulging behind his left eye. "Okay, then. Do we have any wine?"

"I'm sorry!" Roux whispered to me. "You didn't say that your parents didn't know! Are you grounded now?"

"How long have you known about this date?" my mom asked, interrupting Roux. "Weeks, days, what?"

"Um, a good amount of hours," I said. "Roughly

speaking? I just thought it would be a nice way to get to know him better. You know?"

"Yes," my dad said. "It would." He was uncorking the wine bottle at record speed. "Your first date. And it's with Jesse Oliver. Wonderful."

"This is your first date?" Roux squealed. "Oh my God! Then you need to wear this!" She dug around and found a pink sweater. "When I bought this, the salesgirl called the color 'salmon.' Salmon!" She shook it in my mom's direction, and my mom nodded and widened her eyes at me as Roux dove back into her bag. "Can you believe it? I was like, 'Honey, listen. Salmon's a fish, not a color.'" She glanced up at me. "Those are your staying-in jeans, right?"

"Right," I said, even though I had kind of planned on wearing them out. "Hey, why don't you go poke around in my closet and—"

There was another knock at the door, but this time it was all too familiar. So familiar, in fact, that the person went ahead and let himself in. "Hello?" Angelo said, stepping into the loft. "Is this a bad time?"

"Oh, no, this is just peachy," I said. "The more, the merrier."

"Angelo, what are you doing here?" my mom said, going over to him. "Is everything all right?"

"Of course, my dear, of course. I was just in the neighborhood and thought I might stop by."

Both of my parents turned to look at me. "Does Angelo know, too?" My dad gaped. "Really? Did you tell everyone *but* your parents?"

"Hi!" Roux piped up. "I'm Roux! *Love* the suit."

Angelo shook her hand. "Thank you, lovely to meet you, I'm sure. Maggie has told me a great many things about you."

Roux beamed at me. "Well, the good things are better and the bad things are much worse, I assure you. So who are you?"

"Angelo," he said. "A longtime family friend."

"Cool."

I halfway hoped that someone was taking a video of the scene that was unfolding in our kitchen, it was that ridiculous. Angelo and Roux shook hands while my parents and I watched them, mouths open like it was the most amazing tennis match. I was pretty sure that this was going to be one of those situations that was funnier in the past tense. Like Luxembourg.

"And you go to school with Maggie?" Angelo straightened his cufflinks.

"Ugh, yes. Ugh to the school part, not Maggie, of course." Roux squeezed my arm. "She's, like, my best friend. What do you do?"

For several seconds, no one said a word, and then Angelo let it fly.

"Well," he said, "I happen to be a world-class forger."

"Okay, then!" I said, grabbing Roux by the shoulder and practically tossing her toward my bedroom. "Why don't you go find something for me to wear?" I said. "It should take you a while, right?"

Roux was still cracking up at Angelo's answer. "I love

him!" she told me. "Why does everything sound better when a British person says it?"

"Jet lag. Focus on my outfit. Think Audrey Hepburn."

"I'm not a miracle worker," Roux protested, but she went anyway as I turned back toward my parents and Angelo.

"Who," my mother demanded, "is *that*?"

"That's Roux," I said. "My friend, remember? Excuse me, 'friend'?" I made air quotes around the last word. "She just wants to help me get ready." I glanced behind me to make sure that Roux wasn't standing nearby, then I turned back and dropped my voice. "Her parents travel a lot and they're, like, never home. All she has is a housekeeper who doesn't work weekends."

"What about other friends?" my dad asked, but I could tell that my parents were softening. They're big on family and togetherness.

"Um, touchy subject," I said. "There was sort of a scene last year. It got messy. Teenage girls are nuts, did you know that? You really lucked out with me. Anyway, she doesn't have other friends."

"She's quite a whirlwind," Angelo said. "But she seems to have excellent taste in suits, *non*?"

"Are you insane?" my mother said to him. "What were you *thinking*!"

My dad closed his eyes and pinched the bridge of his nose. "Maggie," he said, "explain to me again how you have a date."

"Um, he asked?" No one said a word. "And I said yes?"

"Well, I think it's a wonderful idea. I do," Angelo said as my mother glared at him. "Maggie is merely doing her assignment, and quite well, as a matter of fact. She seems to have assimilated in record time."

"Yes, I have," I said, agreeing, but then my mother glared at me and I shut up.

"Also," Angelo continued, as calm as ever, "let's all remember what it's like to be young and in this job."

Well, that certainly did the trick. Both of my parents grew thoughtful, rather than pissed. "If you want," I offered, "you can give me a curfew."

My parents looked at each other. "Don't look at me!" my mom said. "I have no idea!"

"Midnight?" my dad guessed. "Eleven?"

"Two," I said.

"In Manhattan on a Friday night?" my mom asked. "Uh-uh. No way."

"Most of the kids I go to school with don't even have curfews," I pointed out. "If you make me come home at eleven, I'm not going to get anything accomplished and they're going to think I'm weird. Well, weirder."

"What's Roux's curfew?" my dad asked.

"I'm pretty sure she doesn't know what that is."

"I don't know what what is?" she asked. "And Maggie, is that your closet? Because there are some beautiful pieces in there that are wasting away on some equally beautiful hangers."

I jerked a thumb in Angelo's direction. "He did most of my clothes shopping for me."

"Well done, sir!" Roux raised her palm for a high five, and then, in front of my very own eyes, Angelo high-fived her back.

My dad made a strangled sound and started pouring the wine.

"I don't know what what is?" Roux asked again.

This should be good. "Roux," I said, turning to her, "when's your curfew?"

She pretended to think for a second. "Um, I'm sorry, I'm not familiar with the word. Is it Greek? Latin, perhaps?"

Angelo started to laugh and Roux giggled. "Kidding! I don't have a curfew, Mr. and Mrs. Silver. My parents trust me to do my own thing."

"Twelve thirty," my mom said.

"Do I smell chili?" Roux asked.

Thirty minutes, three near-burns with the flatiron (Roux's mistakes, my scars), two stubbed toes (mine after walking into the bathroom wall), and a bowl of chili (Roux's) later, I was ready to go meet Jesse.

"Okay, I'm just gonna say it," Roux told me. "You look beautiful. Why do our parents send us to private school when we both have all these amazing clothes?"

I didn't answer. I was too busy looking at my reflection in the mirror. Roux had put me in dark jeans, that pink-not-salmon sweater, and leopard-print ballet flats. She even did my makeup, and although she almost blinded me with the mascara wand, the efforts paid off. I looked, for the first time in my life, like myself.

Roux grinned at our reflection in the mirror. "Jesse is going to flip his shit."

"That sounds terrible. Let's hope not."

"And why are you so tall? I feel like a garden gnome next to you." She looked really happy, though, and I knew she was in her element.

"Oh, c'mon," I told her. "You don't look like a garden gnome. You'd never wear that little hat they all wear."

"Yes, but the trousers look comfy."

When my parents saw me for the first time, I swear that I saw my mom's lip tremble, but all she said was, "You look very pretty, sweetie." Then she hugged me, so I knew all was forgiven with the not telling about the date thing.

My dad just squeezed my shoulder and said, "Jesse Oliver's not gonna know what hit him. And if he messes with you, then he's *really* not gonna know what hit him. I'll make sure of it."

"Tone down the violence, Dad," I said, but I was still smiling. It was kind of hard to stop.

Angelo kissed my cheek and said, "As beautiful as always. Roux, you have a talent."

"I know," she said, humble as ever as she leaned against the countertop. "Hey, do you guys ever do, like, family game night? Because I kick ass at Boggle."

"No," we all chorused.

"And I have to go," I added. "I'm late, I have to meet Jesse at the Flatiron Building in, like, ten minutes."

"I'll walk you ladies out," Angelo offered.

" 'Idiotic,' " Roux suddenly said. We all turned to look

at her and I realized she was studying my dad's crossword puzzle. "Forty-nine Down is 'idiotic.'"

My dad and I both zoomed to her side to inspect the grid. "Oh, for Pete's sake," my dad muttered, reaching for his pen.

"I could've sworn it was 'asinine,'" I added.

"Well, my work here is done." Roux sighed. "*Ciao ciao*, parents. Thanks for the chili and good times."

"Bye!" I said as Angelo escorted us into the elevator.

"Be safe!" I heard my mom yell.

"Aww, that's sweet," Roux said.

"Let's get this party started," I muttered.

CHAPTER 23

S o," I said, "are you trying to kill me?"

"What?" Jesse laughed.

"Sharp blades, a frozen body of water. I see what you're up to, and frankly, I'm on to your clever plan."

"Maggie," Jesse said, "it's *ice skating*."

We were standing at Wollman Rink in Central Park. Well, Jesse was standing there. I was standing five feet away with my arms crossed, refusing to move.

"It'll be fun!" he promised.

"Oh, falling on my ass on the ice, what fun!" I said.

"You're not going to fall," he promised. "Look, I'm here, I'll catch you."

The date had started off really well. Not that I had a lot to compare it to, other than every single date I had seen on TV and in the movies, but I had been enjoying myself. Jesse had met me at the Flatiron Building, just as he promised, and I don't want to sound boastful or anything, but he looked damn good. Curly hair everywhere, blue checkered shirt under a gray V-neck sweater, and khakis. I was pretty sure that Roux was going to pretend to slit her throat over the khakis, but Jesse wore them well. He had a peacoat, too, reminding me of the jacket he had put over me on Halloween night, and I couldn't help but smile when I saw it.

"We meet again," he said with a grin, and then he kissed me, and honestly, if the date had ended right there, it would still probably have been one of the best nights of my life.

"We do," I replied. "So what are we doing? Because I'm planning on being impressed."

"Oh, don't you worry about that," he said. "You're going to be impressed. They're going to have to invent a new word because 'impressed' won't even begin to cover it. We're going to start uptown and work our way downtown."

We both paused.

"Uh," I said.

"I am so sorry!" he said. "I was speaking geographically, I swear! Totally not a metaphor for, like, seducing you. I promise."

Seduce away, baby, I wanted to say, but I just shook my head instead. "Don't worry. I always speak geographically."

We took my town car after Jesse had a quick, whispered conversation with the driver, even though Jesse was like, "Um, the subway is right there," which is why I liked him. He'd rather take the subway even though his family probably could have afforded a fleet of cars to drive him around Columbus Circle for twelve hours straight! He's a man of the people!

And then we got to Wollman Rink.

"Um, can't we just say we did this?" I asked him. "I get nervous wearing other people's shoes."

"You do?"

"Yes. Because they're all warm and moist and then I have to *say* the word 'moist' and uggggh." I shuddered. "I hate that word. So that's why I don't ice skate."

Jesse crossed his arms and narrowed his eyes at me. "Ah," he said. "I get it."

I sighed. "Great, thank you so much. Why don't we take a walk and get some of the roasted peanuts and—"

"You don't know how to skate."

"I do know how. I just choose not to."

"You are *such* a bad liar!"

Was there a memo going around the city telling people that? "Well, yes, I am," I admitted. "But I'm not lying about choosing not to skate."

"Oh, so you know how to skate, then."

"Um . . ." I glanced at the ice rink, filled with skaters and impending doom.

"Look," Jesse said. "I'm really good. I play ice hockey in the winter here. I can teach you." He came over and held his hands out to me. "See? We get to hold hands the whole time. Kinda romantic."

"Will it be romantic when I fall and cause a domino reaction that sends thirteen people to the hospital?"

"Has anyone ever told you that you have a real flair for imagining the apocalypse?"

"They have now."

"C'mon!" He shook his hands at me. "What's the worst that can happen? You fall? Big deal. I told you, I'll catch you."

"I have weak ankles."

"I find that insanely attractive in a girl."

"Fine!" I sighed. "Fine, you win! But you can't laugh at me if I fall!"

"Not only will I not laugh," he promised, "but I'll beat up anyone else who laughs."

"Not if I get to them first," I muttered.

Not ten minutes later, I was wobbling out on the ice. "I think these skates are defective," I told Jesse. "They're too wobbly. I need the nonwobbly ones."

"Shut up and skate." He grinned.

I glanced over at the rink's edge, where all the newbie skaters were hanging on to the wall and carefully making their way around the ice. "Look," I said. "That must be where the new people hang out. I'll go over there."

Jesse looked to where I was pointing. "I think the average age of those people is five."

"Don't be ageist," I told him. "Go twirl or whatever. I'll watch and applaud."

"*Okaaaaaaay*," he singsonged as he pushed away, in a tone that told me all too well that he'd be back soon.

Twenty minutes went by and I managed to make it halfway around the rink. I felt sort of sweaty but still managed to smile and wave at Jesse every time he zoomed past. I even watched as he slowed down long enough to scoop up a little girl in a pink snowsuit who had just wiped out.

"You okay?" I heard him say, righting her on her feet, and my heart got sort of fluttery.

But that was probably just a sign of the heart attack I was going to have from the stress of skating.

"Hey," he said, stopping in front of me. "As much fun as it is watching you elbow small children out of your way while clinging to a makeshift wall . . ."

"That kid was hogging all the space!" I huffed. "He had it coming!"

". . . maybe we should skate together now." He held out his hands. "C'mon. Time to be brave."

He was right. For a girl who had always tried to blend in with the crowd, I wasn't doing myself any favors. "Okay," I said, "but—"

"No falling, no laughing if you do fall. I remember the rules."

And you know what? Skating was nice. Like, *niiiiiice*. Jesse went slow, skating backward and holding my mittened hands in his gloved ones. "Push and glide," he kept saying. "Like a hot knife through butter. Don't try to walk, push forward. That's it." In the time that it took me to go ten feet by myself, we had already gone around the rink twice. "Stop looking down at your feet," Jesse told me.

"I can't," I replied. "If I don't look at them, then I'm scared they're going to start zooming in the wrong direction."

Jesse laughed and tilted my face up so I could look at him. "Well, that *is* better," I admitted. "You're a good teacher."

"You're a terrible student." We both cracked up. "Relax, okay? It's just ice skating. It's not brain surgery. I would never take a girl to do brain surgery on a first date."

"How chivalrous." I took a deep breath. "Okay," I said. "Let's glide."

Eventually I got good enough that we could skate side by side, but Jesse kept my hand tight in his. I wasn't about to complain. "I'm sorry I was cranky about this," I told him as we got hot chocolate and waited for the Zamboni to clear the ice. "I'm having a good time."

"Yes, but are you impressed?"

"I am!" I giggled. (I was *giggling*.) "I didn't fall and you're a great teacher."

"Check and check." He pretended to cross things off his list. "Maybe I should have named my dog Zamboni."

"No, that sounds like a type of pasta."

Jesse laughed. "You're funny, Maggie," he said. "C'mon, another round before our next stop."

"There's another stop?"

"I've said too much already!"

"You're such a dork." I grinned. "Hey, guess what?"

"What?"

"Race ya."

When we were done, I got my own shoes back, which were wonderfully comfortable and did not have skating blades attached to them. "Okay," I said to Jesse, "so what's next? Swimming with dolphins?"

"Let me guess," he said as he tugged his Converse back on his feet. "You're scared of dolphins."

"Nope. Love 'em. Especially that high-pitched squealing thing they do. Can't get enough of it."

"Awesome. Because we're not swimming with dolphins."

"Oh."

"Don't worry, I've got a few things up my sleeve. *Impressive* things."

"Of course." I watched as he started to walk back toward where the car had dropped us off. "Hey, where are you going?"

"I thought your chauffeur awaits."

"My chauffeur is probably enjoying his thirty-fifth cigarette of the evening. And he makes too many wrong turns. Let's take the subway instead."

I knew what I was doing. I knew that the Collective wouldn't approve, and I knew that my parents would probably hit the roof if they found out that I gave my car the slip, but I had to start making some executive decisions. No other single spy in the network had a driver taking them around town, and even though I was young, I was still a spy. This was my job now, no one else's.

"C'mon, let's go," I said. "You love the 6 train, admit it."

"Better yet, let's walk." Jesse held out his hand to me. "You're not too cold?"

"I'm tough," I said. "Can't wait to see the next act."

CHAPTER 24

"Are you peeking? You're peeking."

"I'm not!"

Jesse's hands were over my eyes, and my hands were over his hands, and he was doing a craptastic job of leading me through . . . well, somewhere. I couldn't see a thing. All I knew is that we were inside and our voices seemed to echo in circles around us.

"I'm not peeking!" I said again as Jesse laughed. "Please don't walk me into a wall."

"Okay, you can look."

I blinked a few times and saw a haphazard drywall in front of us. We were in the middle of what looked like a construction site, surrounded by bare lightbulbs, Sheetrock, and what I hoped wasn't asbestos dust. "Wow," I said. "Construction."

"This isn't quite the surprise yet," he admitted. "One question, though. Are you afraid of the dark?"

"You realize that that's something a serial killer would say on a first date, right?"

He gave me a gentle shove. "Little Miss Apocalypse. So you're okay if it's a little dark?"

"Just as long as you're not planning on murdering me."

"Great. Follow me."

I held his hand (seriously couldn't get enough of that) and followed him through a plastic sheet and into . . .

"Oh my God." I gasped. "Oh my God."

We were standing under a huge glass ceiling that arched into the night sky, reaching toward the stars. Round art deco doorways surrounded us and I hung on to the wrought-iron railing and kept looking up. "What is this?" I asked Jesse.

"It's an old building that's being turned into a hotel," he said, grinning at the obvious amazement on my face. "My dad's friend bought it, so I asked if we could sneak in. I remembered that you said you missed seeing the sky." He waved his hands toward the ceiling. "I thought I would just try to get you a little closer to it." Then he paused. "Too cheesy again?"

"No," I said. "No, it's *perfect*. It's beautiful, it's so . . . what's the word? Majestic. It's majestic."

We stood next to each other, Jesse's arm around me, and gazed up for what seemed like hours. "You can actually see stars," I told him.

"I think that's a plane."

"No, not that. That one." I pointed up, which really didn't indicate anything, but Jesse nodded anyway. "Maybe it's a planet."

"Maybe." He held me a little tighter and I let him. No guy had ever hugged me before, at least a guy that wasn't my

223

dad or Angelo or someone thirty years older than me. Jesse smelled really good, like shampoo and soap, and I rested my head on his chest and pointed again. "What's that?"

"The Woolworth Building. Where they make woolworths." I could hear and feel him laugh at the same time. "Just kidding, I have no idea what they make there."

"Let's say unicorns," I said.

"Sure, why not? Unicorns for everyone."

"Hooray! Hey, by the way?"

"Yeah?"

"I'm very impressed."

He smiled and then leaned down to kiss me. "I thought you might be."

"I just can't wait for our second date if this is the first one!"

"Well, that's when we do a tour of the unicorn factory," he teased. "Spoiler alert!"

"Hey, can I ask you a question?"

"I have a feeling that my answer doesn't matter."

"True. How did you know all these buildings? This one, the Woolworth one. You're like a weird architecture groupie."

Jesse's eyes dimmed a little and I saw him go somewhere that I couldn't follow. "My mom," he admitted after a few seconds. "She used to take me around after school and show me all the buildings. She wanted to be an architect but then she married my dad and they had me instead."

I wrapped both my arms around his waist and held on tight. "I'm sorry. I know you miss her."

"S'okay. Don't be sorry."

"Where else did she take you?"

"Everywhere. Public gardens, private gardens, old carriage houses. I just wanted to play video games back then and she dragged me everywhere. I was a stupid kid."

"You were a *kid*."

"She used to take me to Gramercy Park but we could never get in."

What?

"What?" I said, looking up at him.

"It's a park that's completely locked. You can't get in unless you have a key and—"

"No, I know what it is." My heart was starting to race. "You couldn't get in?"

"Nope. Not without the key. And you have to live on the park to get one and we don't. Wah-waaaahh." He took his peacoat and pulled it around both of us since it was pretty chilly in the atrium. "One day."

"Maybe," I said, then looked back up at the night sky. "Maybe you should make a wish."

"I thought you could only wish on falling stars."

"I know, but think about it. That's sort of bad luck if a star falls out of the sky. Like maybe your dreams are burning through the atmosphere!" I covered my mouth in fake terror. "Quick, wish on the ones still in the sky!"

Jesse just shook his head, then looked up. "I wish . . ."

"No, you can't say it out loud or it might not come true."

"There's a lot of rules here!"

"Just two."

Jesse sighed and then closed his eyes. "Okay," he said after a minute. "Wish wished. You wanna get out of here?"

"Yes," I said, standing on my tiptoes to kiss him. "And I know just where we should go."

"What? Not to ruin the surprise, but we're supposed to have dinner at a restaurant that serves a kind of food that rhymes with mooshi."

"Awww, that's sweet. You should cancel the reservation."

"But . . ."

"C'mon," I said, taking his arm. "It's *my* turn to impress *you*."

CHAPTER 25

I think," I told Jesse as we walked up Irving Place, "that bread is my favorite food group. It should be the whole food pyramid."

"Do they still have the food pyramid?" he asked, drinking water and carrying our bag from Whole Foods on Union Square. I helped to lighten the load by carrying the baguette and eating it as we walked. "Is that still a thing?"

"I think it's, like, the food rhombus now."

He started to laugh. "It's food geometry. Pick a shape, any shape!"

"They could make it a food dodecahedron and as long as it was filled with bread, I'd support it. Oh look, here we are."

We crossed the street and stood in front of the Gramercy Park gates. "Um, Maggie?" Jesse said. "I've stood at this gate before."

"Oh, you have? Really? Gee, if only you had said something." I rolled my eyes at him. "Dork, I *know* you've stood here. You told me half an hour ago."

"So why is this better than sushi?"

"I liked when you said it rhymed with mooshi. That was cute." I was so excited that I was wiggling around.

"Maggie."

"Okay, okay, turn around."

But he just stood there, eyeing me. "Whyyyyy?"

"Becaaaaause." I took his arm and started to turn him around. "Just trust me, okay? Have some faith. Don't eat my bread, though, for real."

Jesse looked a little nervous, as if it were possible for him to look any cuter, and his turn-around was reluctant. Still, he turned, and when he couldn't see, I fished my old reliable paper clip out of my pocket and popped the lock with almost zero effort, just like Angelo had taught me all those years ago.

"Okay," I said, opening the gate. "You can look now."

Jesse's mouth fell open when he saw what I had done. I had never actually seen anyone be rendered speechless before. "Is this okay?" I asked. "I'm not, like, making you feel bad about your mom, am I?"

"No!" he gasped. "You have a *key*?"

"It's probably better if you don't ask too many questions," I told him. "Just know that I have my ways."

He was looking at me like he had never seen me before. "We can just go in?"

"After you."

"*Maggie.*"

"C'mon," I said, "before we get arrested for breaking and entering."

He walked through the gate like he was afraid it might reach out and grab him, and I followed and carefully shut it behind us. "We probably have to be a little sneaky," I murmured, "since technically no one's allowed in here at night, key or not."

"Sneak away," he replied, and we went and sat on the bench where Angelo and I had sat on my first day in the city, back when I thought Jesse was a Manhattan rich-kid jerk and that this job would be easy.

Nothing had worked out the way I thought it would.

I showed Jesse my favorite pagoda birdhouse ("Is that a pineapple on top?" he asked. "Because if it is, that is cool"), and we watched the city move around us, blinking lights and sounding horns and people who looked like shadows as they hurried past us. No one knew we were there, hidden by wrought iron and trees older than anyone in the five boroughs.

"Impressed?" I asked after we spent a few minutes just curled up next to each other. The bench could have been a little more comfortable, but I wasn't complaining.

"I am," he said. "Impressed and happy. Very, very happy."

I smiled at him and pretended to fluff my hair. "We make a good team," I told him. "You and me, running around town, finding cool things to do. We should market this."

"Nah, let's keep it our little secret." Jesse rested his head on top of mine and passed me some strawberries. "Here, eat up. You earned it."

"You did way more than me," I admitted. "All I did was bring you here. No big whoop."

"No, Mags." He was quiet for a minute, and when he spoke again, his voice sounded shaky. "This means a lot."

Was Jesse crying? I glanced up to see him thumbing at his eyes and laughing a little, like he was embarrassed.

"Um, I'm not sure I was supposed to make you cry," I said. I had never seen a guy cry before. It was weird, like seeing your dad cry for the first time, but also so sweet.

"You didn't make me cry," he said, clearing his throat. "Sorry, sorry. It's just been a long time since something made me happy. And now you make me happy every time I see you. I missed it."

Now I was welling up, too. "No, I know what you mean," I told him. "I know what it's like to just sit and wait for something to happen and think that it might not."

"It's like, I have all this luck and wealth and privilege, but who gives a shit? People expect me to be some spoiled brat, so then I act like some spoiled brat—I mean, I stole that book, what a dumbass—but it's not me at all. And then when I try to act like an upright citizen, volunteer and all that, they accuse me of using my dad's connections to get ahead. But if I *don't* do anything, then my dad gets pissed that I'm not doing anything. And then my mom decides that *she's* the one who needs a break from *her* life. . . ." He sighed and looked up through the trees. "It's like I can't get out."

I had to take a deep breath because I had never heard another person say how I felt. "It's, like, how can you become an adult when everyone wants you to stay a child?"

"Exactly!" Jesse wriggled into his coat some more and I tightened my scarf around my neck. November seemed to be getting colder by the minute, but neither of us wanted to leave. "Oh, shit, are *you* crying now?"

"No!" I said, even as I was blinking back tears. "I just know what you mean about responsibility and living up to expectations. My parents are the same way. If I try to do things my way, then they get pissed that I'm not doing them their way. But maybe their way isn't my way, you know? Maybe I'm supposed to make my own path and not always follow theirs."

"Easier said than done," Jesse said.

"Tell me about it. So what do we do?"

"I dunno. Stand up for ourselves? Make ourselves happy? Screw everything else?"

"Damn the man!" I said as we started laughing. "We're rebels! Get out of our way!"

"Well, we already broke into a park. A life of crime seems to be our only option."

"I'm sorry, *who* broke into the park? There's no 'we' in that sentence, my friend."

"Yes, but I'm an accomplice."

"The Boris to my Natasha."

"Who?"

Jesse obviously hadn't watched hours of old cartoons at Angelo's house when he was a kid. "They're these cartoon characters from *Rocky & Bullwinkle* and . . . you know what? Never mind."

I hated to admit it, but I just realized he'd given me an opening. Jesse was talking about his dad. This was my chance.

"Your dad sounds kind of difficult," I ventured.

231

Jesse laughed through his nose. "That's one word for it. He just doesn't talk. Like, ever. I don't even know what we would talk *about* if we did talk."

I traced a pattern on the edge of Jesse's scarf as I curled up next to him. "Is he a workaholic?"

"That depends. Does someone who works all day and night count as a workaholic?" He sighed and tightened his arm around me. "He's always obsessing about stories. Stories, all the time. He's been working on this one story about these spies. . . ."

I could literally feel the acid start to pool and burn in my stomach.

". . . and he was going to run it and clear everything, but I don't know. Something went haywire and now he's not sure."

The adrenaline was rushing through my body. I was glad it was so dark that Jesse couldn't see my flushed cheeks.

"He's been so pissed off about it. It's like work rules his life. It doesn't matter what I do, only what I don't do. Hey, are you shaking?"

I was.

"Whoa, okay, that was fun, but if you freeze to death, your parents are going to kill me."

"No, they won't," I said, even though they totally would. "Why did the thing with your dad's story fall through?" It was messy, I knew. I was pushing for answers instead of letting them come to me. If this were safecracking, a cobalt wall would have fallen down by now, blocking me out.

But as I've learned, people aren't safes.

"I have no idea," Jesse said as he stood up. "He barely talks, remember? Hey, do me a favor?"

"Of course," I whispered. At that moment, I would have done almost anything for Jesse. Anything except ruin my job.

"Bring me back here again? Maybe in the daytime?" His smile was hopeful and kind, two things I never thought he'd be, and it felt like my heart was beating too hard, aching with every kind word.

"I promise," I said.

"You still crying?"

"No, are you kidding? I'm too busy freezing to death."

We gathered up our food remnants, my heart still pounding in my ears, my hands still shaking a little. What did Jesse mean, *his dad wasn't sure about the story*? Was this whole thing for nothing? Was he not going to run it? If he didn't, would we still have to leave? Would I have to move away from Jesse and Roux?

"Well, shall we?" Jesse said, interrupting my racing thoughts. "Ready for the subway ride of your life? I didn't want to say anything, but I think you're really going to be impressed with the 6 train." He wiggled his eyebrows at me.

I pretended to kick him in the shins and he jumped away. "You're so mean!" he yelped, even though he was laughing. "You have a violent streak and it kind of turns me on."

"Save it for the next date," I said, even though I wasn't sure there would be a next one.

We crept through the gate, shutting it without making a sound, and left the park just as we had found it. Nothing looked different outside the park, either, the city the same as it ever was.

The only thing that had changed, I realized, was me.

CHAPTER 26

My parents were waiting up for me, of course, along with Angelo. I had never gone out this much in my life, so I wasn't used to these little nighttime powwow sessions. And I certainly wasn't ready for this one.

"So did you have a lovely time?" Angelo asked.

"Did you get the files?" my dad asked.

"Was he nice to you? Did he open doors?" That was my mom, of course. I was pretty sure that if Jesse had been anything less than chivalrous, she would have hacked into his computer and deleted his entire hard drive, mission be damned.

"Jesse was nice. And yes, many doors were opened." I left out the part where *I* was the one who had opened the Gramercy Park gate for *him*. "Can we just talk tomorrow? I'm tired." I had never been less tired in my life, but I needed time to sort things out in my head.

"Of course," Angelo said, even though both my parents were already opening their mouths to speak. "I think we all know how exhausting it can be to go undercover for long periods of time, yes? Maggie needs her rest."

"I'm a growing teenager," I added. "You don't want to stunt me."

"Okay," my mom said. "I want a sitrep bright and early tomorrow morning, though!"

I barely slept that night, tossing and turning and trying to figure out what Jesse had meant about his dad and the article. Was he not going to run it? What had changed his mind? If he still planned to run it, would it be delayed? I was so anxious that I spent the early-morning hours googling "Armand Oliver," looking for any clues or signs. There were a few news stories, but otherwise it was the same stuff I had read earlier. The only weak link in Armand's team, it turned out, was his son. I fell asleep in bed with my laptop open in front of me, which explained why I woke up at nearly noon with my face mashed into the left-hand side of the keyboard.

"What happened to you?" my dad asked when I stumbled into the kitchen, bleary-eyed and rubbing my cheek. "Did your computer slap you?"

"I was working late," I mumbled. "The computer won."

"Okay, we're ready for you to report in. How was your date?" my mom asked. "Did you manage to get back into the Olivers' house again? Did you find out if—"

"Mom, please," I said, and I must have sounded crankier than usual because both of my parents looked at me. "Why does it always have to be an interrogation first thing in the morning?"

"Margaret," my dad said.

Great. *Margaret.* That boded well.

"I'm sorry," I said. "I'm just tired and I need to think."

"So you *did* find out something," my mom said. "What was it?"

I sat down at the counter and fiddled with the edge of a manila envelope. "I asked Jesse about his dad, and he said that he wasn't sure if his dad was going to run the article."

"*You told him about the article?*" both of my parents exploded.

"*Of course not!*" I exploded right back. (If you learn nothing else from me, learn this: falling asleep on your computer's keyboard can make you really, really cranky.) "How dumb do you think I am? I was just asking him about his family, and he said his dad's been really upset about this one article getting away."

My parents deflated a little. "Oh, so he didn't say that it was *the* article," my dad said.

"No, but I think it might be. Jesse said it was some big secret about spies, but that a deal had fallen through and his dad was really pissed off."

My mom still looked suspicious. "You like him," she finally said.

"Armand?"

"Jesse."

Busted.

"Well, it's kind of hard not to," I admitted. "He's really nice, he's kind, he holds doors open, and he helps little kids who fall down ice skating."

My mom took a deep breath. "Sweetheart," she said.

"Do you have any proof that Armand might not run the article?"

"Just what Jesse said," I admitted. "But I believe him. He's told me lots of things before, personal things about his family."

"Did *you* tell him anything?"

"What? No! Of course not! We were just sitting at the park last night and—"

"Which park?" Now my dad had joined the discussion, and both of my parents were leaning in, like they were about to ensnare me.

"Gramercy. Why, what—?"

"You went to Gramercy Park by yourself at night?" my mom cried. "Are you serious right now? Where was your driver? I *knew* we should have talked last night!"

"I had to ditch him. It was too obvious!" I continued as both of my parents' tempers seemed to erupt out of the top of their heads. "It was making Jesse feel uncomfortable! And what's the big deal about Gramercy Park? I've been there a million times with Angelo!"

"With Angelo, yes!" my dad said. "Not by yourself! Do you realize how dangerous that can be?"

"To be inside a locked park at night in one of the safest neighborhoods in Manhattan? No, I didn't realize I was in mortal peril."

My mom was pacing again. "This was a bad idea!" She was ranting, but I didn't know if she was talking to me or to my dad. "I told you, didn't I? I said, she's too young, she's not ready!"

"Just calm down," my dad said.

"Will someone please explain to me what's going on here?" I yelled back. "Why are we mad all of a sudden?"

"Maggie, please," my dad said. "Just sit down."

"I *am* sitting! Mom's the one who's standing!"

"You broke into the park, didn't you?" my mom said. "Did Jesse see you?"

"I made him turn around," I admitted. "But he didn't care, he thought it was cool."

My mom looked at my dad. "He thought it was cool," she repeated.

"I just meant that he didn't think it was a big deal!"

"How do you know that Jesse isn't just feeding you information?" my dad asked. "To throw you off? Or that Armand isn't giving him the wrong information so that Jesse won't ruin the deal?"

"What, so you're saying that Jesse works for his dad now? That's crazy!"

"Well, you work for us," my mom said.

"I don't work for *you*!" I shot back. "I work for the Collective! And if you'd listen to what I'm telling you, you'd know that I was trying to do my job! For the Collective!"

All three of us were standing now, each in a different spot in the kitchen, a literal standoff.

"I mean," I continued, "my whole job is to like Jesse Oliver, right? That was the assignment, if memory serves."

"Your job is to *pretend* to like him," my mom told me. "And to stop this article from running."

"Don't you think it's sort of weird to *pretend* to like

someone?" I said. "And sneaky? And maybe not very emotionally healthy?"

"That's the job, kiddo," my dad said. "We're not here to make real friends."

I don't know if it was the lack of sleep, the lack of caffeine, or the fact that the Q, A, and Z keys were now deeply imprinted on my cheek, but that comment pushed me over the edge. "Exactly," I said. "I'm not here to make friends. And that's the problem. How come I don't get to make any friends? How come I don't get to go to a normal school or Halloween parties? How come you just decided all this for me?"

"Because you have a gift!" my mom said. "It's more than a gift. You have this amazing, one-of-a-kind ability to open locks and safes, and you can use that ability to right wrongs in the world!"

"What if I don't want to?"

That stopped the room. Even the clock on the wall seemed to stop ticking. "What do you mean, you don't want to?" my dad said. "This is all you've talked about since you were four!"

"I'm not four anymore! Have you noticed? I'm almost seventeen, I'm almost an adult. Why don't I get to make decisions about my life? What's so wrong with my making a friend? Or worse, dating a boy? I also wanted to be a veterinarian and a cowgirl when I was four, but things change. Maybe *I've* changed, did you ever think of that?"

"You were born into this," my mom said. "That's life. You don't always get to choose your options."

"This isn't the royal family!" I protested. "It's not some blood lineage! This is crazier than the royal family, and *that* is saying something!"

"So, what?" my dad asked. "You don't want to do this anymore? You're done?"

"What if I am? Is that all you like about me, the fact that I can open locks and safes? Is that really all there is? You know, I'll say this for Jesse. He has no idea what I can do and he doesn't care. He *still* likes me."

"Do you think he would still like you if he knew what you were doing?" My mom's voice wasn't angry anymore, just resigned. "Honey, look. Your dad and I love you very, very much. We would love you even if you sat and watched television all day. But this is our job. This is our family. This is what we do. And you don't get to just throw all that away because you got an assignment to like a boy."

"But how can you expect me to make a choice about my life, my future, when I know only one option? All I know is this job. Yeah, I'm good at safecracking, but what if I'm better at being a normal person? What if it makes me happier?"

Neither of my parents said anything.

"Yeah, that's what I thought." I sighed. "This is just a job. It's my life, but it's all about the job for you. I get it now."

"Maggie . . ."

But I turned on my heel and walked away from my dad's voice. "Just let her go," I heard my mom say. And she was right. I needed time to think.

I found my phone and dialed Angelo's number, waiting

for him to pick up. Four rings later, I heard, "Hello, you've reached my mobile. I apologize for not being able to answer at the present time. . . ."

"Damn it," I said, hanging up. That was Angelo's "I'm out on a job" message, not his normal away message. I had no idea if he was in Cincinnati or Zaire and even less of an idea about when he'd be returning.

I knew I was right, though. I *knew* it. Angelo used to always talk about instincts, about following them to see where they led. "People lie," he said, "but instincts do not." I knew my instincts were kicking in about Armand killing the story, and it wasn't just because I liked Jesse, even though that's what my parents thought.

I started to think about everything that Angelo had told me. *Listen. Be beige. Never look back. There is always a choice.*

By that night, I had something better than a choice.

I had a friend.

CHAPTER 27

I came out of my room around six that night, waving my "for civilian use only" cell phone. "Hey," I said.

"Hey," my mom said. "Your dad and I were talking and we just think we need to talk about this more. As a family."

But talking hadn't got me very far. I was ready—very ready—to start doing.

"Can we talk later? Roux just called."

"Roux," my dad said. "The 'idiotic' Roux?"

He was trying to make me smile, but I wasn't in the mood. I was still smarting from our argument, from the idea that I might not be what my parents wanted me to be. Would they still love me, or even like me, if I left the Collective?

Was I even *allowed* to leave?

"Yeah, it was Roux," I said, ignoring his joke. "She just broke up with this guy she met at the Halloween party. She wants me to come over."

"Right now? We were going to order Chinese."

My parents were obviously tiptoeing around me. It was *bizarre*.

"Can I go see Roux instead? She wants me to spend the night."

"Spend the night?"

I sighed the longest, most world-weary sigh in the world. "Yes. That's what girls do. They have sleepovers. Or am I not allowed to do that now?" My lying skills had improved. God knows I had had enough practice.

"What about school?"

"I'll just go with her tomorrow. Look," I added when my parents didn't say anything. "I know I'm not supposed to make friends. But if Roux starts to think that something's up with our so-called friendship, then she's going to be a nightmare to deal with and it's going to mess up everything at school. Trust me, there are serious girl politics going on here. And I told her I'd come over."

My parents looked at one another. "It can't hurt," my dad finally said, just as I knew he would. He was always the pushover. "It's just one night."

"Will you get enough sleep? You've had a long day and you were out late." I let my mom come close enough to brush some hair out of my eyes. "You look tired."

Which is, of course, the least helpful thing to say to someone who's tired, but I let it go. "I don't know. It depends on how upset Roux is. She'll probably cry until about midnight or so." Roux would have pitched a fit if she could hear how I was describing her. "She's on hold right now, I told her I'd ask you."

"Just for tonight," my mom said. "School tomorrow, you come home, we talk in the afternoon. Deal?"

"Deal," I said, then turned around and spoke to the nonexistent person on the other end of the phone. "Roux? Yeah, it's cool. I'll be there soon. . . . Okay, okay, bye."

My mom came into my room as I was finishing up packing. "Honey?"

"What?" I shoved a sweater into my bag, then packed a clean uniform.

"Your dad and I were talking earlier, and we were saying how hard it is to be a spy, but how much harder it is to raise one." She smiled a little. "We're learning here."

"Why don't you just trust me, then?" I asked. The day suddenly felt a hundred hours long. "Why can't you just say, 'Okay, Maggie, we believe in you. Go forth and do your job.'"

"Because when you do this job, it's hard to not have your judgment clouded, especially on your first solo assignment."

"And you think Jesse is a cloud."

"I think . . ." My mom was choosing her words carefully, I could tell. "I think that you want to protect him from whatever his father might do, even if you don't realize that."

She was right.

"You're wrong," I said. "I don't think his dad's going to run the article."

"That may be true, but that's not your decision to make. It's the Collective's."

"What if they're wrong?"

245

My mom shrugged. "Then they'll deal with the consequences."

"But if it affects Jesse's dad, then Jesse has to deal with the consequences, too. You don't understand. His mom . . ."

I stopped myself before I got started. I had promised Jesse that I wouldn't tell anyone about his mom leaving, and I intended to keep at least one of my promises to him. "Can I go?" I said instead. "Roux's waiting, and you can imagine what she's like when she has to wait."

My mom sighed. "Yeah, sure. Got your coat?"

"Of course. It's November." I didn't know a single other spy in the world whose mother felt the need to remind her to take her coat.

The ever-present town car was waiting downstairs and I sent the driver to an address a block from Roux's actual house. There was an alley that connected the two parts of the street, and after he dropped me off, I let myself into one building (no doorman, thank God), walked straight down the hall, and went out the back door to the alley.

Two minutes later, I was at Roux's front door with nary a driver in sight.

"Hey, Harold," I said when I saw her cranky doorman. "What's new? Things good? Wife okay? Kids?" He didn't even blink. "Great, glad to hear it. Do you mind buzzing Roux?"

He turned and pressed a button. Two rings later, I heard, "HELLOOOOO, HAROLD! It's been too long! We haven't talked since this afternoon! Did you miss me? Say yes, you'll break my heart if you don't."

I have to hand it to Harold, he was as stoic as a soldier. A soldier in the Roux War.

"There's a young lady to see you, Scarlet."

"Ugh, Hare-Bear, call me Roux, for the love of God. Why do you insist on being so formal? Oh, by the way, I owe you twenty-five dollars. I stubbed my toe on my bed and let's just say that my language got colorful."

I don't know how much Harold made per year, but whatever it was, it wasn't enough.

"Maggie?" Now Roux was yelling down the phone at me. "Is that you?"

"It's me," I said. "Let me up."

"Is it really her, Harold? You know this crazy city. Imposters everywhere!"

I raised an eyebrow at Harold when he narrowed his eyes at me. "Really?" I said.

"Oh, that's Maggie, I'd know that sarcasm anywhere. Come on up, lady! Harold, let her pass."

When I got upstairs, Roux flung the front door wide open. "I love surprises!" She grinned. "What are you doing here? Why didn't you just call or text? Did you give up technology for Lent?"

"Lent's not until the spring."

"I didn't know you were Catholic!"

"What? No, I'm not." Not even five seconds had passed and Roux had already completely distracted me. "I came over because I wanted to talk to you."

"Excellent." She shut the door behind me and watched as I started to kick off my shoes. "Aww, you're so polite.

Listen, how cool do you think this would be? Next year I wanna make Harold dress up as Gandalf for Halloween."

"The wizard?"

"No, the other Gandalf. Yes, the wizard! How many famous Gandalfs are there? Anyway, this is amazing. I just thought of this while you were in the elevator. He'll dress up as Gandalf and then anytime someone comes to the building and doesn't get allowed in, he can stand there and say, "YOU SHALL NOT PASS!" Roux looked delighted. "Isn't that great? He'll complain, but I think he'd look good in a cloak and a floppy hat."

I could feel a major headache starting to pulse and I wondered if I had made a huge mistake by coming here.

"Uh-oh, what's wrong?" Roux said, reading my face. "Trouble in Jesse paradise? Was the first date that bad? I've been waiting for you to call me, you know. *Tsk-tsk.*"

My date with Jesse felt like it had happened last week rather than just yesterday. "No, it was fine. It was really nice."

Roux waited for me to say more, and when I didn't, she said, "Fine and nice? Wow, those are sexy adjectives. I bet you've waited your whole life to go on your first date to say it was 'fine' and 'nice.'" She shook her head. "If he took you bowling, I'll kill him. Why do guys think bowling is fun? It's not fun."

"No, we went ice skating. And he took me to this amazing atrium and we saw stars."

"Ooooh." She plopped herself down on the couch and tucked her legs against her chest. "That sounds very romantical. Tell me everything."

I sat down next to her, feeling a little ill. My nerves were jangled, to say the least, and it was hard to hold a thought in my head. If this didn't work, I was screwed.

"Do you really want to know everything?"

"Duh," she said, then wiggled her toes. "Do you like the color? Is it too red?"

"It's fine."

She made a face. "Fine, fine, fine. Something's wrong." She sounded like Angelo when she said that. "Tell it to your old friend Roux."

I was scared, though. I had spent most of the day worried about how I had been lying to Jesse, but I was only now realizing that I had been lying to Roux, too. And worse, I had been pretending to be friends with someone who didn't have any friends left. I knew when I started this assignment that I would be digging a few large holes, but now I didn't know how to fill them back up.

"Maggie?" Roux was as quiet as I had ever heard her. "Um, is everything okay? You look . . . well, not great. No offense."

It was the first time I had heard her actively try not to offend. "I . . . I have something to tell you?" I said, even though it came out like a question. "And I'm really scared?"

She scooted closer to me on the couch. "Okay," she said. "Well, just tell me. Let 'er rip."

But I didn't have the words. I had never had to say them before and now they weren't there, leaving me speechless. "I'm not sure how to say it," I admitted. "It's hard."

Roux was growing more concerned by the minute. "You can trust me, I'm your friend. Right? We *are* friends, right?"

That only made it worse, and I could feel my eyes watering. How many times had I cried on this assignment? At this rate I would dehydrate by the time I turned seventeen.

"Okay, Maggie." Roux turned so she was sitting directly in front of me. "I'll say something instead, okay? Is that cool?"

I nodded and thumbed at my eyes.

"Here's the thing. Before you came here, I was a shitty friend. You know that, I know that. I lied, I cheated with guys that were losers—and I'm still not sure why, but I'm going to blame my parents—I spread rumors. I did all the things that girls do on those ABC Family shows. And it made me really, really sad, but I kept doing it because I didn't know what else to do.

"And then you showed up at school and we became friends and now it's like"—Roux's voice was getting wobbly—"you taught me how to be a good friend. You listen to me, you don't tease me about being all crazy sometimes, you made sure that I was okay after the Halloween party. I didn't know how to be a friend until I met you, so if that's why you don't want to tell me whatever it is that you need to say, then I just want you to know that I've learned. I can be a friend to you because you've been a friend to me."

Roux was crying now, too. "Okay? Does that make sense? I know I ramble, just ask Harold." We both laughed a little and then she got up to find tissues. "How many boxes of Kleenex does one household need?" I heard her mutter, but she returned after a minute. "Here, they're the good kind, not those cheap, scratchy ones."

I wiped my eyes and nose. "That was really beautiful." I sniffled. "I've never really had a friend, either, and I'm scared that what I'm about to tell you is going to ruin our friendship."

"Well, since I don't have a boyfriend that you can sleep with, I highly doubt that."

"Ooh, just wait." I got up and started to pace. Apparently my mother's nervous habits were genetic.

"I'll get motion sickness if you keep doing that," Roux said. "Just spit it out. Preach to the choir. You'll feel better and then we can order food and watch movies and you can tell me everything about your date with Jess."

I took a deep, deep breath. "Roux? I'm a spy."

"Honey, Halloween was almost two weeks ago. Time to get out of character."

I had forgotten about my costume. "No, for real. That's what I do. That's why I came to our school. My parents and I are spies."

Roux sat there for almost a full minute without saying a word. (A possible record for her.) I stood there, my heart beating so fast that I thought I might be having my first anxiety attack. "We work for an organization called the Collective. Jesse's dad's magazine is going to publish an article about us, and it's going to name names, including mine and my parents'. So they assigned me to become friends with Jesse Oliver so I could get access to his dad and stop the article from happening."

I wasn't sure if the blood was rushing to or from my head, but either way, it didn't feel good. Roux still wasn't talking. "You need to say something now," I told her. "Please."

She stood up very slowly, then grabbed a couch pillow and hurled it across the room. "Are you *kidding* me?" she cried. "I tell you all this stuff about learning how to be a good friend and you come back with this crazy story about spies? SPIES! You're not even seventeen yet, how could you be a spy?"

"Safecracker," I managed to choke out. "I pick locks and open safes."

"Right. And I can fly. Are you mentally ill?" Roux paused, another pillow clutched in her hands. "You are, aren't you. You suffer from delusions. Great, that's just *great*!" She tossed the pillow down on the ground. "I went from having no friends to having one who's batshit crazy!"

I stood up and went over to my bag. "Good! Leave!" Roux said. "I can't believe I told you all those things about friendship. This is so embarrassing. I trusted you!"

"Roux—"

"No, do not talk to me. Wait, are you recording this?"

"What? No, Roux, I . . ."

"Are you gonna put it on YouTube so everyone can see what an idiot I am?"

"Roux!"

I yelled so loud that she froze with a third pillow in her hands. "Look," I said, then unzipped my purse and dumped all twelve of my passports out on the couch. They lay there in a dark blue heap, each one with my picture inside, embossed with a very real-looking and very fake-being gold logo, courtesy of Angelo's forgery skills. "I'm not lying," I said. "Not anymore, at least. And I need your help."

CHAPTER 28

"So you, like, save the world?"

Roux and I were sitting on the marble countertop in her massive kitchen, all twelve of my passports lying between us. Roux had gone through each one, scanning them like she was a border agent. "Daisy?" she said at one point. "Really? You couldn't call yourself Jennifer or something? Wow, these look so real!"

It had taken a while to convince Roux, even after the big passport reveal. "I think you're on the run from the law!" she had screamed.

"Where's your safe?" I asked her. "Just tell me where it is!"

"What safe? We don't have a safe, we—"

"Roux, your parents are gajillionaires, you live in a penthouse on the Upper East Side, and the artwork in your foyer would be worth $2.6 million if it weren't fake. Tell me where the goddamn safe is."

She paused. "How did you know it's a fake?"

"Because the real artwork is in the Collective's vault in London."

"The safe's upstairs in my parents' closet."

Ten minutes later, the safe was open and Roux's jaw was on the floor. "Do you believe me now?" I said, blowing my hair out of my face. "Or do you need me to break into your neighbor's apartment?"

"No, I think we're good," Roux said.

Half an hour later, we were eating Thai food in her kitchen. I was starving after not eating since breakfast, but Roux was too wound up to eat. "So, you and your parents basically travel the world and stop bad guys."

"In a nutshell," I said, shoveling pad thai into my mouth.

"Have you ever killed anyone?"

"Oh my God, no. I'm a safecracker, not an assassin."

Roux's eyes went wide. "Angelo was lying, wasn't he. He's really an assassin."

"What? No, he's a forger. Believe me, I've met assassins. They're not as friendly as Angelo."

Roux wasn't convinced. "You know an assassin! That means that *I* know an assassin!"

"Roux? Bring it back home. He's a forger, I swear."

"Okay, sorry." She took a deep breath and smoothed her already-smooth hair down. "This is all just really new. Is this why you knew how to forge my mom's signature?"

"Yes. We don't have a lot of time here."

Roux sat up and squared her shoulders, looking like the least dangerous warrior ever. "Well, I'm ready," she said. "Whatever you need me to do, I can do it. Sidekick, assistant, resident ass-kicker, I got it."

"We need to break into Armand Oliver's computer, find out who's been trying to sell this story to him, then go find that person, find out where they're hiding these documents, get the documents, make sure they're not forgeries, and then destroy them."

Roux blinked a few times. "Well," she finally said. "That sounds ambitious."

"It is. So are you in?"

"Hey, remember that time when I gave you a really emotional and heartwarming speech about friendship, and then you told me you were a spy and brought a dozen false passports into my house and then broke into my parents' safe?" Roux gestured at me with her chopsticks. "Yes, of course I'm in. This is the best thing that's happened to me in years. When do we start?"

"As soon as I finish eating."

"Roger that. So, what's my code name?"

Half an hour later, "Redwing" (sometimes it's just easier not to argue with Roux) and I were piling out of a cab in front of the Olivers' building. "This is going to be so bad," I muttered to Roux. "How am I supposed to tell him that this whole thing was an assignment?"

"Well, you still like him, right? Just tell him that. Workplace romances happen all the time."

"He'll kill me."

"Tell him that you know an assassin. I'm pretty sure that'll keep him in line."

I started to feel panicky as we rode the elevator up to the Olivers' private rooftop house. "He's going to be so disappointed."

"You're not breaking up with him, you're just telling him the truth. He'll probably thank you."

I looked at Roux.

"Okay, probaby not," she admitted. "But it's not like you have a choice."

"There's always a choice. I just don't like what I have to choose from."

"Hi!" Roux chirped when one of the maids answered the door. "We're here to see Jesse."

"Roux?" Jesse poked his head out of the kitchen. "Is that you? What are you . . . doing here?" He stepped into the hallway. "Maggie?"

I waved, not trusting myself to speak.

"We're here for the group project," Roux said, loud enough in case Armand was lurking around somewhere and could hear. "You know, for school."

"The what?"

"Can we come in?" I said, finally finding my voice.

"Um, yeah, sure, okay." Jesse looked wary, though, and the three of us stood in the foyer and looked at each other. "Is everything okay? You don't look good."

"Will people please stop saying that!" I cried. "I've got a lot on my mind, okay? Cut a girl some slack!"

"She's having a rough day," Roux whispered, patting my arm.

Jesse glanced back and forth between us. "What's wrong? Are you breaking up with me? Is it because I took you ice skating?"

"Definitely not trying to break up with you," I said.

"I'm just here so we can work on the school project for English class."

"Just go with it," Roux whispered to him. "Trust me."

"Oh-*kay*," he said. "You're here to work on a project. Got it. This isn't weird or creepy at all, by the way."

"Can we go to your bedroom? And work on our *project*?"

Jesse led us upstairs into his room, which seemed a lot more normal than the rest of the house. "There's a *dog*," Roux said, coming to a full stop in the doorway. "Dogs don't like me, and, believe me, it's mutual."

I grabbed her arm and dragged her into the room before shutting the door. "Start forging a peace accord," I told her, "because Max isn't leaving and neither are you."

Roux eyed Max warily. "This is my dance space, this is your dance space," she told him as she planted herself next to Jesse's dresser. As if the dog even cared.

"Will someone please tell me what the hell's going on?" Jesse said. He was wearing pajama bottoms and an old T-shirt and there was a history textbook on his bed next to his laptop.

"I'm really sorry," I started to say.

"Oh my God, you are breaking up with me." He sighed, and the sadness in his voice nearly broke my heart. "Why did you bring Roux with you?"

"Excuse me?" Roux was offended.

"I'm not breaking up with you," I interrupted them. "Here, why don't you sit down?"

Jesse hesitated. "No one tells you to sit down when it's good news."

"That's true," I admitted. "Okay, stand or sit, do whatever you want."

Jesse crossed his arms over his chest and right then I would have given everything to be back in Gramercy Park with him. "I have something to tell you," I began, "but you might not believe it. Roux can tell you it's true, though."

"It's true," Roux said.

Jesse looked from her to me. "Okay, what is it?"

My mouth was trembling but I wasn't crying. "You were my assignment," I whispered.

"I was your what?"

"My assignment. My parents and I are spies and your dad's going to publish an article about us. My job was—*is*—to stop it."

Jesse started to laugh. "Are you nuts?" he said. "You scared the shit out of me!" He came forward and wrapped his arms around me, kissing the top of my head. "You're crazy, you know that?"

As much as it killed me to do it, I stepped away from him, taking his hands and holding him at arm's length. "It's true," I told him. "I crack safes and open locks. That's what I do. And if I don't find out where that article is, my family and our whole operation will be exposed."

The smile started to fade from Jesse's face. "What are you talking about?"

"Last night, when you were telling me about how your dad was upset about that one article? I think that's the article I need to stop."

"Wait, so . . ." Jesse dropped my hands and backed

259

away from me. "You're a spy? I don't believe it. You go to school, you can't be a spy! You take calculus!"

"Do the passport thing," Roux piped up. "That's really effective."

I went to my purse and started pulling out the passports again. "See these?" I said. "These are all mine. All twelve of them." I fanned them out on the bed and Jesse picked one up, looking at it with a mixture of disgust and amazement. "Jess, I need your help," I told him. "I really do."

"I told you things!" he suddenly exploded. "Do you even care what you do to people?"

He looked so upset that I thought he was going to throw something, but instead he just sank down on the bed next to Max. "I can't believe I thought you were for real," he said.

"I was—I *am*—for real!" I protested. "When we were out together, ice skating and talking and sitting in the park, that was all me. I wasn't lying about that!"

"But you were still lying!"

"You know what?" Roux said. "I'm just going to go use the restroom."

We both waited for her to leave before even daring to look at each other. "Maggie, what the hell?"

"I didn't know how this was gonna end," I said. I wanted to sit next to him, touch his hand, his hair, something to bring him back to me, but I didn't dare. "You were just an assignment in the beginning. I didn't realize that I would like you so much."

"So this whole thing? This whole time? The party, the date, everything?"

I gave him a rundown of the whole assignment, starting from my first morning in New York and leading up to the morning after our first date. "So you broke into my dad's safe?" he asked at the end, incredulous.

"Yes," I admitted. "That's why I was here."

He cursed under his breath, then stood up and ran his hands through his hair. "I think you need to leave," he said. "Like, right now."

But I stayed sitting. "Jesse, I know you don't believe me and I get it. I do, I swear. And the last thing I want to do is hurt you. But if I don't stop this article, then everyone in my family will be in jeopardy and our lives ruined. We think it's going to name names." I took a deep breath and shoved my hair behind my ears. "And if the Collective thinks that your dad's going to run this story and I can't stop it, they're just going to send someone else to do the job."

"But you don't even know if he's going to run it!"

"That's why I need your help." I stood up and went over to him, trying to hold his hands again, but he jerked them away from me. "You can be as pissed at me as you want. That's fine, I get it. Hate me. But right now, if you don't help me out, my family and I are going to be destroyed and possibly put in a lot of danger. Then we'll never be able to be together, you and me." I swallowed hard, hoping he would still even want to be with me.

Jesse exhaled and dropped his head into his hands, running his fingers through his hair before they got tangled midway. "So this Collective," he said. "Do you, like, smuggle arms and drugs?"

"More like the complete opposite. We stop it."

Jesse glanced up at me.

"We do things that make the world better. I was in Iceland all summer, cracking the safe of a human trafficker."

He froze. "You were?"

I nodded. "We're not the bad guys. We stop the bad guys. And if we can't do that anymore, you don't want to know what the world will look like."

Jesse looked down at me like he was seeing me for the first time. Which, in a way, he was. "You told me," he said after a minute, "that we would always be honest with each other. Do you remember that? Because I think about it every damn day."

I nodded even as my eyes filled with tears. "I remember. I said that we should be as honest as we could. And I was. And now I'm telling you everything because there's a lot at stake.

"I'll leave if you want me to," I continued. "But if you want to help me, then I need your dad's laptop."

"Why?"

"Because I need to read his work e-mails."

"You're going to hack into my dad's computer?" Jesse cried. "You can't do that, that's illegal!"

"Well, I think we can all agree that bidets are *weird*," Roux announced as she strolled back into the room. "What'd I miss? Are we fighting evil together or what?"

Jesse and I glanced at one another before looking away at the same time. "I'm not sure," I said, trying to keep my voice from shaking. "That's Jesse's decision."

He looked away and started petting Max. "I think you need to leave," he said again. "Both of you. Right now."

No one spoke for a few seconds, then Roux tugged at my arm. "C'mon, Maggie," she said, as serious and somber as I had ever heard her. "Let's just go. It's a lot to take in."

I nodded even as tears swam in my eyes and I gathered up my coat with fingers so nearly numb that they tingled. "I was as honest as I could be," I told him.

"Mags, c'mon," Roux whispered.

Jesse was quiet, and for a minute it felt like my life hung in the balance of his silence. And then he spoke.

"I didn't know that honesty had a gray area."

The tears in my eyes spilled over. "Neither did I," I admitted, and then I let Roux guide me out the front door and take me back to her home.

CHAPTER 29

The next morning I was in study hall, still puffy-eyed and swollen from the night before. Roux had sat next to me in her foyer as I cried and cried about what a terrible girl-friend and horrible spy I was, and she even brought me a small glass of water. However, when I started to sip the water . . .

"Roux! This is vodka!"

She looked confused. "You don't want it?"

I wiped my eyes and handed her back the glass. "Water, please."

"Fine, fine, suit yourself."

Study hall was a more muted kind of misery. My exhaustion was tempered by the espresso that Roux had somehow managed to produce that morning, but my sadness was still raging and had nowhere to go. I had ruined everything and now it was rubble, unable to be put back together.

I was so lost in thought that I didn't even hear the library doors open, so when someone dropped a bag on the table in front of me, I nearly fell out of my chair. "What the—!" I gasped, clutching at my chest, then looked up into Jesse Oliver's eyes.

"You better hurry," he said. "I snuck it out while he was at work. I have to get it back before he comes home."

I blinked at him. "Are you serious?"

"Can I sit here?"

"Um, yeah, of course. Yes, sit, sit." I shoved a chair toward him and he sank down.

"So, you're really . . . ?"

"Yes."

"For how long?"

"My whole life."

"You realize how crazy this sounds, right?"

"Yes." I was so scared he would leave again that I could barely form polysyllabic words.

He chewed on his bottom lip. I've noticed he does that when he gets upset. "I'm still mad at you, you know."

"I know. I'm mad at me, too."

"I'll help you, but I'm not sure I can get over this."

"Can I . . . can I just say one thing?"

Jesse nodded.

"Two things, actually. First, I am so, so sorry that I wasn't honest with you, but sometimes, it's literally a matter of life and death. If I could have told you everything from the very beginning, I would have, I swear to God. But I couldn't."

"And the second thing?"

The second thing was a lot harder.

"My feelings for you," I started, and I could feel the tears rising again. "My feelings for you were not part of the assignment. They were real. One hundred percent, honest-to-God, absolutely real. They have been since that night at the party. I know that's hard to believe, but I'm standing here in front of you, risking every single thing that I have, and I'm telling you that I love you. I'd love you even if you'd never come back and hated me for the rest of your life."

"What about all those other girls on your passports? What would they say?"

"They would say the same thing because they're all just me." I wiped at my eyes before a tear could escape and attract a teacher's attention. "All those girls are me. Different names, same feelings. The same girl who loves the same boy."

Jesse was silent for a long time, alternately looking out the window and down at the table. My hands were shaking so I tucked them into my lap.

"So," he finally said. "How are we going to hack this computer, anyway?"

I looked at him. "Are you saying you'll help me?"

He nodded, his jaw tight.

I flung myself out of my chair and straight into his arms, nearly knocking both of us backward onto the floor. "Um, excuse me!" I heard the librarian protest, but I was too busy clinging to Jesse, and he was too busy hugging me right back.

"I'm still mad," he whispered.

"I know," I said. "It's all right, I know."

I just held him tighter.

"—but not mad enough to let you go." Jesse pulled away after a minute, gesturing toward the now-furious-looking librarian. "She might explode."

"Yeah, okay." It was hard to let go of him, though, and I kept my hand fisted in the back of his jacket, not ready to lose him again.

"So what do we do now?" he asked, as soon as everyone's attention was diverted back to their work and the librarian looked a little less red.

"First things first," I said. "We find Roux."

Jesse sighed. "Why am I not surprised?"

"*Love connection!!*" Roux yelled when she saw us walking in the hallway hand in hand. "Oh my God, I just knew you two wouldn't break up! My psychic friend totally called it."

I held up Armand Oliver's laptop. "We gotta go."

Roux's eyes widened. "Yes. Let's go."

Once we were settled at a Starbucks in midtown Manhattan, we opened the laptop and started it up. "Tell me again why we can't just do this at my house," Roux said. "We have WiFi and our tables aren't so small and sticky."

"Because," I said, "I don't want anyone to trace this back to your house. Whereas there's probably at least a couple thousand people a day who use the WiFi here."

"Crafty. I like."

"Don't you need more gadgets?" Jesse said. "You don't have anything that looks very impressive."

(Honestly, I loved Jesse and Roux dearly, but I was starting to understand why most spies worked alone.)

"Gadgets?"

"Yeah, for hacking."

"I'm not the hacker," I protested. "That's my mom's job."

"Your mom?" Roux said. "Wow, it's always the quiet ones, isn't it."

"And I'm not going to break into his computer," I told Jesse.

"You're not?"

"Nope. You're going to do it for me."

"I am?"

"Yep," I said, then passed the laptop across the table to him. "What's your dad's e-mail password?"

"How am I supposed to know?" Jesse asked. "It's his e-mail, not mine."

"Okay, we'll have to guess."

"E-mail is so archaic." Roux sighed, but Jesse and I ignored her.

"It's usually kids' names and birthdays," I told him. "Or a combination of that. Or maybe an anniversary."

"Can't you just plug something into the computer that'll download it?" Jesse asked.

"That's not exactly how it works," I replied, taking over the keyboard. "Our jobs would be a million times easier if it did."

We tried several combinations of Jesse's name and birth date that we could think of, but they didn't work. "Told you," Jesse said after our fourth attempt.

"What's your mom's name?" I asked him, and he looked stricken. "I'm serious. What is it?"

"Meredith," Jesse said. "Meredith May Oliver."

I typed "Meredith May" and the in-box opened up.

"People are so predictable," Roux said, as if she had spent her life trying to crack passwords. "Good job, Mags."

"Thank you, thank you," I said. "Okay, let's start searching."

CHAPTER 30

We were a trio obsessed.

At first I couldn't find any e-mails about any article. I searched "Collective," "Maggie," "Angelo," "spy," whatever I could think of that might give us a hit. Nothing came up. But when I tried words like "story," "cost," or "secret," it gave me thousands upon thousands of hits. "Your dad really needs to organize his in-box," I told Jesse at one point. "He's an electronic hoarder."

"This is way more exciting in the movies." Roux yawned after the clock passed five and we didn't have anything. Tiny tendrils of panic were starting to wind their way around my throat, and I knew that if we didn't find anything, this whole deal was over. I had blown my parents' cover, Angelo's cover, and my cover, all within the span of a day, and pretty soon, the rest of the world would know who we were. There would likely be government inquiries, arrests, and I'd probably be separated from my parents and put—

"What's that?" Jesse asked, interrupting my depressing train of thought. (I guess he had a point with the whole apocalyptic-thinking thing.) "Go back, go back."

I scrolled back up and saw an e-mail titled, "Re: auction." "My dad was talking about an auction on the phone the other day," Jesse said. "He was angry that someone was trying to sell a story after they said he could have it."

"That would have been good to know two hours ago!" I said, clicking on it as fast as I could.

"Sorry, I didn't think it was important! We don't all do this for a living, you know."

I let it slide because, fair enough. At that point, I was just glad that Jesse was still talking to me.

The e-mail was short and to the point: " 'Due to your request, I can no longer participate in our discussion regarding the International story. We at Meredian Media—' Did he name it after your mom?"

"Yeah," Jesse admitted.

"Awww!" Roux and I both squealed.

"Where was I?" I continued. "Oh, yeah. 'We at Meredian Media have a longstanding policy not to pay for information relevant to our articles. To do so would violate our journalistic integrity, as well as our moral code.' " I paused again. "Your dad has an eloquent way of telling people to take a hike."

"He does," Jesse said. "Where's the trail, though? No forwards, no replies."

We searched for the recipient's e-mail address next and found a slew of e-mails, nearly thirty in all. "Gotcha!"

Roux said, sitting up so she could squint at the screen. "Can you guys even read that? I think I need glasses."

I shoved over and pulled the computer onto my lap so that all three of us could look at it. "He was selling the story," I realized. "Your dad agreed to run it at first, but then the guy turned around and offered it to another magazine to try and get a bidding war going. He wanted your dad to pay for the info."

"*How* much did he want for it?" Roux asked. "That's a lot of zeroes."

"That's *Egalité* magazine," Jesse said. "My dad hates their publisher because he used to work for my dad and then left and took half of his reporters with him. Seriously, don't say *Egalité* around my dad."

"But it doesn't say that he bought the story, just that he wanted to buy it."

"Can't you look at his bank accounts?" Roux said. "See if he made any big withdrawals?"

"I could if I were working at the Collective's headquarters right now." I sighed. "They have all the technology for that. But out in the field, all I do is open the safes." I was starting to realize how far out of my depth I was.

"Roger didn't buy it," Jesse said. "Trust me."

Roux and I turned to look at him. "If he bought it, two things would be happening. One, my dad would be ripping his hair out and swearing up and down the halls. He hates *Egalité* so much that, trust me, we'd know if they got the story."

"I recommend anger management," Roux said.

"And two," Jesse continued, ignoring her, "if they did

already buy the story, everyone would know. He'd be leaking bits and pieces to the press on a daily basis."

"He didn't buy it *yet*," I clarified. "He still might." I saw an attachment on another e-mail and opened it up.

The first thing I saw was my face.

"Holy shit!" I gasped. "That's me." I leaned a little closer to inspect the image. "Is that what I look like?"

It was a dossier about me, I soon realized, and it was just one of about a dozen. My parents, Angelo, different spies that had come and gone over the years—we were all there. Someone had put them all together, and I felt the cold wash of terror start to seep into my skin. "This isn't just someone out to get the Collective," I whispered. "It's someone from *inside* the Collective. Oh my God." I had never considered the possibility before, but now I was looking at old passports, addresses, and birth dates. There were snapshots of me and Angelo outside Gramercy Park—me barely tall enough to reach the lock that I was picking—and a copy of my actual birth certificate. Only a Collective insider could have had this much information.

The e-mail was much worse.

"They have used minors to commit international espionage," I read aloud, "and have operated outside the law for scores of years." I sat back and put my hand to my mouth. I was the minor, I knew it.

"You're shaking," Jesse murmured.

"You think? That's my family they're talking about! They're talking about me! There are a lot of people who could be in a huge amount of danger right now!" The room felt too hot and small. "If this person's selling this

273

information to the highest bidder, he's basically selling a hit list and . . ." I couldn't even finish that sentence.

"Well, you can't be the only one who's gone rogue, right?" Roux said. "Even the best companies have a few disgruntled employees."

"Well, I'm sure people leave the Collective, but no one who does this would sell anyone else out."

And then it hit me.

"I know who it is," I said. "It's Oscar Young."

Roux and Jesse stared at me. "Are we supposed to know who that is?" Roux asked. "Because I'm behind on a few issues of *People* magazine."

My mind was going so fast that I felt a little dizzy. "Angelo told me about him." (I would have to explain Angelo to Jesse at a later time.) "He tried to kidnap me when I was four years old."

It took a few minutes to peel Roux off the ceiling after that revelation. "It was a million years ago!" I assured her as she ranted about the FBI and sloppy police work and the importance of self-defense classes for women. "And Angelo said that his body washed up on shore in South America a few months later."

Jesse looked unsure. "So you think a man has risen from the grave and has decided to sell your story to the highest bidder. Not really plausible."

"People fake their deaths all the time, though!" Roux protested. "Don't you ever watch TV? It's really common, actually." She crossed her arms like she was suddenly the authority on the subject. "Can we go to the police now?"

"No police," I told her. "Spies, remember? We're trying to keep this quiet."

"Right, right."

"Oscar must have the documents and is trying to sell them."

"Oscar is dead," Jesse said. "You said so yourself."

"Nothing else makes sense, though," I protested. "And he's tried terrible things before. Now we just have to find out where the documents are."

"You mean you have to figure out where Oscar *lives*," Jesse corrected me. "And there are about ten billion places where he could be."

You went to Gramercy Park by yourself at night?

Do you realize how dangerous that can be?

He was no knight in shining armor, that much I can assure you.

"I need a map," I said, grabbing the laptop and pulling up Manhattan, searching until I found what I needed. "There," I said, pointing at the screen. "He lives there."

I was pointing at 36 Gramercy Park East.

It was a tall, imposing building with an actual red carpet that stretched down its front steps toward the street, and two oversized suits of armor standing at attention. "Trust me," I said when Roux and Jesse just blinked at me. "I know this is it. I told my parents that we went there on our date and they *freaked out*."

"Your parents are so cute," said Roux, who has clearly never seen my parents freak out.

"Well, if I'm still alive at the end of this, I'll tell them you think so," I said, then started googling Oscar's address. At that point, I would have given a million dollars to see Angelo and ask for his help, but I would have to make do with all the advice he had given me over the years.

"Hey, are you two willing to ditch school tomor—?"

"Yes," Roux said. I knew I could count on her. I looked over at Jesse and he nodded. "Good. Because we're gonna do some breaking and entering."

CHAPTER 31

That night, I was a nervous mess, pacing in my bedroom and claiming that I had a ton of homework. "You know, honey," my mom said at one point, "you don't have to do the homework." Both my parents had been super nice since I had come back home. Our fight seemed like it was eons ago, but they clearly remembered it.

"Just keeping up appearances, Mom," I told her, holding up my graphing calculator. "I can't flunk out. And it's not difficult, just voluminous."

I even waved off dinner, saying that I was swamped, but in truth, I couldn't bear to look either of my parents in the face. They had no idea what I was planning, and I knew that if I were with them too long, I would blurt it out. It was better to hide away in my bedroom and pretend I was a regular, stressed-out student.

At nearly midnight, my civilian phone rang. I glanced at the Caller ID: Jesse.

"Hi," I said, keeping my voice down and pulling the

covers over my head so that my parents wouldn't hear me. "I miss you."

"I miss you, too. Here's my question. Why would Oscar Young still be alive, in the same apartment, and no one in your Collection—"

"Collective."

"—can find him?"

"I know." I sighed. "That's been eating at me all night."

"It doesn't make sense."

"I've been here all this time in the city and he hasn't tried anything?"

"Exactly!"

"Hold on, Roux's calling me." I clicked over to the other call. "Hi."

"Hi. I'm so exhausted that my eyes hurt. Like, my *actual* eyeballs. Does that ever happen to you?"

"Roux, it's midnight. What do you want?"

"Why the hell would Oscar Young still live in that apartment? Like, isn't that the most dumbass thing he could possibly do?"

"Jesse just called me and asked the same thing. He's on the other line right now."

"Three-way me, baby."

So I did. "Jesse?" I said. "Roux's on with us."

"Great." He didn't sound thrilled.

"So, here's my thought," Roux said, and suddenly she sounded wide awake, like she was heading a corporate board meeting. "Oscar Young was working for someone, and when he botched the whole kidnapping thing, they killed him and decided to take over."

"She's right," Jesse said.

"I am?"

"You are."

"She is?"

"Yes. Listen. There's probably a mole in the Collective."

"What? Are you—?"

"Think about it, Maggie! It's the perfect cover! They can still monitor what everyone's doing, including you; they have all this training and these resources; and then when they blow the whistle, they make a shitload of money."

My brain was racing to catch up. "But then why would they even bother trying to sell the story to your dad?"

Roux's voice came down the line. "To make more money."

Thoughts were crashing together like train cars, each one causing a small explosion behind my eyes. I remembered Angelo's words back at the museum. *There is always danger. And there is always money to be made.*

"And then they could just kidnap you afterward," Roux theorized. "Win-win. I mean, um. Win-win for *them*, not win-win for you. Never mind."

"They could have gotten me anywhere, though," I said. "Why didn't they—?"

And then I sat up in bed, a cold sweat starting to form along my spine. Buenos Aires and Luxembourg. Two major cases that had gone completely wrong: empty safes, missing blueprints, my parents and I literally running for our lives and barely making it to the airport.

What if those weren't accidents? What if those were attempts to kidnap me again?

A tiny thought crept into my brain: Colton Hooper was responsible for our safety and new identities on our missions. All of them. He had effectively assigned himself to my family.

"Maggie?" Jesse's voice was cautious. "You still there?"

"Yes. Give me a minute." I put my hand over my mouth, Angelo's words racing through my brain. It couldn't be right, but everything was starting to collide in my brain, a perfect storm of corruption.

Colton was absolutely gutted when he found out about the kidnapping attempt.

He was the one who had brought Oscar Young into the Collective, had sworn that Oscar was one of the best in the business.

I don't think I'll ever forget the look of devastation on his face.

He said, 'I suppose Oscar Young was no knight in shining armor.'

And then Colton's smooth, icy voice rose above everything else.

It's the infamous Maggie.

"Colton," I said, my voice bigger than a ragged whisper. "He's doing this. He set up the kidnapping attempt, and he's been watching my family ever since. That's how he has all this information about me. And he's been sabotaging this case so that I wouldn't be able to stop the article from running."

"Wait, who?" Roux asked. "Colton?"

"I can't explain right now," I said, suddenly realizing

that the entire loft could be bugged. The Collective probably still owned Oscar Young's old apartment. No one would think twice if Colton Hooper came and went from it.

"You can't go to that apartment tomorrow, Mags," Jesse said.

"Are you kidding me?" I said. "He tries to kidnap me when I'm a kid, endangers me and my family in Luxembourg and Buenos Aires. . . ."

"Luxembourg?" Jesse said.

"Buenos Aires?" Roux added.

". . . and now he's trying to ruin the lives of my family and everyone I love?" I was starting to get upset and had to lower my voice again. "You are out of your damn *mind* if you think that I'm not going to that apartment tomorrow."

"Hell yeah!" Roux cried. "No one fu—oops, swear jar—messes with my best friend!"

I tried to tell both Roux and Jesse that they weren't allowed to come with me, that it was too dangerous, but they wouldn't have it. And I couldn't argue with them because suddenly my dad was knocking at the door.

"Mags?" he said. "Are you still up?"

"Gotta go. Tomorrow morning, same plan. Love you." Then I slapped the phone shut. "Yeah, come in, Dad."

He opened the door, letting a sliver of light spill onto the floor. "You okay, honey? I thought I heard you yelling."

"I'm fine. Sorry, Roux just called. She had a nightmare about . . . squid." It wasn't true, but definitely sounded like something that could happen. "Big squid."

"Oookay," he said. "You sure you're all right?"

I hesitated for a flickering second. I wanted to tell my dad about Colton, but I knew neither he nor my mom would believe me. Their faith in my abilities had already been rocked, set off course by my relationship with Jesse, and if I tried to explain my theories, I knew they would reassure me that I was wrong, that it wasn't possible, that I was just trying to save Jesse's family again.

But the only family I wanted to save now was mine.

"Good. Just tired. I didn't get much sleep at Roux's last night." Again, not *technically* a lie.

"You're sure?"

"Yes. We're all good here."

"Okay, then. Go to bed, it's late."

"Dad?"

"Yeah, babe?"

"I love you."

"Love you, too, kiddo. 'Night."

I knew I couldn't tell my parents. They would freak out, try to call Angelo, and . . .

Angelo.

Angelo was on assignment.

Who had sent him?

It could just be a coincidence, I told myself, even though Angelo rarely worked cases out of the city anymore. But what if someone wanted to get him out of the city, knowing that he would protect me at all costs, just like he had done that Halloween night twelve years ago?

I couldn't take any chances. I dug out my civilian phone

and dialed his number. "Angelo," I whispered after I got his voice mail. "I just wanted you to know that the newspaper was delivered but the headline was misspelled. That's all." Then I paused before adding, "I love you."

Translation: *Angelo, the case is bad. Get out now. Run.*

CHAPTER 32

When Roux, Jesse, and I met up the next morning two blocks north of Gramercy Park, my nervous energy had given way to steely focus, and I was bouncing on the soles of my feet. Next to me, Roux was mainlining coffee, her eyes starting to look like slot machine windows. "I need about ten more cups," she said as she passed me the coffee so I could take a sip. "That should put me at normal."

Aside from that tiny sip, I wasn't drinking anything. Caffeine can make your hands shake, and I needed them to be as steady as possible. I wasn't sure what I was going to find in that apartment, but whatever it was, I was going to have to be ready for it.

Jesse showed up a few minutes after us, looking fresh as a daisy, complete with damp hair. "That jerk," Roux muttered. "Why do guys always manage to look good after getting only thirty seconds of sleep? I feel like my eyes are so puffy that people in Philadelphia can see them."

"Let's focus on the big picture," I told her. "Hi."

"Hey," Jesse said. "You guys get any sleep?"

"A little." I shrugged. "Enough."

Roux just held up her massive coffee cup. "Does this answer your question?"

"How about you?" I asked. It was so odd to make small talk with him now, after all the big talks we had had. I couldn't tell if he was still pissed at me or not, but it was a conversation that would have to wait.

"Good, good," he said, even though we all knew he was lying. No one was good that morning. I was pretty sure that if someone harnessed our collective nervous energy, it could power Manhattan through a holiday weekend.

"Are you ready?" I asked them. "Last chance to back out."

"I'm in," Jesse said.

"Me, too," Roux agreed. "I have a bio test this morning that I didn't study for, so there's no way I'm going to school today."

"Okay." I took a few cleansing breaths and forced myself to focus. *You've been training for this your whole life*, I reminded myself. *This is just a job.*

I remembered what Angelo said to me once when I was frustrated by not being able to open a particularly difficult safe: *Let a veil of calm fall around you. Become very focused, very unperturbed by anything around you.* I knew what he meant now.

"Let's do this," I told Jesse and Roux.

Our first obstacle was probably the trickiest: the doorman. I had no idea how we were going to get around that, but Roux had just said, "Leave it to me." That had seemed like a viable plan yesterday, but now that we were about ready to walk through the door, I was wary.

"Roux, did you—?"

"*Hi*, Harold! *Hiiiii*!"

God help me, the poor, put-upon Harold was sitting behind the front desk, hands folded, like he fully expected to see Roux come sailing through the doors.

"Harold, don't you just love Mondays?" Roux sighed dreamily. "A fresh start, a new beginning? Ugh, I'm such a romantic, it's disgusting."

"Do we know this guy?" Jesse whispered to me. "Or is this the beginning of Roux's breakdown?"

"We know him," I whispered back. "It's her doorman. Roux! How did you do this?"

She shrugged. "I can be very convincing." Then she smiled. "My parents' money can be even more convincing."

I looked at Harold, who still hadn't acknowledged that any of this was unusual. "Please tell me that the doorman who's normally here isn't bleeding in a gutter somewhere."

"How ridiculous." Roux shook her head. "He's working at my building. God, Maggie, you've become so dramatic."

Roux was either a genius or an evil mastermind, but I didn't have time to figure out which it was.

"So, Harold. Friend, pal, chum." Roux folded her hands on top of the desk. "Are you going to buzz us in or not?"

We knew we had to go to #11N, since that was the apartment that Oscar Young had first rented back when he tried to kidnap me (he didn't use that name, of course, but I recognized the Collective's all-purpose code name of Joe Miller on the digitized census reports). There were no changes in the name on the apartment, but if you thought Oscar was dead, then you would also think that the Collective had hung on to the apartment and never changed the name on the lease.

"Go on up, miss," Harold said, waving us through the lobby and toward the elevators.

"Harold, you're a gem. A pristine gem honed over years of trial and fire."

"That's how I would describe my job, too," Harold replied.

"Thanks, Harold," I whispered as we hurried past. "Really."

He never even looked in my direction.

"Not the elevators," I said as Jesse reached to press the button. "Never the elevator. Always stairs."

"It's the eleventh floor," Roux protested. "I'll have a heart attack by the fifth floor."

"You'll just have to revive yourself," I told her. "And good work on the doorman."

"Well, shucks," she said, but her grin was a mile wide.

After huffing and puffing our way up eleven flights of stairs, Roux trailing behind Jesse and me, we arrived at 11N. The hallways were narrow and cramped, almost like an architectural version of intense pressure, and when we got to the door, the three of us stood and looked at it.

"It's all you, Mags," Roux said. "Take it away!"

"This is how you got into Gramercy Park," Jesse added. "You really know what you're doing."

"I appreciate the cheerleading," I whispered as I knelt down to examine the lock, "but you might want to save it for whatever's inside."

We knocked first, just in case Colton was home, but thankfully no one came to the door. I didn't know what we would do if he was home, but I suspected that Roux would start pretending to sell Girl Scout cookies, and I wanted to avoid that sort of scene at all costs. "Okay," I said. "Here we go."

I could feel Jesse and Roux breathing over my shoulders as I worked, sticking the tension wrench (otherwise known as a Bic pen cap) in the lock while using my bent paper clip to scrub at the pins inside. It wasn't very loud, but in the quiet hallway, every move sounded like a gun blast.

After two minutes, I got it. "Finally," I muttered. "Took long enough."

"Will you show me how to do that?" Roux whispered.

"Absolutely not."

"That's cool."

We waited a few seconds, just in case Colton came bursting out, demanding to know who was breaking into his apartment, but all we heard was silence. An eerie, terrible silence, but silence just the same.

Jesse, Roux, and I crept in on our tiptoes. It looked messy, like someone had been coming and going and not cleaning up after themselves: dust gathered on top of file cabinets, the parquet wood floors had a few layers of grime on top of them, and there were some copies of the *New York Times* that were from several weeks earlier. "Come on," I said, "the coast is clear."

Jesse followed me as I started to poke around the apartment, looking at antique oil paintings on the wall and crumbs on a plate that sat on top of a stack of old *New Yorkers*. "There's a safe here somewhere," I told him. "We just need to find it."

"How do you know that it's not somewhere in the filing cabinets?" Jesse said.

"Too easy to access," I replied. "These are important files, and without them, he has nothing to sell. No one will buy a PDF file without the source material to back it up."

"Right," Jesse said. "Okay. So once we find this safe . . . ?"

"I'm going to open it."

"Hey, I'm making eye contact with a gargoyle!" Roux said, looking out one of the grimy windows. "I shall name him George."

"Make eye contact with a safe instead. Name it whatever you want."

"Aye-aye," she said. "Later, George."

The three of us poked around the apartment for a few minutes. I couldn't believe no one else could hear my heartbeat, it felt so loud in my ears. If my parents knew I was doing this, they would murder me, bring me back to life, and murder me again. I was going against the Collective, which no one did. Where that put me on the morality scale, I didn't want to know.

"Hey, Mags?" Jesse called from the bedroom. "I think this is it."

Roux and I followed his voice until we arrived in a barren room that held boxes; manila files; and a squat, stout safe. I let out a breath I didn't know I had been holding. "Is this it?" Jesse asked. "It looks old."

"That's it," I said. It was the exact safe Angelo had let me play with when I was younger, before the kidnapping attempt. There was a brass fleur-de-lis etched into the side, and I put my finger in the groove and traced the pattern, just as I had done when I was little.

"Nice to see you again," I whispered. "Let's play."

I unzipped my duffel bag and started to rifle through it. "What the hell is all that?" Jesse asked.

"A diamond core drill," I replied. "It can go through cobalt and it lets me use this." I pulled out a tiny scope camera that had a monitor attached to it. "This lets me see where the grooves are in the lock. Each groove corresponds to a number on the combination and I just have to line them up."

Jesse and Roux looked at me like I was speaking Martian. "Where do you even get this stuff?"

"Sweet Sixteen present from my parents."

Roux shook her head. "I got a Fabergé egg. What a ripoff."

I knelt down in front of the safe and looked at the combination lock. All the blueprints that I had memorized over the years were flooding back into my mind at a terrible speed. "It's a Sargent and Greenleaf," I murmured. "Model 6643. No drilling allowed."

"You're getting all of that just by looking at it?" Jesse whispered.

"Yes. If I try to drill, it'll lock me out. Shit." I took a deep breath and pulled my hair off my face. "There're four wheels, too. Four numbers in the combination."

"How many possible combina—?" Roux started to ask.

"A hundred million," I said.

Jesse muttered something unrepeatable under his breath.

"I've opened this kind of safe a few times before just in practice, but not under pressure. Well, here goes nothing."

I started with the most basic combinations first, the ones that the manufacturer sets. I knew Colton would have changed them, but it was always the first thing I tried. 50-25-50-25. 10-20-30-40. 20-40-60-80. None of them worked.

Jesse and Roux were absolutely silent as I started to turn the knob, waiting to feel the clicks against my fingertips. Angelo had trained me for this, putting toothpicks, feathers, Post-it notes on the gears of my practice combination locks, letting me find the tiniest whisper of a click.

"What—?" Jesse started to say.

"Ssshh," I hissed at him. "I need to hear and feel everything right now."

The first number clicked in: thirty-eight. I could feel the wheel click into place, just a whisper of a sensation that my fingertips had been trained to find. "One down," I whispered. "Three more to go."

Two minutes later, I had the second number. "Twenty-six," I said. "Thirty-eight, twenty-six."

"You're doing great," Roux said. I could feel their collective nervous energy washing over me like waves, which only powered me forward. My legs were shaking from squatting in front of the safe, but I didn't dare move. I didn't want anything to ruin my zone.

"Just so you know," Jesse whispered, "this is a huge turn-on right now."

"Well, I try." I spun the lock, feeling again and again for the third click. I used to get tired at this point, but Angelo never let me quit. All the clicks started to feel the same and I couldn't tell if it was an important number or just a nerve twitch after twisting the dial nonstop for so long. "When it matters," Angelo used to say, "you can't quit."

Fifty-nine.

"Shit, do you hear that?" Jesse whispered. "There's footsteps."

Roux and I both looked up at him and the three of us listened. There were footsteps, heavy ones, like a man's shoes. "It might be a neighbor," Roux said.

"It's not a neighbor," I told her. "He's here." I'll never know how I knew that the mole was coming back to his burrow. I just did. It was instinctual, the way a deer senses a hunter. I turned back to the lock, desperate for that fourth number.

"He's here?" Roux gasped. "Are we going to die?"

"Not today," I told her. "Just get ready to run." I was close, I could tell, so close to feeling that fourth click. "Come on," I whispered. "Where are you?"

"Maggie." Jesse's breathing was ragged. "He could have a gun."

Roux let out a whimper. "*Maggie*," she whispered.

A key was starting to turn in the front door.

Eighty-two.

The safe popped open and I let out a breath as I pried open the door. It looked just as I had remembered it, an old banker's safe with several compartments and a locked drawer. The files were lying on the bottom and I grabbed one and opened it up. My picture smiled back up at me.

I took all of them, leaping to my feet and shoving everything in my duffel bag, leaving the drill and scope behind. "*Run*," I said to Jesse and Roux, and the three of us turned and bolted out of the bedroom.

A man was standing in the foyer, tall and muscular and younger than I had imagined him being, and I don't think I'll ever forget the look on his face when he saw the three of us come dashing down the hall and past him toward the front door. He was so surprised that he just gaped at first, but then he yelled "Maggie!" and the voice hit me like icy water.

I was right. It was Colton Hooper.

Roux flew past him, and he grabbed her wrist, wrenching her backward.

"Roux!" I screamed. What had I been thinking, involving her and Jesse? They weren't professionals, they weren't trained for any of this, they were completely innocent and—

"Let go of me!" Roux yelled, and even though she was half Colton's size, she raised her other arm and brought the heel of her hand down directly on the bridge of his nose.

The *pop* was loud, and he cried out and staggered back as blood started to gush down his face. His grip on Roux lost, she turned and ran out the front door. "Come on!" she cried. Colton hadn't lost his footing, though, and started to follow us as we raced down the hall.

"No elevators!" I cried. "Stairs, stairs, stairs!" We shoved the door open and started dashing down, two at a time, Jesse leading the way. "Roux, you okay?" he yelled as we flew past the tenth floor.

"I'm amazing!" she yelled.

She certainly was.

He clattered above us, going down the spiral with only a floor or so to spare between us, and at one point I almost lost my footing, but Jesse righted me and we made it out into the lobby, shoving through the doors and out onto the sidewalk. I didn't know where I was going, but I ran north, Jesse and Roux close on my heels, and Colton close on theirs. "Maggie!" I heard him scream at one point, his voice garbled from pain and blood, and hearing him say my name only made me run faster.

We raced up Lexington, our feet pounding on the sidewalk. He never gave up chase and we flew through crowds, past drink vendors, running red lights and green lights and everything else in between.

"Weave!" I yelled at Roux and Jesse. "Don't run in a straight line!" I didn't think Colton had a gun—we had taken him by surprise and then Roux had broken his nose, so there probably wasn't time to grab one—but I wasn't taking any chances.

"Look out!" Jesse yelled as a group of tourists came to a sudden stop on the corner of Twenty-Fourth and Lexington. The three of us skidded and ran around them.

"Asshole tourists! Learn to walk!" Roux screamed at them as we dashed past, giving them their first official New York Experience, I'm sure. I was too busy digging my phone out of my pocket, though. I knew I had to call someone for help. We could hail a cab, but that would give him too much time to catch up to us. We could go down into a subway station, but there was no guarantee that a train would be there, and even less guarantee that he wouldn't end up on the same train as us. I couldn't call my parents, not until we were safe.

There was only one person I could call, and I prayed he would answer this time.

He picked up on the second ring. "Maggie."

"Angelo!" I cried. "Angelo, I'm in trouble!"

"Maggie, where—?"

"I got the files. I stopped it, but Colton's chasing us! He's a mole!"

"Who's she talking to?" I heard Jesse yell over to Roux.

"Probably the assassin!" she yelled back.

"*THE WHO?*"

"I didn't tell anyone," I said to Angelo. "My parents don't even know. I broke into his apartment and I got the files and . . ." A huge stitch was starting to form in my side and I was gasping for air. Colton was still after us, but his breathing sounded wet and ragged. He was way too close, only six or seven steps behind us.

"Maggie, where are you? Who's with you?"

"Jesse and Roux, and we're on"—I glanced at a street sign as we ran across the street and almost got decked by two cabs—"Twenty-Ninth and Lexington! I don't know where to go and he's right behind us!"

"Okay, Maggie. Listen to me, darling. Do you remember what we did for your eighth birthday?"

Of all the things I thought Angelo was going to say, that wasn't one of them. "My *what*?" I screamed. "Are you serious right now?"

"Think, love."

"Of *course* I remember! What does *that* have to do with anything? We took a helicopter ride around Manhattan from the East Thirty-Fourth—*oh*." I could already see a helicopter heading down the east side of Manhattan, no bigger than a dot, but I knew that Angelo was on his way.

"I got your message, love, and I'm on my way back into the city right now. I'll be there in six minutes." And then his voice changed into something leaner and more dangerous than I had ever heard from him. "Do *not* let him catch you, Margaret, do you understand me?"

I glanced over my shoulder and saw the anger on Colton's face, the blood now dripping off his chin, and the shell-shocked pedestrians that we were leaving in our wake.

"Got it," I said, then hung up. "Come on!" I yelled to Roux and Jesse, then dashed across the intersection diagonally, barely dodging cars in our wake.

"I am so glad," Roux cried, "that I gave up smoking!"

Ice hockey had apparently given Jesse some generous lung capacity, because he never fell behind, never even looked back. "Where are we going?" he said as we flew past a movie theater on Second Avenue. "Do you even know?"

"Trust me," I said. "Okay? Just trust me."

By the time we got across the FDR Drive, I could see the helicopter in the sky. Just knowing that Angelo was nearby made me feel a million times better, and I sprinted across the road and toward the helipad. I could feel the wind pick up as the helicopter made its descent, and just as it touched down, I turned back to look at Roux and Jesse, who were staring at the helicopter like they had never seen a flying machine before. "So," I said to them. "Show of hands. Who's been on a helicopter ride before?"

The door slid open and Angelo was sitting at the controls, helmet and sunglasses on. The three of us ran to the helicopter, and Angelo put out his hand to help Roux in, then me, then Jesse. We fell into the seats, Roux and Jesse behind me, and I pulled the door shut and put on my own headset as Angelo rose back into the sky, Colton becoming smaller and smaller, angrier and angrier. My stomach nearly dropped out, and I grabbed onto the armrest, shutting my eyes for a second. "Steady, darling," Angelo said. "You're all right now. Safe and sound up here in the sky."

I took a deep breath and nodded. He was right. We were fine.

"May I ask what happened to his nose?" Angelo asked over the headset.

"Roux broke it!" I told him. Behind me, she was panting and pale, but she managed to give the finger to the man, who was still bleeding down on the tarmac.

"You and I still make a lovely team, my dear." Angelo looked at me and smiled. "Are you all right?"

"Fine, fine." I was pretty sure it was going to take a full day for my heartbeat to calm down, but I had the files in my bag. That was all that mattered.

Jesse was panting for air, but when I glanced back at him, his face lit up in a smile and he started to laugh. "What the hell was that?" he asked. "Who *are* you?"

"She's *awesome*," Roux told him. "*We're* awesome."

And the helicopter sailed into the sky.

CHAPTER 33

By the time we landed at Battery Park, my parents were there waiting.

And they were hysterical.

It was sort of hard to hear what they were saying at first because they were squeezing me so hard, but I was able to make out, ". . . you THINKING?" and "GROUNDED FOR LIFE!" and ". . . could have DIED!" I didn't care, though. I was so happy to see them that I just hugged them back as tightly as I could.

And then they were letting go of me and hugging Angelo, then hugging Roux and Jesse, and then Angelo was hugging me, and then I was hugging Roux, and it was such a scene that you would have thought we hadn't seen each other in fifteen years. I was exhilarated, nearly lightheaded with happiness, but that came to an end when I heard Angelo say, "We weren't able to get him."

"The loft is the safest place," I heard my mom say, and pretty soon we were being hustled into a car (my dad kicked out the driver and took the wheel; apparently no one was to be trusted) and heading back to our place.

My parents, Angelo, and I put it on lockdown pretty fast. Lock codes were changed, phone SIM cards were put down the garbage disposal, and my dad yanked all the hard drives out of the computer and dunked them into a sinkful of water, while my mom scanned the rooms for bugs. "Are you two all right?" I asked Roux and Jesse, who were sitting at our table, both wide-eyed in astonishment. "Do you want something to drink?"

They nodded. Across the room, Angelo and my parents were all on pay-as-you-go phones, each speaking quietly and urgently. Angelo's face was especially tense, and he had lapsed into French, which meant that it was serious. My dad was speaking Italian across the room, and I heard "*figlia mia*" several times. *My daughter.*

I poured water for both Jesse and Roux. "Are you in shock?" I asked them. "It's okay if you are. It's a lot, I know."

"Not in shock," Roux said. "Just . . . okay, maybe in shock a little bit."

Jesse reached out and encircled my waist with his arm, then wrapped his other arm around me and buried his face against my neck. I pressed my cheek to the top of his head, smelling his shampoo, realizing just how badly things could have gone and shaking with gratitude that they hadn't.

"Hey," Jesse whispered, low enough that neither my parents nor Roux could hear him.

"Hmm?" I said, closing my eyes and trying to will away the trembling.

"I love you, too."

My eyes flew open as I looked down at him. His face was honest and open and a little scared. "You said it first and I never said it back," he murmured. "I realized that when we were running. I never said I love you, too."

I smiled at him, then gave him several kisses in quick succession.

"You all right?" he asked when I pulled away. "Are *you* in shock? You're shaking."

I shook my head. "Just don't let go, okay?"

He didn't. I reached one arm out to Roux and she scrambled against my side, and the three of us formed a little huddle, staying like that until Angelo said quietly, with as much dignity as he could muster, "It's over. They've shot him."

Everyone breathed a little easier after that, especially my parents, who suddenly noticed Roux, Jesse, and I clutching each other in the middle of the kitchen. "So," my mom said, "who wants a snack?"

"Can that snack be vodka?" Roux asked in the tiniest voice imaginable, but she couldn't keep a straight face, and pretty soon Jesse and I were giggling along with her, and it felt so good to laugh again that I thought I would never stop.

Suffice it to say, a lot went on that afternoon.

My parents met Jesse (I mean, obviously, he was right there), and there was some awkwardness, followed by my dad trying to "bro down" with him (yes, those exact words were used, I'm still mortified), and then finally my mom just made Jesse a sandwich and he said, "Thank you, ma'am," so that earned him points. Still, that was not how I expected their meeting to go, but hey, it could have been worse.

Then my parents and I had a long, long, looooong talk about Trusting Each Other and Being Honest and If You EVER, EVER Take On a Case by Yourself Again We Will Ground You Until You're Eighty-Three. "No matter what, we are a family," my mom said. "We come to each other first."

"But I did come to you!" I protested. "You didn't believe me!"

They exchanged glances. "We have things to work on, too," my dad admitted. "But that doesn't mean we stop counting on each other, okay? We'll *all* make a better effort."

And then there was the whole thing with Roux and Jesse. At first, not even Angelo was thrilled that they had been involved, but after the three of us explained how we had figured it out, and how Roux had been a badass and broken Colton's nose, they started to come around. "I needed help and they helped," I said. "They were *amazing*."

But the biggest surprise of all was Roux. After a few hours, things had calmed down enough so that we could eat something. Angelo was still at our house, as were Roux and Jesse, and my dad was serving up leftover chicken enchiladas when I heard a sniffling sound.

Roux was at the end of the table, bawling. Huge tears

rolled down her cheeks, and when she saw that I was look-ing at her, she held up her hands and waved me away. "I'm fine!" she sobbed, which got everyone's attention.

I immediately hurried around the table and gathered her up in a hug. "It's okay," I said. "Sometimes the shock kicks in late, it's all right."

"It's not shock," she cried. "I'm just . . . I'm just . . . really happy!"

"You don't exactly look happy," Jesse pointed out.

My mom disappeared and came back with a box of tis-sues, but Roux ignored them. "Sorry, sorry," she kept say-ing. "It's just that you're all so nice and, I mean, everything was crazy today and, yeah, it was scary, but I haven't talked to my parents in three weeks and now we're all here eating dinner and it's just nice and I'm really glad I met you, Mag-gie, and if you all move away again I'll be really sad!"

"Oh, Roux!" I said, and then I was crying right along with her. "We're not leaving, okay? You were awesome today; don't worry about everything else."

"Sweetheart," my mom said, "do you want to stay here tonight? You might need a place to rest."

Roux nodded gratefully. "Thank you, that would be nice." Then she glanced at me. "A-am I doing the ugly cry?" She sniffled.

"Yes," I told her.

"Damn it." She sighed, then reached for a tissue.

Angelo leaned across the table. "You were very brave today," he said, "and you have been a wonderful friend to Maggie and her family. We never leave our friends behind."

She nodded, as wide-eyed as a little kid talking to Santa Claus, and he passed her his handkerchief. Underneath the table, Jesse squeezed my leg and I reached for him. Everyone I loved was at one table, together, safe and sound.

I had a feeling things were going to be okay.

Epilogue

I hope he doesn't keep me waiting." Roux tapped her foot on the ground. "Do you wear a watch? Let me look at your watch."

"Angelo is always on time," I said. "And no, I don't, so stop grabbing at my wrist."

"Sorry." Then she sneezed. "Oh, hi, allergy season."

We were standing outside the Chess & Checkers House in Central Park. After a crazy winter that made me feel like I was permanently living in the tundra, the trees were flowering again and the park looked beautiful. "Don't you just love spring?" I sighed.

"Aaaah-CHOO! No."

"Oh, look, there's Angelo," I said. "And not a minute too soon."

"Hi!" she said as he came closer. He was wearing a light gray suit, and his tie matched the rows of purple tulips that lined the path up to the house. That's Angelo for you. Even when he tries to blend in, he still stands out.

After our helicopter extravaganza, things were a little chaotic for a while.

We never told the Collective about Roux and Jesse. I knew they would keep my secret, just as I had kept theirs, and I didn't want to cause any trouble for them. Besides, they had helped save my life and solve the case. Still, some people from the Collective flew out to New York and did a huge debriefing about the files and Colton. By the end of it, I was exhausted.

That's when my parents stepped in.

"I think we need to take a leave of absence," my dad told the representatives. "Maggie has been through a lot and she needs to recover."

I shot a look at my dad when he said that. I wasn't some flailing daisy! I could handle it! Exhaustion was temporary, success was forever!

But then he continued speaking.

"Is it possible that we can stay here in Manhattan? Surely there are enough cases in the city."

Stay in the same city with my best friend *and* the boy I liked? Good plan.

So my family and I took a winter vacation. I went back to school, where I finally began to understand French and not sound like an idiot when I spoke it. Roux and I exchanged Christmas gifts, and Jesse and I . . . ?

Well, we talked. And talked. And then kissed a lot and then talked some more. Only time would prove to him that he hadn't been just another assignment, and now I had time. That was all I wanted.

Angelo walked over to Roux and me and kissed both of us on our cheeks. "Ah, lovely ladies. Are you ready to learn the rules of the best game?"

"I want to be the horse," Roux replied.

"The knight," Angelo corrected her.

"This isn't Monopoly," I said. "And I can't, I gotta go meet Jess."

Roux wiggled her eyebrows at me. "Maggie and Jesse, gettin' busy . . ."

"Oh, be quiet." I gave her a shove, but I couldn't hide my smile. "He's going to take me to meet his mom."

After our huge debacle, Jesse made a great point. "I know how important honesty is now," he told me, several nights after my debriefing ended. "I have to be honest with my mom and she needs to be honest with me." So he sat down and wrote her a long e-mail, explaining how much he missed her, and she wrote back. Things still weren't great between them, but they were trying, and now she was coming into the city for the day.

"Speaking of," Roux said. "WOOHOO! JESSE! WE'RE OVER HERE!"

Angelo winced but continued to set up the chessboard. He would have his work cut out for him today.

I waved at Jesse when he got closer, then wrapped my arm around his waist and kissed him. Even though we'd been dating since November, kissing him never got old. "Hiya," he said. "Ready to meet and greet?"

"Always. Angelo, don't let Roux intimidate you. She likes shiny things, so be careful."

Roux stuck her tongue out at me. "Who are these little guys?" she said, holding a handful of pawns. "They're adorable. I want one."

"Have fun," I said, waving at them as I left. Even as we walked away, I could hear Angelo's calm, measured voice. "You may have many pawns. No, no, not that many . . ."

"Nervous?" I asked Jesse as we walked over to the Boathouse, where we were meeting his mom for lunch.

"A little. Not as nervous as I was that time when a madman was chasing us and we had to jump in a helicopter."

I grinned and squeezed him tighter. "I like to keep you on your toes," I said. "And besides, I was just getting back at you for that whole ice skating thing."

"That seems fair," he said.

"Are you still coming over for dinner tonight?"

"Yeah, of course. Your dad's making chili, right?" Jesse and my dad had really started bro-ing it up, which was good for my dad. He had spent too much time surrounded by women. They even watched the Super Bowl together, which I had never seen my dad do in my life.

"I think so. Guess we'll find out." We stood at the entrance to the restaurant and I saw Jesse scan the diners, his face relaxing as he spotted a tall blond woman. "There she is. You ready?"

"Always," I replied, and we went forward without looking back.

ACKNOWLEDGMENTS

Thank you to Mom, Chris, and John and Barbara Snyder for their love and support, and for not laughing at me when I said I might write a book about teenage spies. I love you right back.

I am forever grateful for the day that Lisa Grubka agreed to be my agent, and even more grateful for her professionalism and her ability to always say the right thing, even when I'm in the middle of a deadline. *Especially* when I'm in the middle of a deadline.

Thanks to the team at Foundry Literary + Media, especially Stéphanie Abou and Rachel Hecht; Anna DeRoy at William Morris Endeavor; and Liza Wachter at RWSG Literary.

Thank you to my friends who read early drafts of this book, offered hilarious wisdom, and generally made everything in my life funnier, brighter, and better: Johanna Clark, Adriana Fusaro, Maret Orliss, Rosemary Orliss, Steve Bramucci, Rachel Cohn (I'm writing these acknowledgments at her dining room table right now, so thanks, Rachel!), Dave Marano, Stephanie Perkins, Jennifer Banash, David and Dara Hyde, Joanna Philbin, Abby McDonald, and Dallas Middaugh.

Thank you to the team at Bloomsbury and Walker for their enthusiasm for this book and for welcoming both me and Maggie with open arms: Emily Easton, Stacy Cantor Abrams, Laura Whitaker, Katy Hershberger, Kim Burns, Patricia McHugh, Donna Mark, and Nicole Gastonguay.

Thank you to Erica Jesonis and Mark Bakula for teaching me how to say "You're grounded!" in Russian and Japanese, and massive gratitude to Céline Charvet at Editions Nathan for translating all of the French dialogue.

Thank you to my dog, Hudson, for being absolutely delightful every single day. (I don't think he can read, but better safe than sorry.)

I could go on and on about how grateful I am for the support of the readers, librarians, bloggers, and fans, but then these acknowledgments would be longer than the actual book. Thank you so much for your notes, e-mails, tweets, comments, and overall loveliness, and for embracing my characters with such warmth. You are the best.

Especially you.